Re-discover a gentler kind of humour

'Quite delightful . . . with an atmosphere of quiet contentment and humour that **cannot fail to charm**.'
Daily Telegraph

'There is **such a gentle humour** in the book . . . Mr Finchley is the ideal Englishman.'
Daily Sketch

'What counts for most in the story, as it did for Mr Finchley, is his **mounting pleasure in vagabondage and the English scene**.'
The Times

'**The longer we travel with Mr Finchley, the better we come to love him** . . . His delight at the beauties of the countryside and his mild astonishment at the strange ways of men are infectious.'
Daily Telegraph

'A swift-moving novel, **joyous, happy and incurably optimistic**.'
Evening Standard

'His gift of story-telling is obviously innate. **Rarely does one come on so satisfying** an amalgam of plot, characterisation and good writing.'
Punch

MR FINCHLEY GOES TO PARIS

MR FINCHLEY, BOOK 2

Victor Canning

This edition published in 2019 by Farrago,
an imprint of Prelude Books Ltd
13 Carrington Road, Richmond, TW10 5AA, United Kingdom

www.farragobooks.com

By arrangement with the Beneficiaries of the
Literary Estate of Victor Canning

First published by Hodder and Stoughton in 1938

ISBN: 978-1-78842-162-1

With grateful acknowledgment to John Higgins

Have you read them all?

Treat yourself again to all three Mr Finchley novels –

Mr Finchley Discovers His England
A middle-aged solicitor's clerk takes a holiday for the first time and finds himself in all sorts of unexpected adventure.

Mr Finchley Goes to Paris
On the point of proposing marriage, Mr Finchley is unexpectedly sent to Paris, and gets into a fine tangle.

Mr Finchley Takes the Road
Finchley marries and explores the countryside in a horse-drawn caravan, attracting more interest than he bargained for.

Turn to the end of this book for a full list of Victor Canning's humorous works, plus – on the last page – the chance to receive **further background material**.

To
R. Percy Hodder-Williams
and
Ralph Hodder-Williams

Contents

I
In which Mr. Finchley's future seems to lack promise

MR. EDGAR FINCHLEY, of Nassington Avenue, Hampstead, regarded his reflection in the dressing-table mirror with a seriousness that betrayed itself in the furrows across his broad forehead and the gentle, caressing movement of his thumb and fingers over a freshly shaven chin. Most men have occasional moods which drive them to a survey of themselves in their mirrors; their reflection assists them to a clear, detached view of themselves which is valuable, if not always flattering. Mr. Finchley was not depressed by his reflection. He was comforted by it, and it is a safe assumption that any man who is in the middle forties and can look at himself in his mirror and find comfort there must be one to whom life has not been altogether unkind.

He was bald ... No, almost bald, Mr. Finchley amended, and his tonsure gave a canonical dignity to his head which was fitting to his well-filled figure and his unhurried carriage. His face was round and a little pudgy, a pudginess which few office workers could escape, but his skin had a healthy colour, although there was now no hint of the tan from his last summer's holiday. That holiday was nine months away and his next soon to come. As he eyed himself in the glass, Mr. Finchley was thinking neither of holidays nor his health; he was trying to see himself as others saw him.

Now this is an exercise more common among women than men, and it needs practice to avoid the obvious pitfalls of under- and over-estimation. Perhaps those who contemplate themselves most in their mirrors are the young—who cannot understand why so much that is fine and intelligent should go unrecognised. But when a bachelor who has an adequate income, who is over forty and has a settled taste in ties and clothes, confronts his image, searching for an objective assessment of himself, there is more often than not only one impulse which has drawn him from the security of his pleasant hermitage—he is thinking of marriage; for the approach to marriage and marriage itself is largely concerned with what another person thinks about one.

Mr. Finchley was no exception to this lax rule. As he eyed himself in the glass he was thinking about marriage. He had thought about marriage increasingly in the last year. So far he had never tried to aid his cogitations by contemplating his image at the same time. This conjunction of thought and imagery marked a very definite advance in Mr. Finchley's attitude towards marriage, for today he was going to do what, in some odd way, he had missed doing twenty years before. He was going to propose, and he was very well aware that, no matter what good opinion he might hold about himself, this would little affect what the other person might think about him.

It was this uncertainty which worried him. A young man could take a rebuff, soothing himself by the reflection that young women often make mistakes which they regret; but a bachelor over forty who is rejected by a widow of presentable person and very good sense has no such balm. He is judged and must take his sentence with good grace and without hope of a reprieve.

Mr. Finchley smoothed his chin for the last time and then, selecting a grey silk handkerchief for his breast pocket, left the bedroom and went downstairs to be met by his housekeeper, Mrs. Patten, who had brushed his felt hat and was waiting with it and his stick and gloves. It was a fine evening in early May and he needed no coat.

There was something in the way with which Mrs. Patten handed him his stick and hat which suggested that she understood what he was about to do. She presented these insignia of respectability as though they were weapon and armour for his coming encounter, watching him take the balance of the stick and draw on one glove, as a squire might have regarded the knight he served. There was also a certain sadness in her manner, an unmedieval disapproval that seemed to say with surprise that even a man of his age could apparently be as foolish as a boy of twenty.

"Will you be late coming back?" she asked.

"That," answered Mr. Finchley, "depends." Then, feeling that he had revealed his anxiety, he added quickly: "That depends upon whether I stay to supper. You need not wait up for me."

"I'll not worry about you," said Mrs. Patten, opening the door for him, and as he went down the garden path she said to herself, for she was very fond of him: "And I wish you luck."

But Mr. Finchley did not hear her. He went up Nassington Avenue and was soon crossing a corner of Hampstead Heath towards Highgate, where was his destination.

It was a warm evening and the Heath was alive with people drawn from their homes by the call of green grass and wind-worked water. In places boys played cricket, while others—refusing to acknowledge summer yet—carried on with their football matches; lovers walked beside the pools, watching the mating play of the ducks; dogs raced, barking, across the slopes, heedless of the cries of their owners, and old men sat contentedly upon seats, glad that another summer was on its way. And through them all walked Mr. Finchley, a neat, shortish figure in a suit which was not too light, his shoes shining, his stick rising and falling rhythmically, and his eyes, constant as a pilgrim's, fixed on the Highgate heights.

As he walked he was rehearsing his proposal speech. Mr. Finchley was old-fashioned enough to believe that the moment when a man asked a woman to share his life was a serious moment, and so little experienced in love that he was unaware of the inarticulateness imposed upon lovers in such moments; he believed that a proposal should be a solemn and fitting expression of the emotion of that moment. He had spoilt several sheets of the expensive notepaper of Messrs. Bardwell & Sprake, Solicitors, in composing his speech, but now he had it perfect, and he was justly proud of his composition. It had enough weight yet was not too heavy, and it was not so long as to make kneeling before a sofa painful to the leg muscles while it was delivered.

Mr. Finchley mouthed it silently as he walked along the gravel paths. It began with a subdued, yet definite, note of self-abasement, listing all his imperfections, cataloguing the many reasons which would presumably make his declaration untenable from the start; touched lightly, yet optimistically, upon the hope which, despite his acknowledged unworthiness, stirred within his breast; emphasised the bounty it was in the power of all women to withhold or accord to man; rose to the peak of his declaration and then died away into a peroration which was portentous in its cadence and subtle with comfort if he should be rejected.

> *Dear Madam, if my suit has no favour in your eyes, I beg you not to clothe your denial with objections and reasons. It will be sufficient to know that you cannot love me as I shall always love you. I will take your plain negative. To be given reasons would probably destroy my hope, and, dear lady, if my love is denied hope, no matter how distant, then my life is barren and I am left a very miserable man …*

"I beg your pardon, were you talking to me?"

Mr. Finchley came to earth rapidly to find that he had halted before a plane tree and had been addressing it with the fervour which should have been rightly reserved for a more auspicious moment. At the foot of the tree sat a young girl, not long left school, and on her lap was an open book. She looked up at him with the frank, open countenance of youth, ready to extend sympathy to a troubled soul.

"I'm sorry," said Mr. Finchley, colouring. "I did not realise I had an audience."

"That's all right," was the answer. "You can go on using me as an audience if you like. I always find it easier to learn poetry if I've got someone to say it to—"

Mr. Finchley hurried away in confusion. The idea of practising his speech upon someone else was almost sacrilegious. Behind him rang out young, pleasant laughter. Young people, these days, thought Mr. Finchley, were far too frivolous, and he walked on perturbed by the accident.

By the time he had crossed the Heath and gained Highgate his thoughts and emotions were more settled, and presently he turned aside from the main roadway down a narrow street of pleasant Queen Anne houses and stopped before a house whose well-proportioned doors and windows were fresh with green and white paint.

As he stood on the doorstep, straightening his tie and mentally priming himself, Mr. Finchley suddenly felt himself seized by a trembling weakness, an enervating efflux of courage and confidence which he had not known since those long moments before the commencement of examinations in his schooldays. He fought to regain his spirit and tugged at the door bell, deciding that the sooner he got this thing over the happier he would be.

A maid opened the door for him and, after taking his hat, gloves and stick, which made him feel even more unarmed and unprepared, she showed him into a long, comfortably furnished sitting-room at the back of the house. French windows looked out to a small garden which was bright with spring flowers.

As he entered the room, a woman who had been sitting by the half-open windows rose and came towards him with one hand outstretched and a smile of welcome on her face. This was Mrs. Crantell. She was a small, dark-haired woman with humorous, restless eyes and a gentle, bird-like habit of moving her head as though her interest in the things around her could never be satisfied. She was a widow, and Mr. Finchley had first met her when she had visited the offices of Bardwell & Sprake after the death of her husband, who had been one of their clients. He had also met her once on his holidays by chance, and it was from that chance meeting had come their friendship.

"Ah, Mr. Finchley, this is a surprise. What have you been doing with yourself? You haven't been to see me for a whole week, and I haven't so many friends that I can afford to let you neglect me for a week. Now then, what excuses have you to offer?"

She sat down on the long settee which was drawn across the window, laughing up at him, and Mr. Finchley knew that this was the moment for his purpose. Here he was in the position he had imagined so often during the last week. Mrs. Crantell sitting on the settee, the light from the garden touching her dark hair and adding a soft warmth to the depth of her eyes, the air moving in through the windows full of the scent of laburnum and wallflowers, and a thick-piled rug before the settee to ease his genuflection as he bent to his purpose.

Mr. Finchley smiled back at her, licked his lips and began to speak:

"My dear Mrs. Crantell, you have called me your friend and I am very proud to be so honoured ..." This, of course, was not in the speech, but her welcome had offered him an easy introduction to his business. He bent towards her and one hand felt for the loose of his trouser leg so that he might give that slight hitch-up which makes bending, for a man of middle-age with a tendency to stoutness, a less clumsy manoeuvre. But before Mr. Finchley could begin to flex his legs a shadow fell across the floor before him and the window opening was filled by a tall, broad figure. A voice boomed into the room:

"Why, why, if it isn't the Right Reverend Edgar Finchley. Dear me, this is a pleasure! How are you, and how are all the torts, malfeasances, contracts, writs and injunctions?"

The moment was gone. In his heart Mr. Finchley cursed this interruption and then straightened himself to meet the newcomer. He found himself facing a man ten years older than himself, a man with a body that still retained the bulk and power of past years. This was Mr. David White, Mrs. Crantell's brother. He had been a mining engineer, but was now retired and lived in the North of England on a small farm from which he descended at times to stay with Mrs. Crantell. Mr. Finchley told himself that it was typical of Mr. White to have chosen this time to pay his sister a visit. He did not like Mr. White for reasons which most people would have found obvious after an hour of Mr. White's company. Mr. White thought that it was humorous to tack odd titles to people's names when addressing them. In his time Mr. Finchley had found himself addressed as Sir Edgar Finchley, Baron de Finchley, the Most Honourable Member for Finchley, and less often by the prefix of an Indian word which, Mr. White explained, meant in South America "he who is the master and must be obeyed"; but Mr. Finchley, who recognised that Mr. White loved him no more than he loved Mr. White, suspected that the word had a very different and uncomplimentary meaning. All this Mr. Finchley could have forgiven, but he could not forgive Mr. White's stories—a mining engineer roaming about the world must have adventures, Mr. Finchley admitted that, but he saw no reason why he should be bored by the same stories again and again.

"David's staying with me for a few days," explained Mrs. Crantell, and Mr. Finchley imagined that he caught in her voice a note of regret that David should have chosen that moment to break in.

"That's right," boomed Mr. White, making himself comfortable in an easy chair. "Every now and then I feel the pull of the metropolis and must come from my retreat in the savage North to sample the effete pleasures of civilisation. It was just the same in the old days. We'd work for weeks, months, and then one day the flesh and spirit would rebel and we'd saddle up and ride, maybe a couple of hundred miles, to the nearest town. I remember a time in Northern Australia—those were the days when tungsten was a new thing—and we'd had about three months of black-faced aborigines, hot scrub land and water that left an inch of sediment in the bucket before you could drink it ..."

There was no stopping him. Mr. Finchley and Mrs. Crantell sat back and let the flood pour over them until the inevitable phrases which ended his stories told them they might come to the surface.

"One day, when I've the time, I really must write my autobiography. Any publisher would jump at it. Yes, sir, I've seen some queer things in my time."

"Would you like to look around the garden, Mr. Finchley?" Mrs. Crantell rose to show him her flowers. It was a dangerous remark, and for a moment Mr. Finchley waited anxiously for Mr. White to take his cue and tell them the story of the man-eating orchid which deserting natives and malaria had prevented him from seeing. The danger passed and they went out into the garden, leaving Mr. White alone with his memories and a pipe.

They walked along the beds admiring the flowers. The dark wallflowers gave off a scent as rich as their colouring, the red and yellow darwin tulips bore their flaming petals on stiff torch holders, forming a heraldic line along the border, and a London pigeon, as plump-breasted as an alderman, rumbled a courting song to his mate in the branches of the sycamore that shaded the end of the garden. They walked in silence until they reached the shade of the tree, and then, as they stood before a clump of purple aubrietia, Mrs. Crantell said quietly, as though she were speaking her thoughts aloud, rather than addressing Mr. Finchley:

"You know, although I like David, there are times when I'm very glad to see him go. As he gets older he gets worse."

Mr. Finchley smiled, and, with an unconscious loyalty to his sex, took Mr. White's part: "As people lose their youth, you know, they get very settled in their habits and it's not easy to shake them off."

"That's true. But how many people realise it? People like ourselves, for instance—do we realise that we are getting on in years and may have formed habits and ways of life which aren't at all acceptable to others? I used to hope that one day David would get married and it would change him. But he didn't, and I realise now that it was just as well, because marriage wouldn't have changed him. Marriage between elderly people is generally not very successful because it comes too late, at a time when neither party is able to change habits and ways of life ..."

Mr. Finchley almost gave away his surprise as he turned quickly towards her, and then he said with a sudden pang striking deeply within him: "Do you mean you don't approve of such marriages?"

Mrs. Crantell laughed at his sudden seriousness, but Mr. Finchley thought he appreciated that beneath her lightness was a purpose and that she had deliberately brought up the conversation for his benefit.

"You can't make hard-and-fast rules about such things, obviously. But speaking for myself, I certainly don't think I should get married again—not even if some handsome cavalier did come along and propose to me. Why should I? I'm very happy as I am. People at my age don't marry for love like youth. It would only mean that I should go and live in some man's house and what had been a pleasant friendship would probably be spoilt because we should find our habits clashing. We should both be happier carrying on in the old way. If you can't have the strong love of youth you must, at my age, have something to take its place before you get married."

Mr. Finchley had no doubt now of Mrs. Crantell's intention. Every word was meant for him, and as she finished speaking he felt a surge of sadness within him and for a moment there was no beauty in the evening. Yet even in his disappointment he could not be angry at the wreck of his hopes before he had more than left the harbour. What Mrs. Crantell had said was true, and to imagine that his was a unique example, exempt from the general rule, needed more conviction than he could immediately summon.

"Marriage is a funny business," he said at last. As a bachelor I don't pretend to be able to speak authoritatively about it."

Mrs. Crantell was a little surprised at Mr. Finchley's docile acceptance of her views. Actually she had wanted them challenged, expected them to be attacked. She had known what had been in Mr. Finchley's mind earlier in the evening, and she had been glad of David's interruption, for it had given her a chance to make her statement. His subdued acknowledgment of her opinion disappointed her even while she recognised that it came from his respect for her feelings. As they went back to the house she laid her hand on his arm and Mr. Finchley was glad of the comfort.

As the evening passed Mr. Finchley's dejection grew and, infecting Mrs. Crantell, disturbed her, so that for the first time within Mr. Finchley's knowledge he heard her speak shortly to her brother, telling him as he began his story of a puma hunt that they had heard it before.

"So you may, my dear," replied her brother, undaunted; "but a good story can stand retelling a hundred times." And away he went, while Mr. Finchley ate his cold meat, momentarily cheered by the warm smiles that Mrs. Crantell gave him across the table. But they were poor comfort for a man who had set out with such high hopes and so much determination, and it was not long after supper that he made his excuses and left the house.

He walked back across the Heath. The night was full of soft, moving shadows, and the reflection of distant lights on the pools sent long fingers of wavering brightness in search of the wildfowl that moved and clucked gently to one another as they settled for the night in the reeds. Overhead a faint wind struggled to move along the high masses of clouds which obscured the stars, and once a laggard gull, haunting the Heath pools when all its fellows had answered the call of spring and gone downstream to seek the coasts and their nesting places, cried with loneliness. The call stirred Mr. Finchley, reminding him of his own loneliness and sending him away to the coasts, to Cornwall and the salty headlands where the spray jewelled the thin leaves of the sea-pinks.

Mrs. Patten was still up when he returned. She took one look at him and said nothing, and Mr. Finchley would have been surprised had he known just how much his face told her of his progress during the evening.

As he undressed, he wondered if he would yet make his declaration to Mrs. Crantell. Then he decided that it would be better to accept her very definite hint and say nothing. He was even grateful, in his misery, that she had spared him the pain of a direct refusal.

He dropped off to sleep, convinced that his life had been bereft of any future he could meet with eagerness. It lay ahead of him, a flat, dull vista. So Mr. Finchley thought.

II
Of caterpillars

THE next morning Mr. Finchley awoke to find that spring had slipped away and winter had returned, lashing everything with a cold rain and blustering about in a fine frenzy of wind. He went downstairs with the air of a man who expects little comfort in the world and finds the prospect of the coming days almost too miserable to contemplate.

Everything went wrong that morning. It always does. When Fate has dealt severely with a man she does not scruple to continue harassing him with petty annoyances and pin-pricks, knowing well that these small troubles will be aggravated by a suffering mind into major calamities. To begin with, the salt was damp in its cellar and refused to run for him, and when he rapped it against the table the bottom came off and he found himself with a lapful of salt.

"Confound it!" said Mr. Finchley, loudly and unashamed, yet even in his anger he remembered to throw a pinch over his left shoulder to keep off bad luck.

His eggs, which he liked soft, were boiled hard, and with the virtuous, injured air of a martyr he refused to allow Mrs. Patten to boil him some more, but ate them with the feeling that indigestion would be the least of his troubles and, if it came, might take his mind from the gloomier meditation of his own unhappiness of soul.

This was not all; Mrs. Patten had run out of coffee and he had to drink tea, which he disliked, for breakfast; the newspaper boy had delivered the wrong paper and Mr. Finchley fussed and fumed as he tried to find his way about the strange columns and, to complete his discomfiture, as he finished breakfast Mrs. Patten came in and stood with her hands crossed before her in an attitude which Mr. Finchley knew meant that she wanted to speak to him about something other than the little domestic details of the house.

He looked up at her and, having his attention, she said:

"I had a letter about my sister this morning. She's no better, and if she gets worse I shall have to go up and look after her. She's got no one else in the world but me."

Mr. Finchley sighed to himself. He was not unsympathetically inclined towards Mrs. Patten's sister, but there were times when he wondered how such a weak and constantly ailing body managed or bothered to live on. Three or four times a year she fell seriously ill, and each time Mrs. Patten, with an affection that was sincere and touching, flew to nurse her, and Mr. Finchley let her go with good grace, for he knew that housekeepers like Mrs. Patten were hard to come by.

"What is it this time?" he asked.

"The old trouble. I told her she ought never to have had that last operation. It did her no good, but her mind was set on it ..."

"Quite!" Mr. Finchley spoke quickly because he did not want to be entertained with the medical history, of his housekeeper's sister, a subject which Mrs. Patten knew intimately. "Well, if she wants you, you must go, of course. I'll go and live at the club for a while. Let's hope she gets better soon, though."

Later, protected by his raincoat and umbrella, he walked down to the tram and sat in a steamy, heavy atmosphere for ten minutes while the man next to him made the comment, which was no doubt overworked that morning, that it was just like winter again. He worked until eleven o'clock listening to the rivalry of the tapping typewriters and the rain against the windows. He looked at his watch for the third time, wondering why the office boy was late with his morning cup of tea, when the boy entered his room and said briefly, "Mr. Sprake wants to see you in his room. He told me to take your tea in there."

Mr. Sprake was the head of the firm, Bardwell being dead. When Mr. Finchley entered, Mr. Sprake was glancing through the pages of an illustrated magazine. Mr. Finchley was not surprised. It was seldom that any of the staff entered Sprake's room and found him immersed in official business, yet for all that it was undisputed that he did more work than anyone else. Sprake was a well-built, well-fed man with the type of face you associate with golf-clubs, whisky-and-sodas and comfortable, fast cars. Moreover, he knew his job and was far from being an amiable fool.

"Good morning, Finchley," he said affably. "Sit down and, drink your tea. I want to have a chat with you. Awful tripe they print in some of these magazines these days. Seem to be full of the mouthings of two-a-penny philosophers and the doings of film-stars."

"I'm afraid I can't pass any opinion as I never read them," replied Mr. Finchley, stirring his tea.

"Neither do I as a rule, but I like to see what sort of stuff they put in the waiting-room out there. Might give the clients a bad impression." He tossed the magazine aside and lit a cigarette. Then he went on: "You remember the Hammerton family, of course?"

"Very well. All brothers, weren't they? This Mrs. Hammerton who has just died—she married the youngest. We've handled her affairs for the last ten years." Mr. Finchley vaguely wondered why Sprake asked him what he already knew so well.

"That's right," said Sprake. "But that isn't all. I was thinking of the family aside from the professional angle. There were five brothers, all of them wealthy and only the eldest of them had any issue—a son. And that son has been very lucky. First he got his father's fortune, and then in turn, as each brother died, another fortune dropped into his lap, and now the last fortune has dropped into his lap—Mrs. Hammerton's. And from what I hear he'll be glad of it. He seems to have run through the other money pretty completely. A man who can so quickly shift four fairly considerable inheritances must be quite interesting to talk to—don't you think so?"

"My opinion of a man like that is that he may be interesting, but he's shown a disgusting lack of self-control. A fortune is a responsibility and should be employed wisely!" Mr. Finchley spoke with some warmth, for he considered thrift one of the major virtues. Also, it was convenient to let out his irritation on the obscure Mr. Hammerton.

"Well," Sprake smiled gently at Mr. Finchley's vehemence; "maybe you'll tell him that when you meet him."

"When I meet him?" Mr. Finchley plainly showed his surprise.

"Naturally. He's inherited a fortune which we are handling."

"But he'll call and see you, Mr. Sprake. He knows all about the affair."

"It's true he has been informed. But apparently he's not the kind of man who chooses to call and see us. We've got to go and see him, or rather you've got to go and see him."

"Where?"

Sprake hesitated before he replied. He was fond of Mr. Finchley, but he could never resist the chance of having some amusement at the other's expense. Mr. Finchley could express indignation and shock in a way which Sprake found a never-ending delight.

"In Paris," he said quietly.

"In Paris!" repeated Mr. Finchley incredulously, and for a moment the firm streak of puritanism which was so much part of his nature forced him to a show of mild horror. Paris! A city whose synonym was sin; a city of volatile immorality. Then, as Mr. Finchley realised that Sprake was having fun with him, he asked seriously

"But why me?"

Sprake gave up his fun and turned to business with equal enthusiasm. "Well, it's like this; this Mr. Hammerton lives in the south of France and he doesn't want to come to England. He'll be in Paris on Saturday. I don't know whether he has French lawyers or not, but there's no harm in trying to keep his business for ourselves. We can handle it for him no matter where he lives. You know there are various papers he must sign and somebody must go and see him."

"But why me?" asked Mr. Finchley again, and added subtly, "I should have thought you would have liked a trip to Paris, Mr. Sprake …"

Sprake sighed and shook his head sadly. "No, I wouldn't. I once had an unfortunate experience in Paris—and I don't like the French. Besides, I've got a golf tournament match on Saturday and I'm not going to miss it. You must go, Finchley. You can talk this Mr. Hammerton into leaving his business with us. What is it today? Thursday. Then you can go over tomorrow and see him Saturday morning. All the details are in the office. That all right?"

Mr. Finchley rose and nodded. "Yes, Mr. Sprake. I'll phone through about the tickets right away." As he spoke he was admiring the foresight which Mr. Sprake had shown by insisting that the senior members of the firm should have passports, ready for an emergency.

"And look after yourself, Finchley," called Sprake as he went out. "Paris isn't like London. You want to watch your step!"

Mr. Finchley left him with the sound of his chuckle ringing in his ears. It was some time before he had settled himself to this new circumstance, and when he did he found that the prospect of going to Paris for the weekend was not so intimidating as he had at first thought. His experiences in France had never taken him so far south as Paris, for he had been stationed for most of the war at Boulogne on transport work. But his French was not bad and, enjoying the novelty of speaking another language, he had kept it exercised by reading, with the frequent aid of a dictionary, an occasional French novel. Anyhow, he thought, Mr. Hammerton was an Englishman and he would only need his French for the journey and in the hotel, which would be straining but not exhausting his linguistic powers.

In half an hour the rest of the office knew of his impending journey and he immediately assumed a new importance in their eyes. The young clerks who came to his room looked at him in a way which invested him with a strange power. Their envy heightened his growing anticipation of the journey. He was rather embarrassed when the girl typist came to his room on some obvious excuse and stopped to commission him to bring her back scent and silk stockings.

"They say they're awfully cheap, Mr. Finchley. It would be so kind of you. *Molyneux, Numero Cinq*, is the scent, and the stockings, I don't mind a bit what they're like—something fawny and size nine. You don't have to worry about the Customs because they let you bring back so much."

"But … er …" Mr. Finchley let his protest die away, realising that it was not easy for him, as chief clerk, to point out that there were certain difficulties in the way of buying silk stockings. The scent, perhaps, but the silk stockings … he got rid of her with the ambiguous promise to do what he could.

When lunch time came, the idea of going to Paris was established with him, and it was with some surprise that he realised his excitement had driven away his morning depression. He lunched with a friend from a neighbouring office, and, as they sat over their coffee, Mr. Finchley brought the conversation around so that he could say without too apparent a break in the sequence of their talk:

"By the way, I'm going to Paris this weekend on business." He said it as though he often went to Paris on business and that the frequency of his trips rather bored him. If he had hoped to impress his friend he was disappointed. The other replied almost moodily:

"Don't like the French. Don't like their cigarettes or their sanitation."

If his friend was not impressed, Mrs. Patten was. His news almost made her forget her sister and she started to collect his things for his bag so that he should be ready for the morning.

"As I shan't be back until Sunday, you might as well shut up the house and go to your sister at Peterborough," Mr. Finchley said, and he went upstairs to change. He was going to call on Mrs. Crantell and let her know the news. He knew that Mr. White would be there, but he felt that he had to tell her of his trip to Paris, and for the time being that event chased from his mind all his disappointment at the way his proposal had been pushed aside.

When Mr. Finchley reached Mrs. Crantell's house, he did not at once tell her of his coming journey. It was not until the three of them, for Mr. White was still there, were sitting at supper that he said quietly:

"I meant to mention it before—I'm going to Paris tomorrow on business. I shan't be back until Sunday."

The two stopped eating and looked at him, Mrs. Crantell showing her surprise and Mr. White's face indicating a quite unusual interest in another's doings.

"Good gracious, Mr. Finchley," cried Mrs. Crantell. "However have you been able to sit there so calmly all this while and keep the news to yourself? I should be bubbling with excitement."

"This is a business trip—"

"Nonsense; business or no business, you should be excited. Now, come on and confess that you are just a little excited about it all."

"Well, perhaps a little ..."

"The way you two talk," broke in Mr. White, "would make anyone think that a trip to Paris was as dangerous as going up the Amazon ..."

"Well, you've never been there," Mrs. Crantell cried, for only a few days before he had been commenting on the strange coincidence that in a life of so much travel he had never been to Paris.

"That is so," admitted Mr. White with a dignity that implied a deprecation of this shrewd blow at his integrity as a traveller, "and that is why Mr. Finchley's remark interests me so, for I have a very strong reason for wishing to go to Paris ..."

Mr. Finchley glanced anxiously at Mrs. Crantell. The last thing he wanted to happen was to have Mr. White's company forced upon him for the journey.

"And what might that be?" asked Mrs. Crantell. Mr. White settled back into his chair, tapped his tobacco home in the bowl of his pipe and said with evident satisfaction: "Well, it's a long story, but an interesting one ..."

Mr. Finchley breathed. For a moment he had thought that Mr. White really intended going to Paris, now he knew that it was only an introduction to a story. He listened patiently as Mr. White unfolded his story, which had the merit of being new.

Mr. White finished his story and the rest of the evening passed pleasantly. Mr. Finchley did not stay long. He had been brought up to the habit of retiring early the night before a journey.

The next morning showed him a bright sky for his trip. A light wind flecked at the thin white clouds and spring was back, all the happier for her day's truancy. A taxi took him to Victoria Station, while Mrs. Patten was left behind to close the house before going off to Peterborough.

Mr. Finchley found himself a corner seat in the boat train and settled down to read his newspaper. The print did not hold him long. The train shook off the straggling London suburbs and was soon rolling through Kent. Mr. Finchley let his eyes wander over the fresh countryside. It was the first time that year that he had been well out into the country, and the spring, which one felt rather than saw in the city, was here colourfully apparent.

The railway embankment was studded with yellow patches of late primroses, and as they swept through the woods of larch and birch he saw the hazy mist of bluebells. The train moved by red-bricked farmhouses, the old roofs a motley company of colours where weather and moss had stained the tiles, and here and there the great cone of an oast house thrust itself upwards like some medieval turret. The hopfields were no more than bare stretches of ground covered with an entanglement of poles and twine. It would be some months before the hop vines reached up and with rapid growth converted the fields into shady bowers so that one walked in a flood of green, translucent light beneath a canopy of stirring leaves and swaying tendrils. Yet, if the hops had no use for spring there were the green lines of young corn, the energetic leaping of young lambs and the wide sweeps of orchard blossom; all these were part of the spring, and Mr. Finchley as he watched them felt something of their vigour and fresh life sweep into him and he forgot his recent disappointment, forgot that this was purely a business trip, and found himself filling with a boyish excitement at the prospect of his journey. It was with something of a shock that he realised that an old gentleman opposite him was watching him with disapproval. Schoolboys may press their noses against the window-pane in their anxiety to miss nothing, but such conduct in a man of Mr. Finchley's years was likely to be misconstrued.

Mr. Finchley hid behind his paper until the train swept into Folkestone Harbour. Here, although the sight of the sea, the cliffs and the black and white Channel steamer made him more excited than ever, he picked up his case with a slow, even restraint and passed carefully along the crowded platform, and on to the steamer.

It was then, as his feet touched shipboard, that Mr. Finchley realised he was leaving England. There was something irrevocable and awful about the movement, a renunciation of the past. As the ship steamed out through the harbour and the white cliffs began to drop behind them and the swell to make itself felt, Mr. Finchley felt himself alone in the world, all his contacts with familiar things broken and, as if to complete the feeling, two nearby passengers began to talk to one another in French, a swift, voluble flow of words that escaped Mr. Finchley's interpretation and filled him with dismay as he thought of his own French.

He moved away from the shelter of the deck structure and found a strong wind roaring into his face and a thin splatter of spray cold upon his skin. A pair of gulls dipped and swung in the wake of the ship, and the throb of the boat's engines vibrated through the planks, communicating to Mr. Finchley a sudden confidence, and he shook off his depression, telling himself not to be a fool.

There was a fair number of people on the boat and it was some time before Mr. Finchley could find a sheltered spot to sit down. He settled on one of the long seats not so far from the little cabin where the Customs official was examining passengers' passports Already there was a long queue outside the door, stretching along the covered deck, of passengers waiting to have their passports stamped. Mr. Finchley decided that he would wait until the queue lessened before he joined it. There was plenty of time.

He sat, dividing his attention between the people in the queue and the moving water which he could see through the window behind him. As he sat there a young man came slowly along the deck and settled on the farther end of the seat. Without a glance at Mr. Finchley, he put his hand into his pocket and pulled out a small, thick book which he commenced to read. He was a tall, intelligent-looking young man, his face a little pale, and his eyes were hidden by horn-rimmed spectacles with which he fidgeted as he read. Mr. Finchley thought he detected about the man a certain hesitancy of manner, a lack of confidence amongst the bustle of the boat which marked one who was accustomed to the even tenor of a scholastic life. He wore an old raincoat and a felt hat which was pushed back from his forehead as though he secretly disapproved of hats and deliberately treated them with disrespect.

For a while, with a curiosity that is common enough to be forgivable, Mr. Finchley tried to get a glimpse of the title of the book which the young man was reading. He was unsuccessful, and after a while gave up the attempt and turned his attention to the sea. Away in the distance a tramp steamer was drawing a smudge of smoke along the sky, and Mr. Finchley watched it until it passed from his vision and then he turned again to the passport queue. As he did so his gaze traversed the young man and he noticed something which had certainly not been there when he had first looked at him.

The pocket of the raincoat which was nearer to Mr. Finchley still gaped where the young man had withdrawn his book, and about two inches above the lip of the pocket was a caterpillar. Its presence there upset Mr. Finchley. Caterpillars were natural enough creatures, with a beauty that made them fit objects of admiration. Mr. Finchley recalled a mass of yellow and black caterpillars which he had once seen swarming over a tall plant of ragwort, turning the yellow weed into an exotic, almost macabre plant which he had not soon forgotten, and then there were the fat, pale green creatures which, no matter how careful the cook, he had discovered sometimes in his cauliflower, and the smaller, jollier, russet caterpillars that let themselves down on gossamer ropes from overhanging trees in the summer to wriggle their bodies before his eyes as though inviting him to applaud their gymnastic prowess. All these seemed natural enough, but Mr. Finchley's insular rectitude was shocked at the presence of caterpillars on a cross-Channel steamer. It was almost as though caterpillars had decided to form a modern movement to discredit established conventions. It was not enough for the butterfly to be a wanderer, the caterpillar had to travel to show its emancipation from old ideas.

He eyed the creature disapprovingly as it arched its body in regular movements and climbed upwards, across the brown folds of raincoat towards the distant shoulder. It was of a species Mr. Finchley had never seen before, its hairy black body marked with a regular sequence of white spots.

For a moment Mr. Finchley watched, astonishment holding him motionless. Then he pulled himself together and was about to make himself known to the young man when from the pocket crawled another caterpillar of a similar kind to its fellow who was now well away up the mountain of raincoat. Mr. Finchley checked himself. His resolution was shaken still more by this new arrival. It was unorthodox. To further his confusion and intimidate him, a third caterpillar emerged from the pocket and close behind it came a fourth, hurrying as though aware and ashamed of its tardiness. One caterpillar Mr. Finchley could have dealt with. It needed only a laughing remark to the young man, a joke and—*flick*—the caterpillar would be on the floor and squashed or allowed to roam in search of fresh pockets to plunder. But four caterpillars made the operation more difficult. A man takes easily the misfortune of having one caterpillar crawling about him. That is an accident which might happen to anyone, but to inform a stranger that he has four caterpillars crawling over him was to suggest, so Mr. Finchley thought, that he was suffering from an infestation which arose from some personal lack of circumspection.

Unfortunately Mr. Finchley was left with little choice in the matter. The first caterpillar was now well on its way towards the region of the young man's neck and all Mr. Finchley's sympathies were with the young man. He knew how he would have felt if he had discovered something crawling about his flesh.

Coughing discreetly he leant forward and, touching the young man on the arm, said gently, for he did not wish to attract the attention of anyone in the passport queue:

"Excuse me."

For a second or two the young man gave no sign that he had heard or felt Mr. Finchley. Then, methodically, as though his brain was functioning slowly and attending to each process in strict rotation and without hurry, the young man turned down the page of his book, closed the covers and swivelled towards Mr. Finchley, saying as he did so: "Were you addressing me?" He had a pleasant scholarly voice.

"Yes, I was," admitted Mr. Finchley. "I'm sorry to disturb you, but I thought you would like to know that you have several, in fact four, caterpillars crawling over you, and one is very near your neck."

As he finished speaking Mr. Finchley slid back along the seat a little, for he could not tell but the young man might explode into a moment of hasty shaking and brushing to rid himself of the caterpillars. The young man did nothing of the sort. He continued to look at Mr. Finchley with a calm unconcern, weighing his words and examining them with evident interest. Then he said quietly:

"That's extremely interesting. I wonder what species they are?"

III
How Mr. Finchley says nothing in a foreign tongue

MR. FINCHLEY had not expected this reply, and he could not help but admire the young man's fortitude. His comment showed a mind which moved more easily to enquiry than to alarm, a condition which would have curtailed his chances of survival in any primitive society.

"I don't know the name of them," replied Mr. Finchley, "but they are rather large black ones with white spots along their backs. If you twist your head around you'll be able to see the one on your shoulder."

At this the young man jerked his head round and found himself staring at the first caterpillar, which had now reached its objective and was looking for fresh worlds to conquer. For a moment the young man squinted at the caterpillar, and the caterpillar, anxious to establish the friendliness of its intentions, raised the fore part of its body and salaamed.

"How extraordinary—they are mine!" The young man made the discovery with some surprise and at once he picked the caterpillar from his shoulder and turning to Mr. Finchley said: "I say, would you mind rescuing the others from me?"

Anxious to help, Mr. Finchley picked off the three remaining caterpillars and held them cupped in his hands, waiting for the young man to take them. The caterpillars wriggled round his cupped hands, seeking escape, then acknowledging their captivity rolled themselves into tight little Catherine wheels. The young man fished in his pocket and pulled out a long white box which had for a cover a piece of thin gauze which had come unstuck at one corner.

"That's how they got out," he said to Mr. Finchley as he relieved him of the caterpillars and put them into the box.

"Hullo!" He peered closely into the box for a moment and then looked at Mr. Finchley as though he suspected him. "There are only four here and there should be five."

"There were only four crawling about you," said Mr. Finchley, and added: "Are they valuable?"

"Well, they're not rare, but they are rather valuable at the moment because I'd promised to take five across to an entomologist friend in Paris and he particularly asked for five. I'm an entomologist," he explained.

"Perhaps that cover has been loose for some time and the other escaped earlier," suggested Mr. Finchley. "Have you been sitting down anywhere before this?"

"I was in the bar for a while and then I sat down on the other side of the boat until it got too draughty there for me. Then I came here."

"Well,"—Mr. Finchley felt a certain amount of gratitude for the young man; it was good in the midst of so much that was new and exciting to be given some definite job of work—"perhaps we can find the missing caterpillar for you. You go and look around the seat where you were sitting and I'll have a look in the bar."

The young man started to thank him, but Mr. Finchley cut him short and turned away towards the fore part of the boat to find the bar. In a world of hurrying humans the existence of a caterpillar was precarious. Any moment might be its last beneath tyrannical shoes.

Mr. Finchley found the bar. It was pleasantly full. He stood by the doorway for a while, filling and lighting his pipe and letting his eyes wander around, taking particular notice of shoulders since that seemed the favourite aspiration of this type of caterpillar. He saw no sign of the missing caterpillar and, his pipe well lit, he went forward to stand by the bar where he could command a better view of the room.

He ordered a glass of beer and found himself standing alongside a man of about his own build with a vinous, jolly face, who said politely to him as he waited for his drink:

"*Bonjour, m'sieur.*"

From this and the fact that he was wearing a beret, Mr. Finchley decided that he was a Frenchman, and he replied with equal politeness:

"*Bonjour, m'sieur*. A nice day for the crossing."

The Frenchman nodded and turned to his drink as though he did not care for the weather as a topic of conversation, and as he did so from the top of his beret a small black body arched itself and signalled momentarily, and Mr. Finchley recognised what must have been the fifth wandering caterpillar. He knew, too, that here was a caterpillar with more daring and determination than any of the others; they had been content to roam over one of their own nationality, ascending no further than a shoulder, but here was one who boldly assaulted a Frenchman and, by way of a turned-up coat collar, made itself at home on his beret.

Mr. Finchley recognised at once the difficulty in rescuing the caterpillar. It was impossible for him to reach up unobtrusively and pluck the creature from the beret, and he felt that a preliminary explanation about the caterpillar might confuse and alarm a member of a nation which is notorious for its insistence that all Englishmen are mad. He had not resolved the problem when he saw the young entomologist come into the bar. He signalled to him.

"Any luck?" the young man asked as he came up.

Mr. Finchley shook his head and then indicated the Frenchman who was standing by him. The young man did not understand. Then Mr. Finchley raised his hand and tapped his hat significantly. The young man watched this action with a wrinkled brow.

"What on earth are you tapping your head for?" he asked.

"I'm not tapping my head," he answered, fearing the Frenchman would hear.

"But you are—"

"No—not my head." He nodded towards the Frenchman and whispered: "His!"

The young man's eyes went to the Frenchman's beret and he saw the caterpillar. Immediately, for the Frenchman had his back to them, he put out his hand to take the caterpillar. For one of his height it was an easy manoeuvre. Unfortunately, as he did so the Frenchman turned round. With a presence of mind that Mr. Finchley could only admire, the young man turned his movement into a gesture to the barman and asked for a packet of cigarettes, and the Frenchman, regarding them both with a placid smile, said gently:

"M'ssieurs, it is ten years today since I was married."

As an opening to conversation it was less orthodox than a comment upon the weather and had distinctly greater possibilities. Mr. Finchley, of the two, recovered himself first.

"Congratulations," he said, and added with the feeling that since the Frenchman was prepared to give strangers intimate information he would not be backward: "I am not married."

"That is a pity," said the Frenchman at once.

"Why?" The young man, forgetting his caterpillar, asked the question with a certain fierceness which proved that here was a subject about which he felt strongly.

"Because the man who is not married is missing the unhappiness of love. In France, m'sieur, we understand love. We do not believe that it is all rapture. We know that the man who is in love is often an unhappy man, and it is good for man to be unhappy—"

"Love," said the young entomologist, breaking in, "may be all right for some men, but for the man of science, for the man of ambition—unless he means to reach his ambition through marriage—it is a great nuisance, taking his mind from its real occupation and disturbing him. Actually I am inclined to doubt the existence of love; admitting only the biological necessity of the mating instinct in men and women. People talk a lot of nonsense about love. I shall never get married. I am an entomologist."

"What is that? A chaser of butterflies, is it not?"

"I suppose," said the young man, "you might call it that, although—"

"That is so," went on the Frenchman. "I, too, am fond of butterflies, but it does not stop me from becoming married. I am very interested in biology, too. I always say it is a pity that butterflies should have to come from caterpillars. I do not like them. A butterfly is beautiful, but a caterpillar reminds me of snakes. It is horrible and makes me shudder. Let us talk of other things."

"Would you," said Mr. Finchley, hiding a smile, "lend me your matches?" He held up his pipe, which had gone out, to show he wished to light it. The Frenchman felt in his pocket and then handed Mr. Finchley the matches. Mr. Finchley took them and then deliberately dropped them. The Frenchman bent at once to pick them up and as he did so Mr. Finchley neatly took the caterpillar from the beret which presented itself to him, and the creature was safely in the entomologist's hands before the Frenchman had retrieved the matches.

At that moment there was a stir in the bar, the word 'Boulogne' floated through the air and through the window Mr. Finchley saw land.

"Ha, we are there," said the Frenchman. "I am a great traveller, m'ssieurs; this is the second time of my life I have voyaged to England, but it is always with joy that I come back to France. You will excuse me, I must go on deck to see …"

He was gone and a few moments later Mr. Finchley and the young man joined the drift to the deck to watch the growing stretch of land which was France, and in the crowd he got separated from the entomologist before that young man could thank him for his assistance.

Mr. Finchley stood on deck watching Boulogne draw closer. It seemed no different from the town he had watched approach so many years before. There was the high bluff of land and the grey and white slope of houses, the coloured funnels of shipping in the harbour, and away on the heights the tall finger of Napoleon's column erected to commemorate the assembly of an army of invasion that never put to sea. Looking at the place, Mr. Finchley told himself there was little to distinguish it from any English town, and it was only when they had passed the dredger working in the outer harbour and were running quietly up to the railway dock that the sensation of being abroad came over him. Men fishing from the quayside looked up and shouted strangely across to the boat, small boys waved their arms and joined the chorus of shouts, and the shop fronts and cafés drawn closer suddenly threw off their vagueness and proclaimed themselves French.

Within the next five minutes Mr. Finchley was subjected to the terrific welcome which France reserves for the unwary traveller. A horde of blue-bloused and baggy-trousered porters invaded the boat, one of whom, an unshaven, degenerate type with a peaked cap, seized Mr. Finchley's two bags and shouting aloud "Venty-eight!" disappeared. Mr. Finchley opened his mouth to protest and then shut it as he noticed that others around him were having their baggage seized by porters who hurried away crying their numbers.

Trusting to the indefinable good sense of the crowd Mr. Finchley followed the passengers off the boat and so to the Customs shed to be met by the babble of porters crying their numbers. Amidst the confusion he was captured by his porter who cried: "Ici, m'sieur vingt-huit!" and thrusting with a powerful pair of shoulders made a way for him to the counter, where he dumped the bags before the officer who looked at Mr. Finchley and asked him if he had anything to declare, and with his feet firmly on French soil Mr. Finchley took a deep breath and mouthed his first, carefully rehearsed words of French:

"*Rien, m'sieur.*"

The officer scrawled with his chalk on the bags, the porter pounced on them, flinging at Mr. Finchley an interrogative: "Paris train, m'sieur?" and Mr. Finchley followed him, determined not to lose his luggage. The porter stopped him in the hallway with a bluster of incomprehensible French, bullied him into changing two pounds into French currency and then hurried him away to the waiting train where he found his patron a seat, placed the bags on the rack and, with a "Merci bien, m'sieur" for the five-franc tip hurled himself away in search of a fresh victim.

Mr. Finchley took out his handkerchief, wiped his brow and shook his head sadly at the thought of the perturbation of the last five minutes. A traveller, he told himself, should be introduced to a new country less vehemently.

It was late in the afternoon when the train drew into the Gare du Nord. Of the journey from the coast Mr. Finchley had little recollection, for after lunching on the train he had returned to his corner and succumbed to an after-lunch drowsiness which kept him asleep until the train was almost in Paris.

At the station Mr. Finchley avoided porters and carrying his own bags walked out and found himself a taxi and directed the driver to take him to his hotel which was in the Boulevard Haussmann. Mr. Sprake had recommended him to stay at the Hôtel Achille—"They all speak English there, so you'll be all right."

The taxi took Mr. Finchley there, cheaply and quickly. He had heard a lot about Paris taxi-drivers, but he soon discovered that his knowledge was incomplete. The driver interpreted Mr. Finchley's desire to reach the Hôtel Achille as a personal challenge that he could not reach the hotel in fifty seconds under the record. He also gave the impression that all other traffic had entered into a conspiracy to hinder him in his vindication of his prowess. He shouldered his way round corners, bullied smaller cars from his path, flashed under the gendarmes' arms almost before their white batons had dropped, kept his hand impatiently upon his horn whenever held up in a block and swept along the less frequented boulevards with a speed which made the taxi quiver and sway and Mr. Finchley blanch. Had he been the only driver out to break a record Mr. Finchley might have felt safer, for other drivers recognising his insanity would have given him a wide berth. As it was, almost every other car seemed in a like hurry, with the result that Mr. Finchley—fond though he was of speed—spent the last few minutes of the ride in a state of frightened paralysis. He was so disturbed by the time the hotel was reached that he over-paid and over-tipped the driver from agitation and found his way to his room to sink exhausted upon the bed, glad of the stability and comfort of its four legs stoutly placed on solid boards.

And lying upon the bed he discovered that the excitement, the train and the taxi had conspired to give him a headache that took away his interest in dinner and Paris.

With a wisdom which no young man could have mustered, Mr. Finchley took a light meal, sat quietly in the hotel lounge for an hour reading and then went to bed, with the result that he was soon asleep and woke next morning to find his head cleared and all his enthusiasm to see Paris returned, strengthened by his self-control of the previous evening. With luck he would finish with Mr. Hammerton that morning and have the rest of the day free. He meant to return on Sunday.

IV

In which Mr. Finchley becomes a commander and retreats from battle

AFTER a light breakfast, during which he consulted the guide book of the city with which he had provided himself, Mr. Finchley took his dispatch case and set out to see Mr. Hammerton. Mr. Finchley knew that the best way to appreciate a city is to go on foot through its streets, and he had decided to walk to the Hôtel Marivaux where Mr. Hammerton was staying, which was close to the Place de l'Opéra, and not far from Mr. Finchley's hotel.

It was a fine fresh morning. The gutters were full, each with a tiny spate of water turned on by the city authorities to clean them and sweeten the air. From the confectioners' shops came the smell of newly baked bread and cakes, a warm, inviting odour. In the cafés the garçons were busy polishing the table tops while the proprietors cast an eye on the arrangement of the outside tables and their wives sat inside writing out the bill of fare for the day. Mr. Finchley walked along, missing nothing and enjoying everything.

Men and women on their way to business jostled by him on the pavement, low omnibuses clattered down the street, their little observation platforms crowded with business folk who hung over the side, surveying the passing world as though they were tourists on some holiday jaunt rather than workers on their way to toil. The whistles of the traffic policemen shrilled, white batons flashed in the bright sunlight, the underground flung out its bunches of travellers and the shopkeepers stood at their doorways sniffing the air. Paris was taking up the business of another day.

To Mr. Finchley came the sudden realisation that he was a foreigner here, an alien surrounded by so much which was strange and, unlike most English people who regard the term 'foreigner' as being quite inapplicable to themselves, he found a great satisfaction in his uniqueness. It was pleasant to be surrounded by a new idiom and to find that idiom only partly comprehensible. The shops carried names unseen in England—Floquart, Baillou and Dupont; and instead of the honest callings of English baker, butcher and ironmonger, there were those names which smacked so much of French lessons—pâtisserie, charcuterie and quincaillerie. The advertisement hoardings held no familiar legends for him. Instead of Guinness, he was exhorted to drink Dubonnet, and the friendly sailor of Players' cigarettes had given place to a brawny, sea-tanned Viking figure who upheld the virtues of Celtique cigarettes. There were no Freemasons' Arms, no Marquis of Granby, no Bull and Bush or Pig and Whistle; instead countless little cafés each with its own picturesque name: Le Tout-va-Bien, La Cigale, Le Boeuf qui Rit, La Belle Savoie, and one, of which Mr. Finchley was suddenly ashamed, that proclaimed itself Le O.K.

Yesterday, he told himself, he had wakened and stepped out into London streets. Today, he was walking along a Paris pavement. It was a translation so novel to him that he was far from anxious to waive its attractiveness by a show of assumed indifference. Experienced travellers might find it easy to be indifferent to Paris, Vienna or London, but Mr. Finchley did not want himself to forget for one second that he was in Paris. He had plenty of things to remind him of the difference. The homely Underground was now the Métro, the traffic kept to the wrong side of the road, housewives hurried along the pavements with the ends of their long loaves peeping from their bags, soldiers in pale blue overcoats and forage caps passed by taking his mind to stories of the Foreign Legion, the newspaper kiosks were hung with magazines and journals of strange title, and the scraps of conversation which floated to him as he walked were not the familiar: "Well, I said to her, I said—'What do you take me for?' And she said ..."—but equally rapid snatches of commonplace, lifted from dullness because they were spoken in another language.

Arriving at the Hôtel Marivaux, Mr. Finchley summoned his best French to ask the clerk for Mr. Hammerton's room. To his annoyance, the clerk replied in English.

"Hammerton? I do not know the name."

"You must do," said Mr. Finchley sharply, for he had not approved of the other's indifference to his French. "I have an appointment with him at this hotel for this morning."

The clerk frowned and then turned to a pile of papers on the desk behind him. For a moment he shuffled amongst them, then he seized one and returned to Mr. Finchley, his face bright with discovery.

"I beg your pardon, m'sieur. It is right. We have a M'sieur Hammerton. But he is not here—"

"You mean he's out at the moment?"

"No—he is not arrived. We had a room reserved for him, but now he does not come until Tuesday. He telegraphed us late yesterday. Is there anything I can do for m'sieur?"

Mr. Finchley shook his head and, disturbed by the news, went and sat down in the lounge for a moment to think out his position. Obviously this Mr. Hammerton was the sort of person who paid little attention to other people's plans. He had known that Mr. Finchley was to see him on the Saturday, and now he would not be in Paris until Tuesday.

Mr. Finchley went back to the desk and wrote out a telegram to Sprake.

Hammerton not arriving Paris until Tuesday. What shall I do? Finchley.

He sent the telegram off and then, his morning upset by this new turn of events, wandered, dispatch case under his arm, down to the Seine. He leaned across the parapet of the Pont Carrousel and did what every Londoner in Paris very quickly does—compared the Seine with the Thames. As he watched, the only movement on the river came from a motor-barge towing a long line of tarpaulined lighters.

He got back to his hotel in time for lunch and, after eating, he sat in the lounge with a copy of *Le Jour*, waiting for the reply to his telegram. Until Sprake let him know what to do he felt too unsettled to make any plans of his own. And as he sat waiting he found himself hoping that Sprake would not want him to return to London and come back for the meeting on Tuesday. Although by staying in Paris until Tuesday meant that he was virtually having a holiday, there was to be balanced against that the cost of the double journey which would be as expensive as waiting on in Paris. They were not very busy at the office just now, he mused, perhaps Sprake would … He dived into his paper, trying to forget his hopes and fears.

He had told the hotel clerk that he was expecting a telegram and, when he saw the page boy coming towards him, he experienced a sudden tremor of nerves which he attempted to calm by telling himself that no matter what Sprake had advised it made little difference to him; he was a paid servant, and his private hopes must not interfere with his business.

He opened the message and read:

Heard from Hammerton this morning. Stay on until Tuesday. We will charge him. Be good. Sprake.

Mr. Finchley folded the telegram happily, more convinced than ever of Sprake's humanity and generosity. The last sentence of the message was a waste of money and unnecessary, but could any man, he asked himself, have a more indulgent employer? It served Mr. Hammerton right to be charged with the additional expense. He should be more accommodating. Then all these thoughts slipped from his mind as he acknowledged that he was a free man, free to enjoy Paris until Tuesday. When he had left London he had hoped for no more than a few hours' hurried sightseeing. Now he had two days to use as he wished. The prospect sent him to his little guide book, and he spent half an hour working out an itinerary.

Mr. Finchley was the kind of man who could enjoy the theory and practice of a guide book without letting himself become a slave to it. The afternoon he decided should be devoted to seeing some of the accredited sights, while the evening he would leave to itself.

That afternoon Mr. Finchley discovered that to make a plan is one thing, to keep it within strict time limits is another. He saw the Trocadéro, he went up the Eiffel Tower, he walked back along the bank of the Seine to stare at the Chamber of Deputies, and he went from there to the Hôtel des Invalides to see the tomb of Napoleon. But he had no time for Notre-Dame, and the Louvre was shut when he reached it. He went back to his hotel for a cup of tea, slept for an hour and then, refreshed, set out in a northerly direction from the river.

The tale of Mr. Finchley's experiences for the next two hours would be too long to detail. Let it be enough that by seven o'clock he found himself in the neighbourhood of Montmartre, and very hungry. Here he found a quiet restaurant—L'Ange de Normandie—and hidden by an angle of boxed shrubs he ate while he watched the people pass on the pavement. It was his first entirely French meal and no word of English passed his lips. He was surprised how easy it was to make himself understood by pointing to the menu items. He drank red wine and ate rich foods and afterwards, emboldened by the success of his meal and his French, wandered away not caring where he was going, happy in the knowledge that he could get on to the Métro at any time and find his way back to his hotel.

He found himself going up a street which was not unlike the Hampstead Road. There was the same Saturday-evening crowd of flashily dressed young men and women, stallholders crying their wares from the gutter, cafés full of customers, and queues outside the cinemas.

Most of the cinemas, Mr. Finchley noticed, were showing English and American films with French sub-titles, but the sound of his own language was no enticement to him.

After a time the road debouched into a large square which was bordered on one side by a tall, municipal building and on the others by a cinema, some private houses and a succession of cafés. Along the gutter were barrows loaded with fruit and vegetables, stalls from which hawkers sold anything from silk stockings to Japanese fighting fish.

In front of the municipal building a large crowd was gathered, listening to a speaker. From the angry cries and turbulent motions that stirred the crowd Mr. Finchley guessed that not everyone agreed with the speaker. As he watched a scuffle began on the fringe of the crowd. Mr. Finchley moved briskly across the square and entered a café. He was not anxious to find himself mixed up in any political unpleasantness.

The café was a place of glistening brass, shining mirrors and comfortable, padded wall seats, into one of which Mr. Finchley sank with gladness.

"*M'sieur*?" A waiter came to take his order and Mr. Finchley, remembering the wine he had taken at dinner, ordered himself a grenadine. In the old days at Boulogne he had been fond of grenadine, though it was too soft and sweet for most Englishmen. He would have liked to try some of the other drinks he saw the customers taking, but his ignorance of their names and his timidness in speaking French kept him from them.

Around him people were sitting talking, nearer the door four men were playing cards, and tucked away in a corner a woman was writing a letter with materials provided by the café.

When Mr. Finchley had finished his grenadine he felt more at home, and catching the waiter's eye, he signalled to him.

"*M'sieur?*" The waiter stood expectantly.

Mr. Finchley steeled himself and said, in French, hesitantly:

"I would like to try some other drink."

For a moment the waiter showed his surprise, then he said:

"*Pardon,* m*'sieur?*"

Mr. Finchley repeated his remark, making it sound stranger than ever in his nervousness.

The waiter, anxious to prove his intelligence, but unable to understand Mr. Finchley's nervous pronunciation, brightly remarked that M'sieur was English, no?

Mr. Finchley nodded and said, resignedly: "Grenadine." Unless his French improved or he found a list of drinks to point to, he looked like drinking grenadine and coffee for the rest of his visit.

But Mr. Finchley was not to have his grenadine. The waiter brought the drink and politely helped Mr. Finchley to ice. Mr. Finchley was about to take his glass and drink when, through the open doorway he suddenly became aware that the hubbub of noises in the square had risen to a higher, angrier pitch, and then he forgot the noises as one of the windows of the café was shattered by a large piece of stone which came flying across the room. It missed the card players by a foot, nearly took the nose off the waiter and landed full on Mr. Finchley's table, sweeping his glass to the floor.

"*Mon Dieu!*" exclaimed the waiter excitedly, and added, fiercely: "*Sacrés communistes!*"

He was gone, forgetting his duties, on some personal mission. Mr. Finchley had no time to speculate on the waiter's political tendencies, for with his going pandemonium broke out all around. The drinkers at other tables jumped up and dashed towards the door, the card players rose and, shaking their fists towards the hole in the glass, shouted curses at this interruption of their game. Then they joined the dash towards the door. The woman writing letters stuffed them into her bag and, with feminine caution, hid under the table, and from the back of the café swept the proprietor, his wife and their four children throwing up their hands in horror at the broken glass and, taking their cue from father, spitting imprecations towards the square. Another stone sailed through the doorway, cracking a large mirror on the wall, and Mr. Finchley decided that he would be safer out in the square than in the café which had become a target for stones.

Circling round the proprietor, who was calling upon heaven to witness the injustice of this visitation, he hurried to the doorway and out into the square. When he had first seen the square it had been full of a pleasant Saturday-night bustle. Now it was in a turmoil. The meeting near the municipal building had overflowed in a tangled, struggling mass of humanity, and the rest of the square had taken up the quarrel with no lack of enthusiasm. Stalls were overturned, women ran shrieking away up the side streets or urged their menfolk on to fierce deeds of valour, hawkers stood over their tumbled goods defending them vociferously, hooligans, quite unaffected by the political issues, seized the opportunity to hurl stones at the windows of cafés whose proprietors had incurred their dislike, and a small knot of policemen advanced in phalanx, with striking batons, towards the centre of the maelstrom, obviously deluded by the idea that once they reached the centre of this fight everything would be quieted.

The moment Mr. Finchley stepped outside the café, although he did not realise it, he forfeited his right to neutrality. All the neutrals had fled at the first whisper of strife. A loud cry of "Sacré bourgeoisie!" on his left made him turn in time to see a long-haired, red-tied youth charging down upon him. The next few seconds held a vindication of the protective instinct that lurks even in the mildest mannered of men. There was only one sensible thing for Mr. Finchley to do, and he did it. He waited until his assailant was two feet from him, then he side-stepped smartly and, as the other passed, gave him a buffet on the side of the head which took the young man off his balance and the skin from Mr. Finchley's knuckles. He had the satisfaction of seeing the other land up on top of a pile of vegetables from whence he was heartily kicked into the thick of the crowd by an indignant hawker.

By that blow Mr. Finchley definitely abandoned all neutrality and called attention upon himself. A small, peak-faced man rushed up to him, embraced him on both cheeks, and calling him "My brave commander!" tugged him off the pavement towards the fray, and at the same time two men, guessing his partisanship from the presence of the peak-faced man, bore down upon him, and Mr. Finchley with his unknown comrade was engaged in a scrimmage before he had time to disentangle himself. The four of them went to the ground in a heap, arms pounding at each other, the air full of excited French and protesting English cries.

For some time they struggled and then the wave of battle passed over them, bearing away Mr. Finchley's assailants and his supporter and he was left, sitting on the pavement, a little dazed and undecided. Around him was the debris of upturned stalls, and encircling him like a dance of wild tribes were the struggling figures of frenzied men. Five minutes ago, Mr. Finchley told himself, his interest in the contrast causing him momentarily to accept his position on the pavement, he had been happily drinking. Now ... he stared at his wide-spread legs that sheltered a bunch of carrots, a cracked bottle of hair oil that oozed peacefully away, and somebody's cap.

As he sat there, from the circle of struggling men a small boy broke away and came dashing along the pavement, and close behind him raced a broad-shouldered hawker, his face twisted into a menacing grimace of rage. The whole scene presented itself to Mr. Finchley with the precision and rapidity of a cinematograph shot and he knew that if the hawker caught him, the boy would get no mercy for whatever had been his sin. It might even be, ran his momentary analysis of the case, that the hawker was going to revenge his political scruples upon the innocent offspring of an opponent. Mr. Finchley did not consider it just to visit the political sins of the father upon the son and consequently, with a spontaneity which arose jointly from his concern with justice and his sympathy for the boy, he allowed the boy to pass him and then thrust out his foot in the path of the hawker. As he did so the boy, knowing himself hard-pressed, doubled around a lamp standard and shot back along his course and, seeing the stumbling hawker and Mr. Finchley's outstretched foot, he understood the whole design.

The hawker, the victim of his own speed and girth, tripped over Mr. Finchley's foot and went flying head-first towards an ironmongery stall which the promethean labours of the stall-holder and his two sons had kept intact. They were no proof against this human thunderbolt. The hawker broke through their defensive cordon, whirling them aside, and struck the stall broadside, sending it toppling to a fine accompaniment of rattling tins, bouncing saucepans and jingling pails and pans.

Mr. Finchley knew at once that it was unwise for him to dally in the neighbourhood. Before the last pan had bounced to silence, he was up and hurrying in the wake of the small boy. Luckily for him, a swirl of the crowd closed behind him, shutting off effectively all chance of pursuit.

Dodging fighting groups, Mr. Finchley worked his way from the square to the comparative peace of the road by which he had entered it. Here was assembled a curious crowd, forming a barricade between square and road, which watched the struggle with technical appreciation, and when any of the combatants threatened to overflow into the road, pushed them back again with the greatest good humour and advice. Mr. Finchley pushed his way through them, refusing to be cast back into the fight. Once by the crowd, he turned aside into a quiet alleyway to adjust his clothes which were disordered. He had lost his hat, his pipe and his breastpocket handkerchief, but apart from this he felt himself sound.

"M'sieur is not hurt?"

The question, in French, came from behind him, and looking round Mr. Finchley met the inquisitive regard of the small boy he had rescued from the hawker. He was a thinnish, bright-faced boy with a well-formed, sensitive mouth and a nose which was tipped upwards at the end to give his face a rather elusive air that set one guessing. It was a face alive with the unconquerable spirit of boyhood, that one moment suggested a timid reserve and the next, in a curl of lip or the wrinkles about his eyes, disclosed a happy-go-lucky fearlessness. His hair was dark and in need of trimming, his face was marked with dirt and his clothes, Mr. Finchley saw at once, were those of a poor boy.

Mr. Finchley nodded to indicate that he was all right and started to brush himself down.

"Ah, m'sieur, I saw what you did," cried the boy. "It was very kind of you. He was chasing me on account of this!" As he finished speaking he brought one hand from behind his back and held up to Mr. Finchley a large haddock.

"Good gracious me!" Mr. Finchley recoiled from the odorous fish. His surprise was so great that he spoke in English. At his words the boy opened his eyes wide and then, still retaining hold of the fish, jumped towards Mr. Finchley, attempting to embrace him and crying in a jumble of French and English

"Oh, you are English! M'sieur is English! What joy! Me, also, I am English like m'sieur. We are two English people together. Gosh! What a thing to happen to me. Listen, m'sieur, I will show you how English I am. London stands on the Thames, the Thames rises in the Cotswolds and there are always pretty girls at Hen … Hen … I have forgotten. But there is the other which my father taught me to remember. The best cider is in Somerset, the best cheese in Cheshire, the best drinking is in Flea Street, and the finest county is Devon, because that is where my father was born …"

The boy's words came tumbling out in a rapid spate and Mr. Finchley recognised beneath the French accent the unmistakable tones of an English voice.

V
Of ice-cream and escalators

THERE are some minds which, far from being thrown out of gear by unexpected excitement, seem to draw from a crisis a motive power that enables them to work with more than normal ease and precision. The reaction of individuals to the unexpected can seldom be gauged beforehand. Some achieve the superb omniscience of Sherlock Holmes, others the conventional banality of Dr. Stanley, and some are submerged in a flurry of inarticulate nervousness. Mr. Finchley's reaction acknowledged a little of wisdom, a touch of convention, and a dash of nervousness.

"If you are English," he said, covering his agitation with a show of sternness, "why did you steal that haddock?" From his manner an impartial observer might have assumed that, for an Englishman, haddock stealing was one of the major crimes, a violation of a taboo surviving from the barbaric days when the rough islanders drew their living from the encircling sea.

The boy, obviously perplexed by the conjunction of haddocks and Englishmen, and impressed by Mr. Finchley's sternness, gave an answer which Mr. Finchley, his presence of mind returning, had to admit to himself was as good in France as it would have been in England.

"Because I was hungry, m'sieur, and wanted something to eat, and because it was lying on the ground with lots of other fishes. I did not think he would mind, but he did. I am sorry if I have done wrong and annoyed m'sieur, but when one is hungry …" He shrugged his shoulders expressively.

For a moment Mr. Finchley wondered whether he should venture into a forensic explanation of the boy's wrong, but seeing ahead of him the old tangle about the woman who stole bread to feed her starving children, he conciliated his sense of justice with the sensible thought that the hawker would not miss the haddock very much and the boy had to eat.

"When did you eat last?" he asked.

"This morning, very early, m'sieur."

That settled Mr. Finchley. Although he knew little enough about children, he remembered from his own childhood the often-repeated maxim that a young body needed regular and plentiful feeding to help it in its growth. He disengaged the haddock from the boy's hand and tossed it away up the alley to await some marauding cat and led the boy across the road to a small café which displayed a board on which was announced boldly:

Plat du Jour—Choucroute Garnie

6 Francs.

He took the boy inside and ordered him the meal of the day, and no word was spoken until the proprietor brought the steaming plate of cabbage and sausage.

For a second or two the boy was incredulous of this hospitality. He looked at the plate and then at Mr. Finchley and said: "This is for me, m'sieur?"

Mr. Finchley nodded and said: "Get on with it, youngster. I've already had my dinner."

He sat back and watched the boy eat, and for the first time in his life knew the pleasure of watching a child enjoy food which he had provided. Mr. Finchley had made very few contacts with children in his life. For him they were suspect, they had untidy habits, peculiar manners and an occasional frankness which could be most embarrassing. As he watched this boy he found himself stirring with a growing curiosity. What was an English boy doing roaming about the streets of Paris at night? For a moment his mind toyed with the romantic convention of a homeless, unwanted waif, but a glance at the boy's clothes and his manner proved that he had some anchorage in the city, and he had spoken of his father.

The boy finished his choucroute, sighed in the long-drawn way of children acknowledging a full stomach, and pulled towards him the coffee which Mr. Finchley had ordered for him.

He smiled at Mr. Finchley and said pleasantly: "You are very kind to me, sir. Are you my friend?"

Mr. Finchley chuckled and answered: "I think you'll want a few friends if you're going to make a habit of stealing haddocks, young man."

"Oh, I won't do that again, m'sieur," the boy assured him seriously. "Not now I know you don't like it."

"What's your name?" Mr. Finchley asked, a little ashamed of his curiosity.

"I am called Robert … Robert Gillespie." He pronounced the name in French fashion, and volunteered: "I am English, m'sieur. Oh, I am very English, too, in my ways. All my friends call me the Englishman because of my ways. I am ten years of age and I live with my guardian, Pépé Rivel."

"But what about your father?"

"He is dead," the boy replied with a calmness that showed he had suffered no recent loss. "So is my mother. That is why I live with Pépé. What is m'sieur called?"

Mr. Finchley told him, and found that this was only the preliminary to a series of questions.

"M'sieur is staying at the Hôtel Achille? That is a magnificent place! M'sieur must be very rich? And m'sieur comes from England? From London?"

"Haven't you ever been to London?"

"No, m'sieur. I have never been to England. But some day I will go. My father talked always of England." His dark eyes shone with a swift memory, and Mr. Finchley was suddenly resentful of those circumstances which had set this young boy down in France, denying him the simplest of birthrights, a knowledge of his own country.

"One day, perhaps you will go," said Mr. Finchley. "But it's getting late and you should be going home. Where do you live?"

"By the river, near the Quai de la Rapée, but I will walk back with you."

"You'll do nothing of the sort at this time of night. I'll put you on the underground for the station nearest your home. We're a long way from the Seine and from my hotel."

"But Paris is very interesting at night. I could repay you for your kindness by showing you all the things on the way …"

"Home for you!" said Mr. Finchley stoutly, and, despite all the boy's protests, he marched him to the nearest Métro station and journeyed with him as far as he could before he had to change stations for his hotel. His last sight of the boy was the lad's thin, excited face pressed against the window of the carriage as the train moved out of the station, a dirty hand waved at him and a nose wrinkled in a friendly gesture.

Mr. Finchley smiled. Then, realising how tired he was, forgot the boy, and went on towards his hotel with an unfeigned thankfulness at the thought of bed. His sleep was troubled that night with phantoms of arguing, fighting Frenchmen wearing red ties and the coming and going of small boys waving haddocks at him.

He awoke late to find a strong sun touching the edge of his bed. He got up, shaved himself leisurely, and, eschewing the French breakfast, did justice to eggs and bacon and marmaladed toast, and afterwards spent a quarter of an hour in his bedroom choosing himself a hat from a selection which the hotel management had sent up for him. The hat problem had worried Mr. Finchley for a while on waking until the hotel clerk had pointed out, with a wink, that although it was Sunday there was always a way to get such things. Mr. Finchley did not enquire into the way. He accepted the service gratefully.

A little conscious of his new hat, and with his pipe going well, Mr. Finchley went out to enjoy the morning air and find his way to the Champs Elysées, which was next on his list of places to visit. He stood for a moment on the hotel steps, puffing at his pipe and surveying the morning. It was a warm, golden day; the soft light from the sky filtered through the leafy trees to touch the grey stones of the street with mellow tints. From where he stood Mr. Finchley had a view along the boulevard, a fine stretch of trees and pleasantly constructed shops and houses. There was a feeling of space and leisure seldom found in London, and Mr. Finchley decided that Paris was a beautiful city, a city which managed to be a capital without being ugly and too busy for beauty.

He lingered for a while, obsessed with the fanciful thought that if he moved, everything about him would be spirited away and he would find himself back in Hampstead with the clink of a milk-cart going up Nassington Avenue in his ears. Then his eye caught that of the porter, who was watching him with some curiosity, since few of the guests of the hotel practised the habit of coming to the vestibule steps on a fine morning and sniffing the air like a pointer while they beamed good humour at the passing world. The porter wished there were more such people.

Mr. Finchley, hating to be conspicuous, descended the steps and moved away up the pavement. He had not gone far when he felt a tug at his arm and a familiar voice said:

"*Bonjour, m'sieur*. I hope you have slept very well? Pépé says that the world does not properly appreciate the blessing of sleep."

Mr. Finchley looked round to find the boy, Robert, at his side.

"Where on earth did you spring from?" he asked in surprise.

The boy smiled. "I have been waiting for m'sieur. I have discussed the matter with Pépé and he agrees with me that as you have been so kind and are my friend, then I must repay you. But how, we asked ourselves? Then I have an idea. I said: "'M'sieur is an Englishman and although he speaks French better than you speak English, Pépé, he is a stranger in Paris, so I will go to him and offer him my services.'" Then Pépé makes me wash and put on these clothes and I have been waiting for m'sieur to come out."

Mr. Finchley looked at the boy. His hair was glossy with water, his face bright from a scrubbing and he was wearing a clean, open-necked blue shirt and a tight red jumper which, being short in the sleeves, gave his arms a queer anthropoidal lengthiness. He wore no stockings, and on his feet were a pair of brown sandals. Mr. Finchley saw at once that although Pépé might not be well-off, he appreciated the virtues of cleanliness and tidiness. Then he frowned, a little disconcerted by this reappearance of Robert. He was far from pleased at the prospect of taking the boy as a guide. He had been looking forward to a day's sightseeing by himself and was in no mood to alter his plans.

The boy saw the momentary clouding of Mr. Finchley's face and understood. He said very quietly, "But perhaps, m'sieur, you would wish to be by yourself? I shall understand."

Mr. Finchley did not have to understand children to know what it had cost the boy to make his declaration. His voice betrayed the disappointment he was fighting to keep down, and as he stood there, looking down at this dark-haired youngster, he felt suddenly ashamed of himself. No one with any humanity would have disappointed a boy who had come with such good motives and open friendliness. For a moment he hesitated—there was still time to tell the boy pleasantly that he was not wanted and to send him away with a five-franc tip to keep him happy. Yet, somehow, Mr. Finchley had an uneasy feeling that a tip would not salve this boy's disappointment. He scratched his chin with the tip of his thumb-nail and eyed Robert in perplexity. The boy, anxious, made no sound or move for fear of prejudicing the decision he guessed was being made. Had Mr. Finchley realised just how much his decision would sway the unravelling band of his future, he might have taken longer in reaching a decision. He was a traveller in the night, aware of a fork in the road but denied the light to read the signpost.

"So you want to be my guide, do you?" he asked, his mind made up.

"If you will allow me," said Robert, his eyes brightening at this hopeful opening. "Pépé said I was not to worry you if you did not wish it, and I shall understand if you wish me to go …"

"Of course not!" cried Mr. Finchley heartily. "You are engaged as my guide for today. But," he added seriously, "there is one thing which worries me—"

"What is that, m'sieur?"

"Well, if you had not come along I should have had to get another guide to show me around, and I should have paid him, of course. Now, even though we two are friends, I cannot allow you to give your services for nothing. I have no doubt that were you not coming with me you would have found work as a guide with someone else. I must not impose upon our friendship to that extent. What are your charges?"

The boy's eyes opened at this, and for a while he stared at Mr. Finchley. Into his eyes came a look of pride and delight.

"Do you really mean that, sir? "he asked.

"Of course. Before we set off we must settle the terms. What do you charge?"

For a moment Robert deliberated silently, his mind torn with an anxiety not to overcharge, his pride delighted by this recognition of his value as a guide.

"Would five francs suit, m'sieur? That," he added with less conviction, "is what I usually charge my ladies and gentlemen."

"Excellent," agreed Mr. Finchley. "Five francs for the morning and five francs for the afternoon. That's settled."

"And now," said Robert, assuming his duties as guide, "what had m'sieur in mind to see?"

"Well, I want to go to the Louvre."

"M'sieur!" Robert raised his hands in horror.

"What's the matter? "asked Mr. Finchley quickly.

"M'sieur—you cannot want to see the Louvre, and on a Sunday morning when it is so crowded. If you must go you should go some time in the week when there are fewer people and you can be sure of getting a seat to sit on when you are tired."

"Perhaps you're right," agreed Mr. Finchley. "I did intend to see the Champs Elysées."

"You did? "Robert's voice had a livelier tone.

"Yes, I've heard a lot about it. Do you approve of that?"

"Of course, m'sieur, but it is only an avenue. We should really have a place to visit. Do you like escalators, m'sieur?"

"Lifts?"

"That is it—I knew there was another English word. Do you like them?"

"Why, yes. But—"

"Then that is good. We can walk up the Champs Elysées towards the Arc de Triomphe. That shall be our place to visit. There is a lift there, m'sieur—it is a little dearer than walking up the stairs, but what is that? We can go up in the lift to the top and you will see Paris beneath you."

Their itinerary decided, they set out; Mr. Finchley, his little red guide book in hand, and Robert bouncing happily at his side, his voice pouring out a stream of information.

"See, m'sieur, outside each Métro station there is a map and the station is marked with a red circle. That soldier—he is one of the African Battalion, they are very famous. The name of that church? I am afraid I don't—But, of course, it is the Madeleine. You are quite right, m'sieur; that is a very clever book you have."

They turned into the Place de la Concorde.

"And what," said Mr. Finchley, turning the leaves of his book, "is that?" He pointed to the tall Egyptian needle that dominated the centre of the place.

"That?" Robert frowned, eyeing the needle seriously. "Well, that, that, m'sieur, is a monument. Yes, it is a monument," he declared happily. "And it was here that there were the riots recently. Ha, if you could have seen the bloodshed and the tyranny of the Guarde Mobile. It was here that Pépé himself was injured in the fight. Come, I will show you the very spot. Many times has Pépé pointed it out and told the story."

And Mr. Finchley, who was more anxious to read about the needle, was hurried across the place to the spot where the fabulous Pépé had valiantly opposed three guards only to be battered into a patriotic stupidity by their batons.

"See, it is this very stone where he fell and was rescued by his compatriots before the firing and murder began." Robert spoke with great heat, putting into his story all the vigour which belonged to Pépé. "Even now he treasures the tunic button of the guard he first vanquished."

They turned up the Champs Elysées. Up and down the road spun an endless succession of cars, and along the pavements, under the shade of the flowering chestnuts, walked a gay, holiday throng. The gardens were fresh and coloured with blossom-loaded clumps of shrubs; the fountains sent great sprays and fans of misty water into the air, iridescent moments of beauty that played a second in the sunshine and then dropped away in the breeze to wet the pavements, or met the brown water held in the wide, ornamented basins. Nursemaids played with their charges in the gardens, young lovers sat on the seats and watched the fat pigeons strutting across the gravel, grave men with pointed beards and black cravats shook out their papers and read, indifferent to the hubbub around them, smartly dressed men and women went by, chattering and laughing, and about the feet of the crowd trotted the oddest assortment of dogs that Mr. Finchley had ever seen. There were diminutive French bulldogs, poodles carrying their puffs and bareness with a haughty disdain for vulgar comment, midget black-and-tan dogs with mousy ears and mincing gait, and once an English mastiff, slouching along with bowed head, its great eyes full of mysterious sadness and gloom.

"Now this, I suppose," said Mr. Finchley, stopping to consult his book as the bulk of a building showed through the trees, "is the Grand Palais."

"Yes, that is so," Robert assured him.

"No, it can't be," said Mr. Finchley, unfolding his map. "It must be the Petit Palais, or have we passed them both and is it the Palais de Glace. Which is it, Robert?"

Robert looked first at him and then at the building. "Well, I should say—oh, m'sieur, there is a most beautiful motor-car going by."

"The name of the palace?" said Mr. Finchley stubbornly, refusing to be drawn.

"Does it matter, m'sieur?" Robert defended his ignorance with a show of logic. "You have seen it—what does it matter about its name? Besides, there is the lift waiting for us."

"I want to know its name," said Mr. Finchley, and he sat down so that he might manage his map easier. Robert stood by, kicking pieces of gravel and waiting impatiently. It was some time before Mr. Finchley got the map oriented and settled the name of the building.

"You will understand, m'sieur," said Robert as they moved on, feeling the need to vindicate himself, "it is not possible for a guide to know everything. Now there are hundreds of other places … It is sad that you should have picked upon the one place I did not know. But apart from that I have satisfied you so far as a guide, have I not?"

"Yes," said Mr. Finchley, his reply long-drawn with doubt. Then smiling to banish the boy's fears, he went on: "Of course, there are some questions even the best guides cannot answer."

As they entered the higher slope of the avenue, a stretch which has now lost its old residential beauty to an invasion of glittering shops and cinemas, where highly polished cars, gay dresses and the groomed smiles of film-stars tout for the attention of every pedestrian, Robert forgot his dragomanic worries and the conversation passed away to generalities.

"Are the streets like this in London? "he asked.

"A few," replied Mr. Finchley; "but there are no cafés, of course."

"No cafés!" Robert was astonished. "And are there no ice-cream barrows?" He pointed to a white and gold stall presided over by a dark-skinned Italian.

"Oh, yes, we have ice-cream barrows."

"And do English boys and girls buy ice-cream and eat it as they walk along?"

"They do."

"That is good. If ever I went to London I should be unhappy if there was no ice-cream. Pépé and I are very fond of it." He was silent for a moment, and then went on, tentatively: "I suppose, m'sieur, you would not object if I used some of my wages to buy myself ice-cream? If you have no objection, perhaps you could make some arrangement, for you see ..." His sentence tailed away.

Mr. Finchley helped Robert from his embarrassment.

"I should have no objection at all, Robert. Only I insist that it is part of my privilege to supply my guide with refreshment. That is the arrangement with all the best guides."

"You are very kind. I am very fortunate in having you for my friend."

They went up to the stall and Robert asked for an ice.

"*Chocolat ou vanille*?" enquired the ice-cream man.

"Vanilla, please," said Robert.

"And for m'sieur—" the Italian looked at Mr. Finchley.

Mr. Finchley shook his head. Robert said urgently "You must have some, too. It is so hot."

"No." Mr. Finchley was adamant, and added quite untruthfully: "I do not like ice-cream." Robert uncovered his little cup and, digging at the firm ice, walked soberly away, enjoying the coolness of the sweet, entirely oblivious of the life of the avenue, and Mr. Finchley followed him, feeling very self-conscious. He was not used to the company of small boys who ate ice-cream vigorously and noisily. The thought worried him for a time, until he consoled himself with the reflection that in France there was more freedom of expression and few French people would have found anything incongruous in his conduct.

Robert finished his ice and gaily threw the cup into the roadway.

"You should not do that," said Mr. Finchley, finding a way to salve some of the uneasiness that came from his loss of dignity. "It creates a litter and"—this was a shrewd shot—"it is most un-English."

"Oh, m'sieur! "Robert was contrite at once.

"I am so sorry. Of course, it was wrong of me." And he turned towards the roadway to retrieve the cup. Mr. Finchley caught his arm in time. In his eagerness the boy would have gone charging into the stream of traffic.

"Let it be this time," he said. "But remember in future. Never make litter."

Robert, conscious of his lapse from grace, was subdued for a while, and even passed the interesting dog shop where he had planned to stop, without more than a look over his shoulder towards it. But by the time they had reached the Arc de Triomphe his spirits had returned. All the way up the avenue the great archway had been before them, a four-legged colossus. Now they were standing in its shade.

"This is it," said Robert unnecessarily. "We will go up in the lift and see Paris from the top." In his eagerness he tugged Mr. Finchley across the open circle of traffic, dodging taxis and buses, bringing Mr. Finchley panting and thankful to the haven of the Arc.

They went up to the small entrance to get their tickets for the lift. At once Robert's face expressed annoyance.

"What's the matter? "asked Mr. Finchley.

"It is the lift," said Robert. "It's out of order." He pointed to a notice.

"That doesn't matter, we'll walk up," said Mr. Finchley, anxious to be at the top.

"But, m'sieur, it is a long climb. Perhaps we had better not go. It would have been so much pleasanter in the lift. You will be so tired climbing—"

"You're making the fuss about climbing, not me," said Mr. Finchley, laughing. "I believe you only brought me here so that you could have a ride in the lift."

"Oh, no! I want you to see the view. It is magnificent."

"Then come along."

They began their climb, Robert running ahead and Mr. Finchley taking it easy. The stairway was dark and echoing with the voices of other climbers. Occasionally Robert came running back to encourage Mr. Finchley.

"It is not far now."

Mr. Finchley reached a long vault-like room directly under the roof of the Arc which had been turned into a museum. He would have liked to stay here a while to rest, but Robert would not let him, and a few moments later he came out on the top and was glad that he had not dallied in the museum.

He went to the parapet, which he considered dangerously low, and sat down. His head was not good for heights. Robert stood by him. In the clear morning light all Paris was beneath him. Radiating like the spokes of a gigantic wheel stretched the great avenues that ran so straightly from the tall archway, bearing names famous in French history: Wagram, Friedland, Kleber and Foch. Floating out of the grey mist of roof tops and the green islands of trees rose the milk-white cupola of Sacré Coeur, the slender pylon of Eiffel Tower and the tall façade of the Trocadéro.

Mr. Finchley leaned on the parapet, enchanted by a view which few other cities could equal in breadth and variety. Beneath him was all Paris, a city whose name was a magic to wake a thousand different emotions, through whose heart looped the Seine, serving the city as the Thames served London, as though to prove that all great cities must stand by water since man cannot make a home if he has not the sight and sound of running water to capture his affections.

The climb had made Mr. Finchley's legs ache, and he was glad to sit down, and the view held him, his eyes continually discovering fresh pleasures. There was a joy in being so high, lifted above the city, that floated through him like a wine, filling his head with fancies. Had he ever been part of the ant-like movement below him? Traffic, people and houses seemed so toy-like; the only real things were the distance and the stone parapet. He revelled in his isolation, forgetting the people about him, conscious only of the city spread out for his enjoyment, and Robert, seeing his interest, left him quietly to wander away.

This Mr. Finchley was his friend, but he did not fully understand him yet. He was sure, however, that just now Mr. Finchley wanted to be left alone, and Robert respected that desire.

It was some time before Mr. Finchley discovered that Robert was no longer with him. He was not alarmed. The top of the Arc was wide and a structure in its centre hid the other side from him. He got up and walked around to the other side. As he had thought, Robert was there. Seeing the boy, he quickened his pace, for Robert was leaning well over the parapet, so far over that Mr. Finchley felt a faint stirring of vertigo within himself.

He was within three yards of the boy when he stopped suddenly, every instinct of decency within him repelled by what he saw. Robert was leaning well over the parapet, industriously spitting to the ground far below, and the wind, blowing from behind, was helping him.

VI
In which Mr. Finchley bumps into a friend

MR. FINCHLEY was justly shocked. Expectoration is not a pleasant habit for an adult, and it is little excuse that the habit has been indulged by the worthiest of men, generally seafarers. The civilised code implies an abhorrence of the habit. But small boys seldom have a great deal of respect for conventions and they find it hard to restrain the instinctive homage which all bridges and great heights demand of them. There is, for a child at least, something tragically beautiful in the slow curve and quickening drop, excitement in the wind-frayed passage and the violent annihilation on pavement or the gentle absorption into mother river. Salivation at the sight of food belongs to men and dogs, but in the salivation evoked by heights and unrepressed by children lies a sign denoting man's growing divergence from the animal world.

There was no ill-will in Robert. He intended no harm towards any pedestrian. We are all brought into this world to accept our share of bad luck, and it is a mark of humanity to accept bad luck with a smile. And it could be said in vindication of his pleasure that the wind had dissipated his spittle into fine spray long before it reached the gravel.

Mr. Finchley was, however, in no frame of mind to seek any justification for Robert. Into his head flowed a medley of words—decency, self-respect, orthodoxy, vulgarity—and he hurried forward angrily, crying "Robert!"

At the sound of his voice Robert turned from the parapet, his face heavy with a swift guilt.

"M'sieur—"

Before he could say more and before Mr. Finchley could do anything, someone passed Mr. Finchley and seized Robert sternly by the shoulder, and a torrent of French swirled around Mr. Finchley as he watched a uniformed attendant shaking Robert and speaking excitedly to him.

"Robert, what on earth is he saying?" Mr. Finchley drew nearer.

The attendant looked at Mr. Finchley and then at Robert. Obviously restraining himself for a moment until he was sure, he asked Mr. Finchley

"Is this your boy?"

Mr. Finchley understood him, opened his mouth to explain their exact relationship and, because it was easier, said "Yes." That was enough. The attendant dropped Robert's arm and approached Mr. Finchley. Thrusting his face close to him, so that a warm smell of garlic and stale cigarette enveloped Mr. Finchley, he let loose a spate of French which sailed turbulently by Mr. Finchley's uncomprehending ears and was whipped away by the wind to be scattered into space.

Robert stood uncomfortably, witnessing everything, his one relief the knowledge that Mr. Finchley would be far from understanding all that was being said to him. The attendant was expressing, on behalf of the city authorities and the citizens of Paris, exactly what he felt about a man who was so degraded, so lost to human decency that he deliberately brought his son to the top of the most venerable monument in Paris, the archway dedicated to the glory of Napoleon, the last resting place of the Unknown Warrior, and from the top encouraged his son to befoul the pavements below and besmirch the innocent pedestrians with his filthy ejaculations. And when he had finished his remonstrance on behalf of others he added an equally long tirade on his own behalf in which he speculated sarcastically and rudely about Mr. Finchley's antecedents, the probable vileness of his ancestors and the ultimate fate which must lie in store for one who was so sunk in vice and sacrilege. He outlined one or two appropriate ends for such a man and then, putting on the brakes, slowed down and came to an end with the slow, magnificent question:

"*Et, voilà*! What have you to say to all that?" And Mr. Finchley, who, apart from a word here and there, had understood nothing but this last remark, which had been spoken clearly and slowly, decided upon a policy of politeness and said in French good enough for the man to comprehend his meaning:

"Do you mind repeating what you've just said? You spoke a little too quickly for me to understand everything."

As Mr. Finchley finished speaking there was a little pause, during which there rose to the top of the Arc the thin, gnat's noises of the world below. Then the attendant exploded. He flung his arms in the air, turned his face to the skies and cried aloud his agony, and to him there came hurrying the few people who were on top of the monument. They gathered around, eager-faced and expectant, and turning to them the attendant recited the whole story, volubly, gesticulating, passion marking his face in twisted lines.

He was only a man. He was human and he had a duty to perform. The crowd knew it, he told them to make it quite clear. But how could he do his duty when confronted by such stupidity and such people? These Germans—Mr. Finchley caught the word Allemands, and vaguely wondered why he should be talking about Germans—what could one do with them and their dirty spitting habits? When he had finished and was assured of the crowd's sympathy and support, he turned to Robert and Mr. Finchley, and flinging one arm towards the exit, cried out for them to go, and Mr. Finchley needed no understanding of the language to discover his meaning.

Deciding that discretion was the wisest move, he took Robert's arm and moved towards the stairway, and as he passed the crowd drew back from his contamination as though he were a leper discovered in a healthy city. The gloom of the stairway rose to meet him and behind him rang out the words "*Sacrés Allemands*!" And Mr. Finchley felt that not to be recognised as an Englishman was even more humiliating than to have been cast out of the Arc de Triomphe.

Mr. Finchley was hurt at the injustice he had received and annoyed because he had been denied an explanation. He descended the stairs, growing angrier every moment, and Robert, who was ahead of him, knowing how he was to blame, kept turning a woeful and tearful face back to him, protesting his sorrow.

"M'sieur, I am so sorry. I am so desolated. It was all my fault."

"Yes, it was your fault!" cried Mr. Finchley sharply. "I thought you were an English boy and knew how to behave. And don't keep waving your arms about and telling me how sorry you are—"

"Oh, m'sieur, how just is your anger. I deserve to be spoken to so harshly. I am very unhappy." And Robert really was very unhappy, and the tears that trembled at the corners of his eyes were genuine enough. Before they reached the bottom of the stairway Mr. Finchley had begun to lose some of his anger and had realised that he was less angry with Robert than with the attendant.

"Don't say anything about it!" he ordered tersely, as Robert began to make a fresh admission of sorrow when they were in the daylight. Robert was silent and followed Mr. Finchley into the Avenue Foch where they found a seat and sat down in the sunlight. Mr. Finchley pulled out his pipe, turned his back on the Arc de Triomphe and began to smoke. In five minutes he felt calmer, and another five minutes found him able to review the incident dispassionately.

Robert watched him anxiously, taking great care not to fidget. Mr. Finchley knocked out his pipe and turned to him.

"Listen to me, Robert," he said. "I intend to say little about your bad behaviour, except that I hope you will never allow yourself to be so naughty again. That's all, and now let's forget the whole affair. It's too fine a day to be bad-tempered."

Robert accepted the forgiveness gratefully, and a little while later they were walking into the Bois de Boulogne, carrying under their arms rolls and sausages which Robert had bought.

"A lot of people in Paris do this," explained Robert. "It is pleasant to take food into the Bois."

The Bois was a wilder, untidier Hyde Park. Dotted among the trees and by the edges of the lakes were family parties picnicking.

Mr. Finchley and Robert found a spot in the shade of some bushes by the lakeside and sat down to their meal. Robert chatted merrily and Mr. Finchley let him run on, taking a pleasure in the boy's eager talk and untiring interest in the things around him. To him, it was a new experience. In the centre of the lake moved low skiffs and canoes, and inshore, ducks made their way from one party to another, squabbling over the food thrown to them. The birds excited Robert and he threw most of his roll to them, scolding when a fat drake, with a neck that changed colour like cooling metal, greedily captured most of the bread.

"It is as Pépé says," he remarked seriously. "When charity is given it goes, not to the poor and weak, but the big and strong who can fight for it."

Mr. Finchley did not contradict this axiom. He found himself growing curious about the philosophical Pépé and a little disturbed by the occasional grown-up remarks of Robert. He saw in them an indication that the boy had spent more time than was wise in the company of adults, and he was dimly worried at the thought that the boy should not have had his proper share of young companionship. Yet, he could not deny the evident happiness which animated Robert, even in his wisest moments.

After they had eaten, Mr. Finchley lay back, with a sigh of contentment, and closed his eyes, and when Robert next looked round he was asleep.

Mr. Finchley slept for half an hour and when he awoke it was to find Robert stretched out beside him, propping himself up on his elbow and reading an old newspaper he had retrieved from a litter bin.

"M'sieur has slept well?" Robert enquired, glad that he was now awake.

"Very well," said Mr. Finchley, yawning a little as he stretched himself. He was glad that the boy had not wakened him or interrupted his sleep. It was a good sign that Robert knew how to keep still for a while. That, he understood, was a virtue few children possessed. To reward Robert, he suggested that they should go for a row on the lake.

The afternoon was carrying on the promise of the morning and Mr. Finchley was glad of the peace and beauty of the lake. Robert sat in the stern with the rudder rope and Mr. Finchley pulled away from the landing stage, his arms moving a little awkwardly at first to the unaccustomed exercise. The lake was long, its banks lined with pleasant walks and a variety of trees, and in its centre were two islands, thick with shrubs and marked in places by patches of wildfowl sunning themselves. Over the water moved other craft and a few swans, propelling themselves out of the way of the boats with an air of resentment at this intrusion of humanity.

They had not gone far when another boat drew up abreast of them. In it was a red-faced, perspiring man, his jacket off, his head surmounted by a tiny beret that made his heat and energy seem ridiculous. In the stern sat a boy about Robert's age, but a boy dressed in a neat, rather feminine sailor suit, and wearing a red-tasselled sailor's hat. As they drew level the boy suddenly leaned over the side and shouted a stream of rapid and, to Mr. Finchley, unintelligible French at them. Mr. Finchley saw Robert start. Then, from his boat, there volleyed back another stream of undoubted acrimony and taunt which Robert capped by placing his finger to his nose.

"What is it? What is it?" cried Mr. Finchley, not wishing to be involved in any disagreeable altercation.

"It is him," explained Robert. "He says his father is a better rower than you are. And he said other things I will not repeat."

"And what did you say?"

"I told him you were the best rower on the lake, m'sieur, and I also added some things I do not wish to repeat, m'sieur. And now he says he and his father will race us to the end of the island. I know you do not wish to race, m'sieur. That is natural. But it was necessary for me to say you were such a good rower to defend your honour. We will pull away from them. They will think, of course, that you are afraid ..." Robert noted the effect of this anxiously. "But I shall know it is not so. M'sieur must think of his dignity."

Mr. Finchley looked from Robert across to the other boat. The French papa, the slave of his son, beamed at him affably, unaffected by the scurrilities which had passed between the boys, and patted his oars significantly.

"Do you think I wouldn't beat him?" enquired Mr. Finchley.

Robert shrugged his shoulders. "M'sieur may be good, but the other gentleman—he looks good, too. It would be wiser not to race than to race and be beaten."

Mr. Finchley snorted. If he couldn't beat ... He pulled himself up. No, it would not be—he saw the French boy make a grimace towards him, and at the same time he noticed that the Frenchman was flabby and out of condition, though obviously enthusiastic for the race. Mr. Finchley made a swift resolution.

"Very well, we'll race them. And bother my dignity!"

Robert's face broadened to a delighted grin, and in a few seconds the arrangements were made. The two boats jockeyed into position, a manoeuvre not effected without further comments from the younger members of the crews, and then Robert held up his hand, chanting slowly:

"*Un! Deux! Trois!—Allez donc*!" And they were off.

Mr. Finchley dipped his oars, tugged long and hard, and the boat glided away. For some seconds he rowed with short, jerky strokes to get the boat under way, and then he settled down to a long steady pull. He saw that he had not gained on the Frenchman.

For fifty yards the two boats moved abreast, their rowers lunging and straining, the boys shouting encouragement to them. Waterfowl scattered from their path and other boaters shouted to them. Mr. Finchley dipped and pulled, swung and tugged, his face flushing, his breath going in fierce grunts.

Then as the shrubbed bank of the island slipped by he saw with gratification that he was taking the lead. At first he went ahead slowly, and then more rapidly, until from the French boat he heard an explosive outburst from the boy and saw his father bend more urgently to the oars. Mr. Finchley increased his pace to take this challenge, and then with the confidence of one who knows his own powers he settled down into a steady stride that would keep him his two lengths' advantage, for he did not wish to make the victory too crushing.

Robert, overjoyed at their lead, spent his time leaning backwards over the stern, shouting encouragement of a derisive nature at the other boat. At first Mr. Finchley was tempted to order Robert to cease this display. It was, he felt, not English, and scarcely the way to treat an opponent. Then remembering the French influence which had claimed Robert, and recalling the rancorous challenge of the other boy and his rude comments, Mr. Finchley decided to let Robert alone. He did so, feeling somewhat depressed by the knowledge that even to know a language is not enough if one does not understand the slang. Most of Robert's comment was unintelligible to him.

The end of the island appeared on Mr. Finchley's left, and he eased his oars and let the boat glide along. The race was done. Robert still hung over the stern watching the other boat, and it was thus with the boat floating under its own momentum, deprived of a watchful coxswain, that disaster overtook them. There was a sudden jar, a harsh scraping of wood, and Mr. Finchley looked round to be met with a cry of alarm and the sight of a young man, who had been standing up in his boat to take photographs of some wildfowl, toppling backwards. The man hit the water with a splash.

Mr. Finchley, forgetting the race, jumped to his feet and waited for the waters to subside. A head was thrust from the disturbed lake and a pair of angry eyes surveyed him.

"I say, I'm terribly sorry about this." Mr. Finchley hesitated for a moment between making his apologies and helping the man out. There was a warning shout from Robert, and Mr. Finchley looked round in time to see the other boat bearing down upon him, the perspiring papa still tugging hard at his oars and the small boy obviously dismayed and incapable of steering the boat clear of the obstruction before him. The bow hit Mr. Finchley's boat amidships and the jolt knocked Mr. Finchley forward from his uncertain balance to land in a heap on the bottom boards.

Mr. Finchley picked himself up and saw that the man in the lake was wading towards the island.

Calling to Robert to make fast the empty skiff to theirs, Mr. Finchley rowed towards the island with the other boat in tow.

They landed in time to be able to help the man ashore. He was standing in water to his waist, trying to scramble up the steep bank. As he pulled him from the lake and the man looked up into his face as his feet slipped on the bank, Mr. Finchley nearly let him tumble back into the water, for he found himself staring into the mildly inquisitive eyes of the young entomologist he had met on the cross-Channel boat.

VII
Of Mr. Finchley and a determined madame

THE young man, proving that youth can adapt itself to a changed situation quicker than the middle-aged, was the first to recover his equanimity. He slipped off his jacket to wring it out, and accompanied this operation with the remark:

"I think it is Plato who says that there are in this world people whose souls, unknown to them, are constantly seeking out one another. Hitherto, I had supposed that this was a theory, of no interest at all, except to novelists, who used it as an excuse for the succession of coincidences one finds in many books. It seems I was wrong."

"I don't know about Plato," said Mr. Finchley, distressed; "but I should be glad to think that I could blame this unfortunate accident upon my soul rather than on my clumsiness. I really am most terribly sorry about it. Can I—"

"But it was not your fault, m'sieur," Robert interrupted him. "It was my fault for not steering the boat properly. I am to blame, m'sieur." He turned to the young man gravely. "It was I. I beg your pardon, and I hope you will not believe that Mr. Finchley was to blame at all."

"Well, there's no point in fighting for the honour of having tipped me into the lake, and, anyway, I'm used to taking a wetting occasionally."

He smiled at Robert through his glasses, and then turned to Mr. Finchley. "Perhaps in order to satisfy our souls and finish with their search for one another, I ought to introduce myself. My name is Hume, Laurence Hume."

"And mine is Finchley, and I would like to thank you for the nice way you have regarded this accident."

"Not at all—"

"M'sieur must change his clothes." Robert was hopping around them anxiously, not sure whether he was forgiven and eager to help where he could.

"Yes, that's right," said Mr. Finchley. "You must get out of those clothes as soon as possible."

"Well, I'm staying not far from here, so it won't take long," said Hume.

They got into their skiffs and rowed back to the landing stage. They avoided the curiosity of the boatman and stopped a taxi on the road which skirted the side of the lake.

Hume nodded cheerfully to Mr. Finchley and Robert to show he bore no malice and then climbed into the taxi, calling his address to the driver. Mr. Finchley and Robert were left standing on the roadside.

"We were lucky," said Mr. Finchley, "to have capsized such a good-tempered person."

"He was very pleasant," answered Robert. "Oh, m'sieur!" he cried out. "I have forgotten. Look, here is the gentleman's camera which he dropped in his boat. What stupidity! I meant to give it to him—"

"Now what are we to do?"

For a moment Mr. Finchley was inclined to be annoyed at Robert's forgetfulness.

"We can take it to him, m'sieur. I heard the address he gave to the driver. It was in the rue Chalgrin, which is not far from here."

They walked leisurely towards Hume's lodgings, not wanting to arrive before he had had time to change his wet clothes. They found that the road was one leading off the Avenue Foch, and the house, a tall block of apartments. From the concierge Mr. Finchley found the floor on which Hume was staying and, leaving Robert in the hallway talking to the concierge, he went upstairs, ignoring Robert's plea that he should use the lift. Hume was staying on the second floor.

He rang the apartment bell and the door was answered by an old grey-haired woman with bright, grey eyes and a puckered mouth. Her face had a shrewd, severe expression. She wore a black dress with a tight collar held by a black ribbon which was fastened by a gold brooch.

Her severity relaxed a little as Mr. Finchley, in his best French, said that he wanted to speak to Mr. Hume, and she greeted him with a flood of words, grabbed him by the elbow and pulled him into a long hallway which was dark and full, or so it seemed to Mr. Finchley, of hanging curtains and spindly-legged cupboards and chairs. A faint smell of food lingered in the air.

Madame conducted him down a long corridor to Hume's room, knocked fiercely on the door and pushed it open.

Hume, who was sitting by the gasfire in a dressing-gown, rose quickly, saying:

"Well, here we are again. What brings you here?"

Before Mr. Finchley could answer, Madame flung a volley of French at Hume, who answered less adroitly, and then she disappeared.

"Sit down," said Hume. "Madame is going to bring us some tea. Would you like a cup?"

Mr. Finchley nodded. "I brought along your camera. The boy picked it up from your skiff."

"Thanks, I'd made up my mind that it was gone; thought I'd dropped it in the water. I was taking some shots of the wildfowl on the lake. You interested in birds? Surprising the variety of species you find on these public waters."

By the time Madame came back with their tea, Mr. Finchley had learnt quite a lot about Laurence Hume, and had told him how he came to be in Paris.

"Your landlady seems kinder than she looks," he said when she had left the room.

Laurence sipped his tea and then smiled. "Madame Mignard's all right," he said. "I always stay here when I come to Paris. It's better for your French to live in a totally French atmosphere. Hotels speak too much English. But don't let Madame's generosity deceive you. She is French—and that means she thinks all travelling Englishmen have plenty of money. But she's all right it's just that she has to make a living, and that's not too easy in France at the moment. She doesn't usually answer the door and serve tea; but being Sunday afternoon I expect the house-boy is out."

While they talked, Mr. Finchley looked around the room. It was one of many that took up one floor along the wing of the building. Outside it ran a small, dark corridor that led, through the hallway, to a large lounge and dining-room. The windows of the room looked out into the well of the building and across to the windows of the rooms of the opposite wing. The room was furnished as a bed-sitting room.

There was a knock on the door and Madame Mignard entered. She spoke to Mr. Hume and after a while he turned to Mr. Finchley, smiling.

"Madame wants to know whether you are stopping for dinner, and I've a shrewd idea she thinks you've only just arrived in Paris and might be looking for rooms. Watch her face when I tell her you're stopping at the Achille."

He turned and spoke to Madame. At once she threw up her arms in alarm and addressed Mr. Finchley directly, and he understood her meaning clearly enough.

"Oh, la, la!" Madame Mignard cried. "M'sieur is stopping at the Hôtel Achille. M'sieur must indeed be a very rich man—"

Mr. Finchley shook his head hastily to assure her that he was not a very rich man. Robert had been impressed when he learnt that Mr. Finchley was staying at the Achille, and now Madame was showing surprise; Mr. Finchley began to feel that perhaps he was being extravagant by stopping there. After all it was, indirectly, Mr. Hammerton's money he was spending.

"I am not rich, I assure you," said Mr. Finchley. "I simply went there because it was recommended."

"But there are many cheaper places, if m'sieur is not very rich," insisted Madame. "Look at M'sieur 'Ume, now. He is wise, for when he comes to Paris he does not waste his money on hotels, no matter for how short a time he stays. He comes to me and is comfortable, and my charges, m'sieur, I assure you, are such that cannot be beaten anywhere in Paris. The food is of the first class and there is always hot water. Tell him it is so, M'sieur 'Ume, for you should not want to see your fellow countryman robbed by the wretches who run Paris hotels." As she spoke Mr. Finchley saw that her face had changed expression, her eagerness giving place to a determination with which was mixed a strange solicitude for Mr. Finchley's purse, and Mr. Finchley realised how different was the French conception of money from that of the English. Madame in ordinary matters was undoubtedly generous and possessed of a sense of humour. Let the subject be finance and she was everything of French economy—not meanness—with money. It was, Mr. Finchley reflected, the effect of living in a country where monetary values waxed and waned between moon-like extremes.

"But Mr. Finchley likes the Achille and anyway he is only stopping until Tuesday," said Laurence.

"That is nothing. Two days at the price of the Achille—that is a lot of money. I have a room like this one to which m'sieur is welcome if he wishes it. I should not like m'sieur to leave Paris with a bad impression of the French because of his bill at the Achille."

"What do you say?" Laurence turned to Mr. Finchley.

Mr. Finchley considered the suggestion for a moment. He was not opposed to the idea. It would be cheaper, and although he felt he did not like Mr. Hammerton, that could not dispel his natural love of thrift. Apart from that he would be, if only for two days, living in a completely French atmosphere which was, he knew, the real way to get an understanding of the people. Also he felt that it would be difficult to give Madame Mignard a refusal without affronting her and branding himself as a man blind to his own interests.

"All right," he nodded. "I'll come—"

"M'sieur will be very happy!" cried Madame Mignard, her face softening with pleasure, and she began at once to make arrangements. When she had left them Laurence turned to him ruefully.

"I'm sorry, you know, if you've been rushed into this. It was my fault. I forgot for a while that Madame never lets the chance of a fresh lodger go by. And I must warn you that the water is frequently far from hot."

Mr. Finchley was surprised to see Robert in the concierge's office, waiting for him. He had forgotten about the boy. Robert did not seem to consider that Mr. Finchley had been unkind to keep him waiting.

When Mr. Finchley explained that he was going to leave the Achille, Robert asked to accompany him to the hotel and help him pack; and Mr. Finchley, realising how thrilled the boy would be to go into the hotel, gladly gave his permission, and as gladly used the lift to reach his room. The glory of the lift was forgotten for Robert before the wonders of Mr. Finchley's room as he helped him to pack.

"Does m'sieur sleep in these?" he asked as Mr. Finchley placed his best silk travelling pyjamas in the case. "They are superb. I am resolved from this minute that some day I will have such a pair."

But it was Mr. Finchley's toilet case that evoked his greatest admiration.

"Such hairbrushes, sir! Pépé and I always use a comb—but these! Would m'sieur permit me to use them?" And before Mr. Finchley could give or withhold permission Robert was standing in front of the glass brushing his hair and crying aloud with pleasure at each stroke. After a while he stopped his toilet and looked gravely round at Mr. Finchley, his dark eyes big with thought. "It is a pleasant thing to think," he declared, "that there are so many good things ahead of me in life. Pépé says it is wise to think well of the future. Some day I shall have pyjamas like that, hairbrushes like this and a little case with my initials like yours, and I shall live in a room like this and ride in the lift often."

Mr. Finchley coughed gently to hide his amusement, and then said kindly, "One day, Robert, you will. But you must not imagine that such things represent all that the future offers you. There are more important things which you must not forget."

"Such things as what, m'sieur?" asked Robert eagerly.

"Well, such things as . . ." Mr. Finchley hesitated, feeling himself slipping into deep water. "For instance," he said quickly, remembering the haddock, "it is more important for a man to be honest than to acquire hairbrushes."

"Do you mean that dishonest people do not have such lovely brushes?"

"No," Mr. Finchley laughed. "Generally they have much better brushes than that. What I mean is that you must not reckon success in terms of worldly goods. Do you understand what I mean?"

"Oh, quite, sir. Pépé often says that the poorest men are mostly the happiest because they have so little to lose. We both laugh at that, for he as often says that he would take on the cares of any rich man for half his money. But I understand what m'sieur means. There is a curé who visits us and talks like that. Pépé says he is a good man but ignorant of life."

As he spoke his eyes found Mr. Finchley's automatic razor.

"Mind you don't cut yourself," cried Mr. Finchley as his small hands began to examine the case. But Robert would not put it down until he had been shown how it worked, and for some moments the room echoed to the regular *slap, slap* of the razor on its leather as the boy operated the strop. Mr. Finchley watched him as he worked the razor and he wondered what kind of a man was Pépé, wondered whether he was the right person to have charge of this young boy. From some of Robert's remarks he had his doubts of Pépé, and he found it disconcerting to hear Robert repeat with childlike sincerity the gentle cynicisms of his beloved Pépé.

"Such an instrument is expensive, sir?" asked Robert as he finished stropping.

"In France it would cost nearly a hundred francs," Mr. Finchley informed him.

"One hundred francs! That's a lot of money. But I will begin to save my money for such an instrument. I am dark and when I am eighteen I shall have a beard and I shall cut it with just such a razor."

"Well, you've got plenty of time to save the money," said Mr. Finchley. "And now I think you'd better be getting back to Pépé. I shan't want a guide any more today. Here's your ten francs—that ought to give you a good start towards the hundred!"

Robert took the money and his dismissal soberly.

"Thank you, m'sieur. But first I will help you down with your cases."

Outside the hotel, with a taxi waiting, Robert surrendered the case he was carrying, looking up at Mr. Finchley seriously:

"Although I behaved so badly, and it was my fault that M'sieur Hume fell in the lake you are still my friend?"

"Why, of course!"

The boy's face brightened. "Thank you, sir. And you were pleased with my services as a guide?"

"You were excellent. If you want a recommendation I'll give you one at any time. And now, good-bye and good luck."

As the taxi drove away, Mr. Finchley leaned back against the upholstery, thinking. He could not help deciding that his advice to the boy had been pompous. He was so unused to the company of young people that he found it hard to accommodate his manners to their moods, and this lack of versatility on his part made him vaguely dissatisfied with himself, awaking within him a consciousness of incompleteness of character. Robert, it was true, was not like most small boys. He carried himself with a precocity that Mr. Finchley regarded as dangerous, and he was, Mr. Finchley guessed, not restrained by the usual conventions of childhood. That was Pépé's fault. Yet underneath it all he was a boy, interested in boyish things, and his pathetic eagerness to have Mr. Finchley's assurance of friendship stirred Mr. Finchley to a disappointment in his own lack of adaptation. He sighed heavily, shaking his head at his thoughts, and then told himself that he could not go through life expecting to find himself ready for every emergency that crossed his path. Robert had crossed and disappeared into the side thickets. It was enough to have been awakened to his deficiencies.

Some time before seven, which was the hour for dinner, Hume came wandering into Mr. Finchley's room to see that he was settled comfortably.

"Everything all right?" he asked cheerfully.

"Yes, thanks," replied Mr. Finchley.

"Good. I came along, too, to put you wise about the people in this place. It might be a bit of a shock for you otherwise—"

"Good heavens!" Mr. Finchley looked at him, perturbed. "What's the matter with them?"

"Nothing … I mean nothing to be worried about. It's merely that they are French, and until you've got used to them they might seem a little strange. There's five of 'em, and they're all different in politics, religion and sentiment. That doesn't seem possible, but it is. Then there's the family. You've met Madame. There's her husband, he's a doddery old retired army man, and her widowed daughter who has a small child, a girl, whom you won't see because she's packed off to bed at six each night—"

"But I have seen the child. She was in the hall when I came back, and I suppose it was her mother with her. She seemed very young for a widow, and quite pretty—"

"Then it wasn't Madame's daughter," said Hume decisively. "She's not pretty. It was probably Marie, the child's governess. I forgot to mention her. Between ourselves I think Madame comes the martinet a bit with Marie. Surprising thing is that she's English and—if I know anything—probably saving every sou to get back to England. But I don't know much about her. She wasn't here the last time I was over."

For one who professed not to know much about Marie, Mr. Finchley thought that Hume was very well informed.

"She's a very pretty girl," said Mr. Finchley, with one eye cocked towards Laurence. "I remember, I was surprised that for so fair a girl she should have such dark eyes, almost black—"

"No, they're not black. They're really a very deep blue, but they have a peculiar quality of appearing very dark, almost black sometimes."

"You seem to have made a study of them," observed Mr. Finchley.

"Not at all," replied Laurence, strolling towards the door, his casualness not disguising the fact that he was not anxious to continue the conversation. "It's merely the observing habit which is bred in any capable naturalist. You've got to be able to memorise exact colours to be any good, and I merely noticed the quality of her eyes as I should notice the coloration of a moth's wings—"

"And which do you prefer," asked Mr. Finchley, jokingly; "moths or young women?"

"Moths," said Hume definitely as he went out.

"And I think I know why," Mr. Finchley said to himself as the door closed; "you can't stick a pin through a woman and neatly label her as you can a moth. It needs more practice before you can handle and catalogue them properly."

From wondering about Hume and Marie he found himself thinking about Mrs. Crantell. Had he any real claim to accuse someone else of a lack of understanding women while he himself was so much in ignorance of many of Mrs. Crantell's feelings?

The sound of the dinner gong from the end of the corridor brought him from the consequent reverie, and going to the door of his room, which was at the top of the corridor, Mr. Finchley witnessed a strange sight. The notes of the gong had scarcely died away before the doors along the corridor began to open, and from each, like a lot of trap-door spiders tempted by the desire for food, emerged a lodger. One by one they came out and hurried towards the dining-room. Mr. Finchley felt that it was scarcely good manners to show so much eagerness for dinner and he let them get a good start on him.

When Mr. Finchley entered the room, every eye turned towards him, and Madame, flanked by her husband and daughter, indicated his place to him and then announced impressively to the company: "Mesdames et Messieurs, this is Mr. Finchley, an English gentleman, who is staying with us for a few days."

Then, like a schoolmistress in a hurry with her register, she rattled off a reel of names, introducing Mr. Finchley, and after each name Mr. Finchley received a polite bow or smile.

The introductions done, he found himself sitting between a young man with a spotty face whom he knew as Monsieur Perret, and Marie, the governess, who smiled at him pleasantly. Across the table was Hume.

Madame rang a bell and from somewhere behind her appeared Jean, the house-boy, who began to serve soup. The bell served the double purpose of signifying that the dinner was under way and the moment its echoes had died away they were followed by a mounting noise of conversation. It began with a quiet remark by Madame's daughter which was taken up, tossed and jostled along the table until it reached Monsieur Perret, by which time the nature of the remark seemed to have changed to a personal challenge which M. Perret had to answer. He waved his arms, twisted his head and rolled his eyes, and finished by dipping his spoon savagely into the soup and imbibing a noisy mouthful to a chorus of approval from the rest of the table.

"Did you get it?" asked Marie quietly of Mr. Finchley as she saw him knitting his brows, perplexed.

"Well, not quite," admitted Mr. Finchley. All he had caught were the words *magnificent*, *incredible*, *frightening*, and a jumble of other words which did not make sense.

"I thought you didn't. Well, they've just decided that it has been a lovely afternoon and the Bois was very crowded. Now they're off again—watch the bearded gentleman up by Madame. It's politics and he's a Communist." She grinned at him and her nose wrinkled merrily, so that Mr. Finchley decided he liked her.

While the bearded man and a placid-faced man wearing a butterfly bow made of a plaided material were leaning across the table shouting at one another, the soup plates were removed by the imperturbable Jean and Mr. Finchley found himself with a plateful of crisp, beautifully fried potatoes. For a time he left these on his plate, listening to the rattle of talk, waiting for the fish or meat which would accompany them. Then he noticed that no one else was allowing conversation to interrupt their eating, so he ate his potatoes.

At this point M. Perret turned to him and with a gracious smile loosened a spate of words at him. They poured by Mr. Finchley, enveloped him and he was left with the one word 'Baldwin' ringing in his ears.

M. Perret smiled and waited. Mr. Finchley gulped and felt his neck grow too big for his collar. M. Perret's smile faded and a belligerent look began to spread over his face.

Mr. Finchley was saved by Marie's voice whispering to him—"He's just said how he admires Mr. Baldwin and he wants to know whether you don't think he's a marvellous politician. Better agree, he doesn't like to be upset."

Hastily Mr. Finchley nodded his head and self-consciously said, "Yes, yes, I agree."

M. Perret's smile returned and Mr. Finchley recovered himself to find a helping of braised cod on his plate and his potatoes gone. He applied himself to the fish, avoiding the eyes of the other lodgers for fear of being drawn into a conversation. As he finished his fish there were three separate altercations going on. At Madame's end of the table she and the bearded man were discussing and disagreeing about infant mortality, the spotty man and M. Perret were glaring at one another and throwing the names of Clark Gable and Sacha Guitry at one another, while Laurence Hume, his mild eyes sparkling behind his glasses, was mediating in slow but excellent French between a white-haired man with a dewlap that shook with each movement of his head and a dark-skinned man who punctuated his remarks with violent scoffs of laughter and noisy visits to his glass of red wine.

"Jolly lot, aren't they?" said Marie. "But you get to like them. There's no harm in any of them."

As Mr. Finchley laughed and turned resolutely to the helping of leeks in lukewarm oil which had been placed on his plate, the same plate he had used for fish, he heard Madame call down the table to Marie and from the tone of her voice he guessed that she was issuing some reprimand.

Madame's comments did not repress Marie for long. "M'sieur Perret is now telling his friends exactly what he thinks of American films; and Madame's husband has not passed out, but he's an old man and he always goes to sleep at meals. The noise soothes him. Have some of this chicory and endive salad. You'll like it."

Mr. Finchley's conception of a pleasant meal was mainly ceremonial; slow ceremony, with time for reflection and digestion. But here he was battered and assaulted from all sides and his head began to ache with the effort of trying to catch at meanings. He felt he had eaten a great deal, but he was still hungry. His plate never held more than one thing at a time and, according to some undefinable rule, some plates were used for a variety of dishes.

He was glad to see the coffee served, though its excellence was lost upon him as he stood in the path of a heated stream of vituperation which flowed between M. Perret and the bearded man. Some of their phrases he caught and turned to Marie for help.

"Who is this Alphonse Reims they're talking about?" he asked.

"He's a boy millionaire who's staying at the Marivaux Hotel. M. Perret thinks he's a nice little fellow and the bearded one would like to boil him in oil and distribute his wealth to the poor. My sympathies are with the beard, if the child's anything like the one I have to look after."

The meal ended suddenly. Madame glanced at her watch, rapped hard on the table, kicked her husband to wakefulness with an unobtrusiveness born of long practice and announced graciously that they had her permission to withdraw.

The signal was obeyed instantly. The lodgers tidily replaced their napkins into their sachets and, forgetting their animosities, scuttled back to their rooms.

"Well, I warned you," said Hume as he followed Mr. Finchley out of the room. "Madame rules this roost all right. I was sorry I couldn't help you out much, but those two on either side of me kept me busy acting the umpire.

To them I am the impartial Englishman. But I noticed Marie rescued you when it was necessary."

"Yes, she was very good to me. I like her." Hume did not pursue the subject. Instead he asked:

"What are you going to do now? Like to come out to a café and have a drink? I'm free this evening."

Mr. Finchley accepted his offer gladly.

VIII
Of a collision and a confession

MARIE came out of the apartment, pulled the door firmly behind her and breathed a long sigh. It was a sigh that expressed many things, her relief at escaping from the apartment, from the watchful Madame and an irritating charge. She was not, she felt, intended to be a governess, she lacked the patience. She was a prisoner, her cell behind her, freedom before her.

She stood outside the door for a moment, pulling on her gloves and thinking about her duties, and her pretty face frowned. Then, with a shrug of her shoulders, she cast the whole of Madame Mignard's family into limbo. The frown went from her face, her lips puckered into a gentle whistle and she hurried towards the top of the stairway. Here, careless of being seen, she hitched up her skirt and, sitting upon the wide wooden balustrade rail, began to slide down the stairs, her whistling increasing with her speed. There were two turns to be negotiated before she reached the long slope down to the main hallway, and she took these corners with a skill that betold practice. And she was practised, for this sliding was a ritual she performed every time the apartment door closed behind her and let her out to the freedom of a night or an afternoon off. It was undignified, but it helped her into a gay mood to enjoy her freedom. It was a pleasant sensation. She could imagine she was ski-ing or going down a toboggan run, the cold air striking her face and wrestling with her breath.

Sliding down banisters is an art in which the young are most accomplished, and any small boy will tell you that once you are fairly started down a slope there are only two ways of stopping yourself. One is by using the hands as a brake, and this can take the skin from the palms or mess up a pair of gloves easily, and the other method is to swing the body outwards from the rail and jump for the stairs, a procedure which involves the risk of a broken leg or twisted ankle.

Marie had never contemplated the possibility of having to stop half-way down a slope. Only once had she ever encountered anyone on the stairs, and that had been M. Perret, and as she slid by he had politely, without any surprise, raised his hat to her and wished her 'Good evening.'

But now, as she gathered speed down the last slope, slipping quickly towards the dim shadows of the hallway, from below her came the quick spurt of a match and she saw, standing a few feet from the end of the railhead, a man. His head was bent over the pipe which he was lighting, innocent of the menace that was hurtling towards him.

Instinctively Marie's hands dropped to brake on the rail, and as quickly she renounced the idea—she had no intention of ruining her best pair of gloves. The prospect of jumping for the stairs was as quickly flouted by the reflection that if she did not break her leg she would probably ladder her stockings, and they were dear enough these days. The only thing to do was to warn the man. She opened her mouth to scream, and as quickly shut it. If there had to be an accident it would be well to keep it quiet. It was only when she was two feet from the end of the rail that her humanity got the better of her base desire to avoid a noisy scene, and then she had little time to do more than call frantically:

"Gangway there!"

The sound of her voice made the man look round, but gave him no opportunity to dodge her flying figure. Legs wide spread, arms thrown high, she cannoned into him. His pipe went rocketing into the air, trailing a wake of sparks; his hat, cartwheeling like a boomerang, looped over the hanging light and fell softly to the carpet, and he collapsed silently and heavily as the girl struck him full in the chest.

Marie had her wish. Except for her one shout, there had been no noise. The man had succumbed like a wrecked airship, flabbily and ponderously.

For a moment Mr. Finchley lay prone on the floor, staring dazedly into Marie's face. Then as his breath came back to him, he gasped brokenly: "Do you mind? You're sitting on my chest ..."

Marie shook herself free from the bewilderment which had seized her and, rising to her feet, bent down and gave Mr. Finchley a hand.

As she saw him frown, she said, "Now you're going to be angry with me. And it was my fault, I know ..." Her words tailed into a faint chuckle which she suppressed at once, and at the sound Mr. Finchley, who had been more surprised than hurt, forgot to be indignant and smiled.

"It's all right," he assured her, "I'm not hurt. Please don't worry about it."

"You're sure you aren't hurt? I could kick myself for being so clumsy."

"I'm quite all right," Mr. Finchley said, and he added quietly: "Is that the way you usually come downstairs?"

"Only when it's my night off," she informed him, picking up his hat and pipe. "You see, I feel so darned glad to get away that I have to do something to celebrate—"

"Hullo, what's happened?"

Hume, who had been in the concierge's office to see whether a letter he was expecting had come by the last mail, came out to see Marie holding Mr. Finchley's hat and brushing him down.

"Oh, just a little accident," said Mr. Finchley, smiling. "Miss … um—"

"Peters," Marie helped him.

She was glad that it had been Mr. Finchley she had upset. Not Hume. Mr. Finchley she felt was ready to forgive her, but Hume, with his detached air and far-away superiority, would have made her feel so ridiculous.

"Miss Peters and I got in each other's way."

"I can guess," said Hume, "sliding down the banisters. Unknown to Miss Peters I had the privilege of watching her perform the other evening."

"You did!" Marie felt herself blushing.

"I did," said Hume, wondering why she blushed at a plain statement of fact. "I admired your skill, but I felt that some time you would certainly have an accident." His tone was almost reproving.

"It's easy to be wise like that," said Marie. "I suppose you've never slid down a banister in your life?"

"I seem to remember," put in Mr. Finchley gently, "that I was very good at it once." It would never do to let these young people quarrel. What a curious thing it was, he felt, the way young people refused to admit their interest in one another and covered it by deliberately inviting argument. The thought prompted an idea, and he said casually: "Mr. Hume and I were just going out to a café." He glanced at Hume. "Would you care to join us, Miss Peters? I don't know whether that's a proper invitation to make, but after our recent meeting I feel we could both do with something to … to … um—"

"I know what you mean," Marie put in. "It's nice of you to ask me. Actually I'm on my way to the pictures, but if I'm not butting in, I'd love to join you." Hume said nothing, and Mr. Finchley hoped that he was pleased with the arrangement.

They entered a nearby café and found a table in a corner.

"I'm glad that you two are with me," Mr. Finchley said happily, the onus of conversation upon him. "I know nothing about all these French drinks, and now you can help me out. I've had to stick to grenadine and beer so far."

"Well, I think we can do better than that for you, Mr. Finchley," said Marie. "Can't we, Mr. Hume?"

"It shouldn't be hard," admitted Hume.

So Mr. Finchley was initiated into the mysteries of French drinks, syrups made from blackcurrant and oranges, flavourings of gentian and curaçao, and—though only one glass—a cloudy yellow liquid which Marie assured him was the nearest he could get to absinthe in France these days. And while they drank Marie talked. She was, even Mr. Finchley had to admit that, a talker, but her talk was interesting. At least, it was interesting to him, though he could not speak for Hume. That young man took his drink and was polite, so that it was impossible to tell his thoughts.

"If you dislike being a governess so much," said Mr. Finchley, "why are you a governess?"

Marie eyed them both for a moment, and then she said casually, "I'm not a governess, really. I'm a fraud!"

"You're a what?" Mr. Finchley was beginning to be a little confused with his medley of drinks.

"I'm a fraud. You see"—it was evident that Marie was glad to have someone to confide in—"I've only been with Madame for four months. But before that I was never a governess. I came to France three years ago with a cabaret troupe from England. You know the kind of show. *Les Girls*. I used to dance and sing. Then when the engagement finished I stopped on. I knew French and got a solo cabaret engagement—the other girls went back home. For two years I did very well. Then I hit some bad luck, and you'd be surprised how soon your savings go. It's not a pleasant feeling, so when I saw that I didn't seem to be going to get that kind of work, I answered Madame's advertisement. And—isn't it terrible?—I gave her several references which I'd written myself. She's never found out and, honestly, I've been quite a good governess. Only it bores me. Still, I'll soon have enough money to get back to England with a little over to keep me for a while until I get an engagement."

This confession, so unexpected, took them both by surprise. From the way it had been delivered they realised how glad Marie had been to find someone to share her secret. Hume was the first to recover himself.

"Do you mean you're an actress?" he asked.

"That's it. You know, a show girl. But I have really acted. I had small parts in West End shows before I came over here, and when I get back I'm not going to touch cabaret work—unless I have to."

"But those references—that's forgery!" Mr. Finchley was shocked.

"I know," Marie giggled. Then seriously: "But Madame wouldn't have given me the job otherwise, and you ought to hear her talk about the stage, never mind cabarets. You'd have forged, too, if you'd been in my position. And now, I suppose, you'll go and tell her—" She was defiant.

"Don't be ridiculous," said Hume. "Of course we shan't." He looked at her curiously and shook his head. "What an extraordinary creature you are," he said. "I shouldn't have imagined that you were capable of it—"

"And why not? And any way, who are you to call me extraordinary?" Marie's mouth tightened.

"Now, now—there's no need to quarrel about it," Mr. Finchley came soothingly to the rescue. He hurried the conversation away to safer topics and, as though Marie's confession had increased their intimacy, they became friendlier and she forgot she was going to the pictures and Hume forgot his first annoyance at Mr. Finchley's inviting her to the café.

She told them about her engagements in Paris cabarets, and fished from her bag a collection of postcards showing her in the various costumes of her act. Once she felt they had accepted her she showed no reticence and Mr. Finchley was continually amazed at her frank run of talk. He had never met such a girl before.

When she had finished talking about herself she turned to him, demanding to know what he had seen in Paris, and before he knew where he was she and Hume were making an itinerary for him. For some time he let them enjoy themselves arranging his sightseeing the next morning, and he accepted with gratitude an invitation to accompany Marie to Malmaison the following afternoon which she had free. He promised to meet her after lunch at the bus terminus of Porte Maillot.

"Won't you come, too?" he asked Hume. But Hume shook his head.

"No, thanks," he said. "I shall be busy all day tomorrow," and Mr. Finchley caught the nervous, hesitant note that had been in his voice early in the evening.

They let Marie enter the apartment before them, for she did not wish Madame to know she had spent the evening with them.

"The old trout's peculiar that way. Like all these righteous people, she's got a long nose for goings-on."

She said good night and left them, and as they waited to give her five minutes' grace, Hume tossed his cigarette into the gutter and said wonderingly

"What a girl! I'd always thought her type belonged purely to fiction. Her mind has no place for anything but cabaret shows. She'd probably think that the Rotifers were a comedy act—"

Mr. Finchley loyally defended her. "She's got courage, anyway, and as much common sense as anyone. You can't expect everyone to share your own interests in life. I like her—don't you?"

"She's amusing," admitted Hume.

Back in his room, Mr. Finchley found that he had no inclination for bed. He took out his pad and began to write a letter to Mrs. Crantell. Since coming to Paris he had thought of her only at odd moments, but this evening had put her into his mind. For a second or two he was tempted to put into the letter something of his feelings for her, but a moment's deliberation showed him that this would not be wise, and he set down the things which had happened to him. It was the nearest Mr. Finchley ever got to writing a love letter, and he had to be content with the expression of the sentiment that she might have been with him on this unexpected holiday and with the termination, which ran—Your affectionate friend, Edgar Finchley.

Had he been able to see Mrs. Crantell's face when she received the letter and noticed its change when she found it concerned almost entirely with the doings of a boy named Robert, Mr. Finchley might not have considered his decision to curb his feelings so wise.

IX
In which Robert enlists the aid of Saint Xavier

THE next morning Mr. Finchley had his breakfast in bed. It was brought to him by Jean, who wakened him effectively by banging back the window shutters and shouting some derisive comment to a friend in the courtyard below. He pointed to the tray on the table by the bed and said proudly, with all the fervour of the limited but enthusiastic linguist—"Breakfast, O.K." And as he left the room he added with a smile that gave his words a villainous intent—"Good-bye."

Wondering if Jean's good-bye might not contain a sinister reference to poison in the coffee, Mr. Finchley attacked his croissants. He wondered if these would sustain him until lunch time. He decided that if every other male in Paris could be satisfied by such a breakfast, then he had no real cause for complaint.

His breakfast finished, Mr. Finchley leisurely washed and shaved himself and made himself ready to go out. That morning, he decided, he would see the Louvre. If he put it off, or allowed himself to be put off much longer, he would never see it.

He went from the gloom of the apartment—Madame seemed always to keep her curtains drawn for fear of the sun fading her carpets and chair tapestries—into the sunshine of the street.

At the head of the street he could see the green lawns and shrubs that lined the Avenue Foch. Mr. Finchley wandered along the avenue, his face wrinkled by a happy smile of contentment with the weather and himself. A wave of perfume from a flowering shrub swept into his nostrils, and his eyes moved along the pleasant walk, contrasting the beauty of the place with the noise and heat of the Camden Road and the unlovely office of Bardwell & Sprake where, on this Monday morning, his fellow clerks were working at their desks. He felt a guilty apprehension at his freedom and their bondage, but it did not last long and was completely forgotten as he stopped to watch a fat pigeon waddle from his path across the grass. As he stood there a voice called his name and, looking up, he saw a small, familiar figure racing towards him across the grass.

"Oh, m'sieur, I was afraid I should miss you. I am so late!" It was Robert, panting and flushed with running.

Mr. Finchley had thought that he had seen the last of Robert and this sudden appearance found him unprepared. He was not sure that he was pleased to see the boy. He frowned and said severely:

"What are you doing here? Why aren't you at school?" The last question he felt to be a shrewd one, for surely Robert should have been at school and not at large in the streets.

"At school, m'sieur?" There was no doubt of the boy's surprise.

"Yes, at school. You go to school, don't you?"

"Of course, m'sieur." There was little conviction in Robert's tone, but he went on with a sudden access of assurance, a little too much assurance Mr. Finchley thought: "But one does not go to school today, m'sieur. It is a holiday for the feast of Saint Xavier."

"Saint Xavier?" Mr. Finchley was not versed enough in the calendar of saints' days to tell whether Robert spoke the truth or not.

"That is right, m'sieur. And I said to Pépé, what shall I do today? and he said: since your English friend was kind enough to have you for a guide yesterday, and he no doubt wants something to do today, go to him. But this time do not let him pay you. This day you must go together as friends. So I have told Michel and Gaston to meet us at the Concorde Métro Station and we are all to go to the Chatelet Station. I have told them what a good friend of mine you are, and they are very anxious to meet you. We have arranged to visit the Quartier Latin this morning. I said that you would certainly want to go there. You will accept our invitation, will you not, m'sieur?"

Robert's words came tumbling out between his gasps for breath from running, and his fresh face held an anxious expression, as though he were not sure of his reception by Mr. Finchley. The question of schooling had given him the feeling that he might be unwanted.

At first Mr. Finchley was for telling Robert kindly that he could not accept his invitation. He did not want his morning ordered for him. For many years he had been accustomed to living his own life and making his own arrangements, and the selfish method of the past made it difficult for him to change his attitude quickly. He also disliked the breathless haste with which Robert came pouncing upon him with his plan. An expedition, if he wanted to make one to the Latin Quarter, should be thought about first and planned in leisure. But seeing the boy's anxious look, his readiness to take a dismissal yet his pathetic hope that it would not be given, made Mr. Finchley ashamed of his first terseness. He even regretted the question of the school. What did the boy's schooling matter for one day, and why should he, he asked himself, disappoint the lad when this obviously meant so much to Robert? He could find time to see the Louvre as well that morning. This boy, so glad to acknowledge an English friend, had laid a claim to Mr. Finchley which it would have been brutal to ignore. And there were Michel and Gaston waiting—whoever they were—he could imagine the boy's chagrin if he had to go back to them alone. He decided to go with Robert, yet nevertheless he felt it his duty to make one point clear.

"I shall be glad to come with you, Robert," he said; "but there's one point you must understand. You're an English boy and you should understand more about English ways. It may be all right to come rushing up to a Frenchman without warning to carry him away to some jaunt, but all Englishmen—especially when they are on holiday—like to have some time to think over what they will do. So, if in future you make other English friends in Paris, you should remember that. They will think more highly of your friendship, too, if you try to understand them to such an extent."

Robert received this reprimand soberly, but his gloom had a temporary cast as he struggled to control his joy at Mr. Finchley's acceptance of his invitation.

"M'sieur is too kind to me. I do not deserve such a friend, and I will remember what you say. But, m'sieur," his face brightened; "it is all right, because I have remembered. We go on the Métro from the Etoile up there"—he pointed up the avenue towards the great archway—"and it is some way to the Concorde and all that way I will not say one word and m'sieur can think about the plans. You will have plenty of time and then when we reach Michel and Gaston it will be as though I had asked m'sieur yesterday to come. Oh, I am so glad I thought of that. It is all right now, is it not? Come on, m'sieur. From this moment I am silent until we meet my friends."

And without another word he pulled at Mr. Finchley's arm, leading the way towards the Métro station, and Mr. Finchley, perplexed at this apparently simple solution to his insular lack of accommodation, was glad of the boy's silence to ponder the mystery of children. Not one word more did Robert say. So rigidly did he keep his vow that when, at the Etoile, Mr. Finchley took the wrong train he indulged in a frenzied dumb show trying to explain the mistake. They had travelled two stations along the wrong line before an embarrassed Mr. Finchley rightly interpreted the boy's excited pointing at the map of the route and his continual shakings of head and backward pointings along the line. When they quitted the compartment it was to leave behind a collection of travellers who were all plunged into profound sorrow at the sight of so pleasant a gentleman cursed with an idiot son. It was the unspoken commiseration of the travellers rather than Robert's mute appeals which had embarrassed Mr. Finchley.

Only when they reached the Concorde did Robert break his silence, and then, as the train slid into the station and the compartment doors drew back he rushed to them and hung dangerously outwards looking for Michel and Gaston. Mr. Finchley knew when he had discovered them, for the boy began to shout—"*Michel! Gaston! Par ici. Nous voici. Michel! Venez rencontre mon ami anglais.*"

The train stopped, a few passengers pushed their way by the excited boy, and then Michel and Gaston entered the carriage. Mr. Finchley had expected to see two boys of Robert's own age. Instead he was confronted by two men who nodded politely to him as Robert introduced them. They sat themselves down on the seat facing Mr. Finchley.

Michel was as old as Mr. Finchley. He had a pleasant face which was made more interesting by a suggestion of disappointment underlying the good nature, and he wore a little pointed beard whose darkness was touched with a sprinkling of white hairs. On his head he wore a wide-brimmed black hat, and his body was clothed in a shabby velvet-collared coat and dark blue trousers, and he carried in one hand a violin case. Gaston was a young man of middle height, a warm brown complexion and a face wrinkled with a perpetual grin. His chief features of adornment were a large green cap pulled rakishly over one eye and a red-and-yellow muffler of an exotic Paisley pattern. In his hand he, too, carried a case, but it was not a violin case, and Mr. Finchley was quite unable to decide what it might contain.

"*Bonjour, m'sieur,*" said Michel.

"'Ow do you do," said Gaston, and for a while Mr. Finchley was deceived into thinking that he could speak English. He soon found out that Gaston had no more English than the phrase he had conferred on him.

"Here we are, all together," said Robert happily. "This is going to be a happy day."

"You are both musicians?" Mr. Finchley asked the two, with a nod at their cases.

Michel nodded. "We are musicians, m'sieur. For us the music is life and we go nowhere without our instruments. When we are separated from them, we are separated from life."

"They play excellently, m'sieur," volunteered Robert; "and when they play I sometimes sing for them. It is a happy thing to do."

What a happy, musical, carefree race the French were, thought Mr. Finchley.

"M'sieur is not embarrassed by music?" asked Michel as the train rattled along. It was a curious question, but Mr. Finchley decided that it was Michel's way of asking him whether he liked music.

"Not at all," Mr. Finchley replied. "Not at all. I like music. Frequently in London I go to the concerts and operas."

"Then m'sieur has seen Toscanini, Sir Thomas Beecham and Adrian Boult?"

"Ha, the joy of music!" cried Gaston fervently; "I am not hungry when I can hear the great works of Wagner, I forget my thirst when I am with the noble Bach—"

"*Et n'oubliez pas le grand Beethoven*," insisted Michel, which set the two off to a quarrel over their favourite musicians which made them quite oblivious of Mr. Finchley and Robert.

"They are frequently like that, m'sieur," said Robert. The arrival of the train at the Chatelet, where they descended, put an end to the argument.

From the Place du Chatelet they crossed the Seine bridge to the Ile de la Cité, and—at Mr. Finchley's request—made a detour that he might see Notre-Dame. But he was not allowed to enter. They were anxious to get to the Latin Quarter.

Mr. Finchley was disappointed with the Latin Quarter. He had expected wild-looking students, queer twisted streets and a scene of bohemian profusion. All he saw was the wide, busy thoroughfare of the Boulevard St. Michel, and shops and cafés such as were found all over Paris. The people were no different, and the students he passed were serious young men with books under their arms and dressed quite soberly.

"It is not," said Michel, sensing Mr. Finchley's disappointment, "what it was. Everything changes."

Half-way up the boulevard, they stopped. "We have business for half an hour. M'sieur will excuse us? We will return to m'sieur, here," said Michel.

Mr. Finchley found himself sitting at a table outside a café, a glass of coffee ordered for him and the two men gone up the street, and with them Robert, leaving an assurance that he would return soon. It was business, and Mr. Finchley would understand.

Mr. Finchley did not understand, but after the walk he was quite glad to sit down.

He sipped his coffee, wondering what was their business, and what Robert had to do with it.

When the half-hour was done, he had drunk three glasses of coffee and was tired of sitting. The three did not return. He waited a little longer, then deserting his post, he walked up the boulevard, looking back occasionally at the café, expecting to see Robert and his friends arrive from the other direction perhaps.

The pavement was crowded, the road noisy with traffic. Suddenly, ahead of him, above the noises of the morning, he heard music, the treble of a violin and the husky blare of a saxophone, and on the pavement, a hundred yards in front of him, he saw Robert and his friends.

Michel was fiddling, Gaston breathing into his instrument and between them stood Robert. As he watched, Robert began to sing to the gay tune which was being played.

Mr. Finchley was horrified. The blare of the saxophone, the trembling of the violin and the sweet, youthful notes of Robert's voice all conspired to increase the agitation in Mr. Finchley's mind. As the trio performed Robert smiled happily at the passers-by and Michel and Gaston beamed at Robert as though he were their mascot and must bring them luck. The song finished and Robert left the two and ran along the pavement from one person to another holding out his hat. Gaston and Michel began to play a waltz tune.

Mr. Finchley was so disturbed that he remained standing on the pavement, and Robert saw him.

The boy came trotting towards him. "Oh, m'sieur—you have grown tired of waiting? It is understandable—today things are not going well. We have still ten francs to get. Michel and Gaston always play until they have twenty and then they finish."

Mr. Finchley caught Robert by the arm. "Robert," he said severely. "Are you sure Pépé likes you to sing in the streets in this way?"

Robert's eyes opened wide in a puzzled look. "But why not, m'sieur? Pépé does not mind. Whenever we are in Paris he lets me go with Michel and Gaston. I like it, too. Do you not like my singing? Michel says I have a good voice. It is not wrong, is it, to help Michel and Gaston like this? They are my friends. But perhaps it is the song m'sieur does not like. I will ask them to play an English one for you."

He moved away but Mr. Finchley held him by the arm.

"What is wrong, m'sieur?" Robert asked.

The young voice, fresh and innocent, held such a quality of simplicity that its frankness hurt Mr. Finchley, and he felt himself growing angry. It was all wrong that a child like Robert should think it fun to sing in the streets, it was inhuman that his guardian should not stop him. There he was, a small, eager boy, untouched by any of the baseness of the world, standing in the gutter singing like a bird, and not one of the passers-by saw anything wrong in the picture. Another two years of that kind of life … Mr. Finchley tried not to think of what might have happened to his young innocence. Then, to soothe his indignation, his common sense returned. It was no good allowing himself to become sentimental about Robert. Had it been a French boy standing there he would have felt no indignation; had he been walking on Hampstead Heath and seen an English boy doing the same thing, he might have passed by unaffected. It was because Robert was an English boy, isolated in this French surrounding, that the appeal of this small exile impressed him so vividly. The boy was happy and his friends really were friends. It was useless, Mr. Finchley felt, to quarrel with the obvious inequalities of life.

He caught hold of the boy's arm. "Come along!" he said firmly. "You're not going back to them, not for this morning, anyway—"

"But, m'sieur ..." Robert's protest died as he was hauled along the pavement. Behind them Michel and Gaston jigged away at another dance tune, and as the music grew fainter so Mr. Finchley's pace slowed up until they were walking normally.

"I am sorry if m'sieur is annoyed," said Robert after a time.

"I am not annoyed," said Mr. Finchley. "We will say no more about it."

"Then where are we going, m'sieur?"

"We are going," said Mr. Finchley definitely, "to the Louvre—"

"Oh, m'sieur, you do not want to go there. It is—"

Mr. Finchley silenced him. "We are going to the Louvre," he repeated. "It will do us both good."

Afterwards Mr. Finchley was not sure that it had done them both good. They wandered through gallery after gallery, Mr. Finchley beginning in a spirit of excitement which gradually dwindled away to a curious lethargy and repletion. There was too much to see, and when he reached the Mona Lisa, nothing in the world could have provoked from him more than a mild stare or driven from his mind the pressing thought that his feet ached.

"Is it not beautiful?" he asked Robert, feeling that it was his duty to open the boy's eyes to this cultural world. But Robert was not impressed.

"There is a woman like that who sells crayfish near the Place de la République. Sometimes the fish are bad. Can we go out now?"

But Mr. Finchley would not let him go out. He explored three more galleries first. It was good for both of them that they should see these paintings and sculptures, he thought, and even as he thought it he felt it to be a lie, and he was sure of it when they were out of the Louvre and sitting quietly in the freshness of the Tuileries Gardens with the traffic roar faintly around them. And sitting there the memory of the singing incident grew fainter and Mr. Finchley began to feel at peace with the world, and Robert, seeing him grow responsive, asked him questions about England, questions which Mr. Finchley took a pleasure in answering. He told Robert about the country he had never known. He took him to Stratford-on-Avon, described the Berkshire Downs, the beauties of the Thames, and sent him deep into Devon and Cornwall. And with this small boy beside him as he talked Mr. Finchley began to be aware of the narrowness of the groove he worked and lived in, and for a while there opened up before him the vision of a larger, wider experience which he had denied himself all his life, which he had denied himself so long that now it was too late.

He and the boy had lunch together in a small restaurant and then, to make sure that Robert did not go back to his friends, he told him about his intended trip to Malmaison that afternoon, and Robert was enthusiastic to accompany him.

"It is the right weather for the country, m'sieur. I love the country."

They met Marie at the Porte Maillot. Mr. Finchley had been nervous of her reception of Robert. This was her afternoon away from children, but Marie soon reassured him. Her dislike of children was apparently based upon her dislike of one particular child. She and Robert, as they waited for the bus to come in, soon became friends.

As the bus came in and they were about to climb aboard, an exclamation from Robert checked them.

"Why, M'sieur Hume!"

They turned to find Hume just come up to the bus stop.

"Hullo," said Mr. Finchley, "what are you doing here?"

"My friend was called away on business this afternoon, so I thought I'd come along after all," he said, with a show of unconcern.

"Well, come and join the happy party," Marie greeted him pleasantly. "The more the merrier. I hope your conscience doesn't prick you for running away from your birds and butterflies in the museum?"

"If it does," called Mr. Finchley happily, as they took their seats, "he can make up for it by working overtime tomorrow." He sat with Robert at his side, and only then wondered what chance had arranged the party so that Hume sat with Marie.

The bus started away on its bumpy journey through the Paris suburbs towards the house where the unhappy Josephine had lived, the house which had held her sorrow at the loss of Napoleon to another woman.

He had expected Malmaison to be in the country, but to Mr. Finchley it was no more than a pleasant mansion whose grounds were islanded in a growth of untidy houses. All around it stretched the lusty, unlovely growth of outer Paris. Here and there a field stood bare against the march of houses, and the river, twisting and looping, threw ineffective salients to block the rapid victory of the suburbs.

Only in the grounds of Malmaison itself did the country linger, a gentle, refined country. Thrushes sang, the sun struck a soft light from the flower petals and the wind whispered a quiet chatter of consolation to the branches of the old trees as they bent towards the shallow pools where dull carp moved slowly. And the guide, who showed them over the house, soon destroyed any real pleasure they might have taken in the house. It was not his fault. He had been a guide so long, he could not be expected to recognise the moods of the many visitors who claimed his days, so he had resolved his difficulties by working out a humorous line for each faded brocade, a quip for each pathetic insignia of past splendour. All the world loves a joke, he must have argued, and no doubt he was right, but the jokes must be good and his were not. He must have suspected this, for he led the laughter himself after each witticism and Mr. Finchley and his friends laughed with him, feeling uncomfortable.

"Poor Josephine," said Marie when they were outside and had left the guide with his tip. "How unhappy she must have been." But the troubles of Josephine did not depress Marie for long.

On the way back she had Hume sitting with her, and Mr. Finchley, from behind, could see that she had become a listener, and he hoped that she would be a good listener as he heard Hume explaining seriously:

"You see the bearded titmouse has become almost extinct now, and this pair we found in Norfolk meant a lot to us. We rigged up an old punt as a hide in the reed bed and we spent days out there in turn, photographing and making a study of them …"

And later—

"And these little flies, the Drosophilidæ, breed so quickly that they have been used in experiments on heredity. You can study generation after generation for inherited characteristics and the arrangement of their chromosomes ..."

Apparently Marie could be a good listener, Mr. Finchley decided as they rattled back to Paris.

The afternoon had passed quietly, almost uneventfully, yet Mr. Finchley was glad of that. Against a background of green lawns, cold, pathetic rooms, he had been given a revelation; he had seen Hume drawn towards Marie, noticed their reluctance to admit what they felt, and smiled at the eager talk with which they had disguised their interest in one another. At once he felt curiously wise and indulgent—and then he remembered Mrs. Crantell and was chastened.

Before the bus reached Porte Maillot Robert was making tentative suggestions for an expedition that evening to the fair which was being held in the Place de la République, but Mr. Finchley was safe from his bait.

"Mr. Hume is taking me to the Casino to hear Maurice Chevalier, and tomorrow, after I have attended to some business in the morning, I am returning to England."

"Then I shall not see you again?" Robert's face trembled.

"Cheer up," Mr. Finchley encouraged him. "I will write to you from England sometimes and you shall write to me. I'll tell you what—if you like to come up to the apartment about four o'clock in the afternoon tomorrow, you shall help me pack and come with me to the station. How's that?"

It was a little better, and Robert did his best to smile. It was a smile which kept swimming into Mr. Finchley's memory all that evening as he sat in the Casino, and which made him at times oblivious of France's most famous smile.

X
How Mr. Finchley spends an evening out

AT nine o'clock on Tuesday morning, Mr. Finchley rang up the Marivaux and found that Mr. Hammerton had arrived the previous evening. Mr. Hammerton's man informed him that Mr. Hammerton would be glad to see him at eleven.

At half-past ten Mr. Finchley gathered his papers into his brief case and started to walk to the hotel. It was a fine morning and he felt like walking. In order to be on time he finished his journey by taxi. He never kept a client waiting. But the same feelings had no place in Mr. Hammerton's philosophy, for when Mr. Finchley reached the Marivaux he was told by the man that Mr. Hammerton had been called out and would not be able to see Mr. Finchley until four o'clock.

Mr. Finchley, with difficulty, restrained his annoyance before the man and left, his only solace a sense of satisfaction that he had been right about Mr. Hammerton, a thriftless, inconsiderate waster. He did not look forward to the interview at four o'clock.

For a while he walked along the street, trying to work out his best plan. Then he telephoned the apartment, told them he would not be in to lunch and asked Madame to tell Robert to come back at seven and he would take him out to dinner. Now that the interview was made later there was no need for him to catch a late boat train and travel through the night. He would go back early the next morning. This done, he finished the morning by climbing to the Sacré Coeur, enjoying the view of Paris. He lunched at a snack bar, keeping an anxious eye on his brief case, and then passed the time left to him at a newsreel cinema. He felt it was a weak way to pass the afternoon, but his annoyance with Mr. Hammerton had bereft him of the initiative to make better plans. Inside the cinema he was considerably embarrassed because the girl attendant, on showing him to his seat, had waited by him mysteriously for a while, and when he showed no signs of acknowledging her presence, broke into a whispered protest that could be heard all over the theatre. Her rapid French and his confusion made the whole incident unintelligible to him, and finally she had gone away muttering. Later, from an examination of the behaviour of the other attendants as they showed people to their seats, he discovered that it was the custom, even in cinemas, to tip the attendant. The discovery made him hot with shame and he paid little more than perfunctory interest to the pictures of the President of the Republic making a speech, the whirling dervishes of a bicycle race and the glimpses of wealthy little Alphonse Reims taking an outing in the Bois.

At two minutes to four Mr. Finchley entered the lift at the Marivaux. He had never seen this Mr. Hammerton, yet already he disliked him, and he did not feel that his antipathy was illogical. Here, if ever there was such a man, was one who had wasted his opportunities.

This time Mr. Hammerton was in, and Mr. Finchley found himself facing a tall, thin man with a high forehead and dark hair combed severely back with the faintest path of a parting slipping down the sharp slope of his temple. His face was long, his mouth strong and big and his cheekbones large, and he carried an expression of weary resignation, as though there were few things which interested him in life. Mr. Finchley found it difficult to believe that this man was fifty—he looked much younger.

"I'm sorry to have kept you about," he said politely. "Still, I expect you found something to do in Paris. If I know lawyers you'll charge me with the expenses." He laughed dryly and lit himself a cigarette after Mr. Finchley had refused one.

"The wait has certainly not been unpleasant, sir," said Mr. Finchley, and without waiting for comment he brought out his papers and continued: "Here are the various documents relating to the inheritance, all of which I presume you will want to have a little time to look through. Some of them need your signature—duly witnessed, of course. If there are any points on which you would like advice I shall be glad—"

"Yes, of course," said Mr. Hammerton. "I'll have a look at them later. The old girl died just in time, didn't she? I've been fortunate in my relatives. They never seemed to have kept me waiting when I was in need."

"There is one further point, sir," Mr. Finchley went on as the other paused, and as he spoke he thought what a pity it was that a clerk must never be allowed the indulgence of a human being. He would have given a lot to speak frankly to Mr. Hammerton for five minutes.

"What's that?"

"As you will see when you go through the papers, most of your aunt's securities and investments were English and Bardwell & Sprake, of course, acted for her during her lifetime, and—unless you have already decided otherwise—we should be very happy to perform the same duty for you."

Mr. Hammerton looked over his shoulder from the window, and said tersely—"Why not? I don't care who looks after it, as long as I have the spending of it."

"Thank you, sir. We very much appreciate the honour and I assure you —"

"Don't assure me of anything," said Mr. Hammerton fiercely, turning from the window and coming towards Mr. Finchley, "and stop talking like something that's been wound up. Here—" he pushed Mr. Finchley firmly into a chair, "sit down there and be human for a moment. Fill your pipe, scratch your head—do something to show you don't move by a spring."

Mr. Finchley sat down, fearing for a moment that the man was going to be violent with him. Then, as though their familiar shape would give him back his equanimity, he took out his pipe and pouch and began to tap home the tobacco.

"That's better," said Mr. Hammerton, sitting opposite him. "Go on, light it!" He watched the operation, and not until Mr. Finchley's pipe was going strong did he speak, and then he said seriously:

"You haven't a very high opinion of me, have you, Mr. Finchley?"

Mr. Finchley's surprise was too great to be hidden entirely. What Mr. Hammerton said was true, of course, but he had not imagined that his feelings were so apparent. It was disloyal to his firm to obtrude his personal opinions into a business matter.

Mr. Finchley did what any good clerk would have done—he hedged.

"Mr. Hammerton, I assure you that you are—"

"Please!" Mr. Hammerton implored. "You don't have to be polite with me. I'm asking you not to be polite, but truthful. I shouldn't think much of you if you didn't think I was a pretty worthless creature. Do you know what I have done with my life? I'll tell you. In the last thirty years I've wandered from one country to another and managed to spend three fortunes doing it. I've spent carelessly the money which other people have worked hard to make. And what have I to show for it? The money brought me nothing worth remembering, except a string of hotel names. No adventures more exciting than missing a boat or having my pocket picked. I used to think there was some virtue in the money, something that would attract adventure and excitement to me because I had it—but it didn't; and here I am at fifty with this new fortune dropped into my lap to save me from a string of debts and set the ball rolling again. I'm a selfish, worthless creature." Mr. Hammerton finished his self-denunciation vigorously, and Mr. Finchley could not help feeling that the man obtained some satisfaction from his savageness against his own faults. And yet Mr. Finchley recognised his sincerity. That, at least, was a sign of grace. He began to feel sorry for the man, and when he felt sorry it was hardly possible for him to go on disliking Mr. Hammerton quite so much.

"Yes, I think you are," said Mr. Finchley slowly. "But there's nothing to get dispirited over. None of us is perfect. You can hardly regard yourself as too old to make a fresh start. You wouldn't be the first."

"That's what I keep telling myself," admitted Mr. Hammerton bitterly, "but you don't know how much easier it is to say than do. Change your life! What could I do?"

"Are you seriously asking me to suggest things you might do?"

"Yes, of course. What would you do? Suppose you'd been in my position and suddenly realised you wanted to get a clean new grip on life?"

"What would I do?" Mr. Finchley poised the question lovingly. For a moment he said nothing, thinking; then he spoke simply and honestly as he felt: "I'd grow some roots, that's what I'd do. I'd go back to England, buy a farm, get a good foreman to help me and I'd make a place for myself in my own country. I'd forget hotels and have my own four walls, my own fire, burning my own logs, and I'd take a pride in pigs and sheep, not motor-cars, and as long as I had a field of corn to look at I'd forget the best views in the world ..." He broke off, suddenly self-conscious, looking at Mr. Hammerton.

Mr. Hammerton's face was alive now.

"I was right," he said. "The moment you came in through that door, do you know what I said to myself?"

"I haven't the faintest idea," confessed Mr. Finchley.

"Well, I said—'Here's a nice, honest sort of fellow who thinks I'm about as much use to the world as a piece of dried putty. And he's right. But before he goes out of this room I've got a feeling that he's going to help me.' And you have. You've told me to do the very thing I've been thinking about for weeks. I've got to talk about this with you. Won't you come and have some dinner with me to-night? I'll have those papers ready for you then. We can talk about this idea—you must come. It's important to me. You can travel back tomorrow. How does that suit you?"

Mr. Finchley hesitated before he replied. He had promised to take Robert out to dinner that night, yet it was his duty to please his client. He looked across at Mr. Hammerton and seeing the other's anxious face, he decided to be straightforward with him. In the short time they had been talking, Mr. Finchley realised that he had witnessed a change in the man, his guard of weariness with life was gone, leaving him a pleading, intensely human figure. Mr. Finchley knew there need be no hesitancies between them now. Very simply he told him about Robert and how disappointed the boy would be if he let him down.

"The travelling back tomorrow is quite all right, of course. But you can imagine how the boy would feel."

Mr. Hammerton waved his hands, indicating his relief.

"If that's all that is worrying you, you can consider your troubles over," he declared. "Bring the boy as well. He sounds a nice little fellow and I haven't talked to an English boy in years. He ought to get a thrill out of dining at the Marivaux."

Robert did get a thrill. When he was told that he was to dine with Mr. Finchley and a friend at the Marivaux, his eyes opened wide and his verbal appreciation of the honour took the form of a request to use Mr. Finchley's brushes in order that he might look his best.

"I must not disgrace you with your friend, m'sieur. In England, Pépé says, they do not care how they look, but in France we must always look well for the sake of our honour."

He brushed his hair neatly and then looked across at Mr. Finchley, neat and important in his dinner jacket, his bald head shining, his face fresh and rosy from a shave, his stout body bearing the white shield of his shirt front bravely.

"How magnificent m'sieur looks. I am so proud that you are my friend."

Mr. Finchley stopped any further eulogies and they went out to get a taxi, and later, hand in hand, for Robert was seized with a sudden nervousness before the gleaming entrance of the Marivaux and the Olympian splendour of the commissionaire, they entered the hotel.

Mr. Hammerton was waiting for them in the lounge. Mr. Finchley's respect for him increased as he observed the way in which he treated the boy. His manner towards Robert was that of one man to another, an attitude which Robert, too, appreciated.

"So you are Robert Gillespie? I am honoured to make your acquaintance."

"M'sieur is very kind," replied Robert.

A waiter led them to their table in the restaurant. It was a large saloon with gilded wall panels, hanging candelabras, sparkling glass and silver, and a soft expanse of white cloth and brilliant flowers. At one end of the room an orchestra played.

As they sat down Mr. Hammerton said: "Because the three of us are Englishmen, far from our native land, I have ordered an English dinner. Does that please everyone? Good. There is vegetable soup, Dover sole, to remind us of the white cliffs and Shakespeare—"

"He is the gentleman who said 'To be or not to be,' is he not?" asked Robert. "Pépé tells me often that that was papa's favourite quotation."

"Quite right, Robert. To follow the fish we have roast beef, baked potatoes, brussels sprouts—do not let the word brussels deceive you, they are honest English vegetables—and Yorkshire pudding—"

"Ha, Yorkshire. That is another county I know. They are so good at cricket, which is a game the French do not understand. In all the English papers which I find I read first the cricket scores—"

"That's the right way to read a newspaper," observed Mr. Finchley. "A true Englishman always turns first to the cricket scores."

"And to follow we have baked apple pie and Cornish cream. For drink there is beer and Somersetshire cider. Does that make us all homesick, gentlemen?" This was a gay, animated Mr. Hammerton, altogether a more pleasant man, Mr. Finchley decided.

Robert nodded his head, and then said: "Some day I shall see all those places. But when I am bigger I shall go to England. Since I have known Monsieur Finchley, I have been thinking that I should like to go soon. I like the French, but it is not the same as my own country people."

"There is plenty of time," said Mr. Hammerton. "You must not lose heart. Living abroad will strengthen your mind, give you vision and tolerance. At one time every young man was sent abroad for a few years to complete his education and that is what you are doing. You will return to England knowing another language than your own, and with such experience that most Englishmen would gladly have."

For the next half-hour there was little talk, for they were all busy eating and drinking.

Over their coffee Mr. Hammerton talked about the farm. Since Mr. Finchley had last seen him he had made up his mind. He was filled with an exuberant enthusiasm. His enthusiasm, Mr. Finchley felt, was a little too overwhelming to give any warrant of longevity. But he repressed the suggestion, telling himself that we all register enthusiasm differently and it was wrong to judge without the evidence of time.

He was going to England at once to begin his search for a farm. It was to be in Kent, with plenty of pasture for sheep, fruit and corn land and enough wood to give him pheasants for shooting and logs for his fire.

"Gaston comes from a farm," said Robert. "He has promised to take me there some day. How good it would be to live on a farm with all the animals. I am sorry that Pépé does not like animals. There are many dogs I could have had, but he always says no and I have to take them back to the Bois ..."

Mr. Finchley guessed that Robert's dogs were obtained as he procured haddock, and he was glad of Pépé's embargo.

When dinner and farm conversation was done, Mr. Hammerton suddenly demanded what they should do that evening.

"We must not take up more of your time," said Mr. Finchley.

"Nonsense, we can't break up the party so soon. Let's see, what could we do?"

Mr. Finchley made no argument. He could see that Mr. Hammerton had made up his mind, and he himself—after the excellent dinner—was in no mood to raise objections.

"If m'sieur is determined," said Robert, "there is the Foire de la République. It is a very good place to spend the evening."

"The fair! The very thing!" cried Mr. Hammerton. "We'll go there. I haven't been to a fair for years. Come on—we must lose no time."

He marshalled them out and they were soon in a taxi on their way to the Place de la République.

When they reached the fair the two men surrendered themselves to the guidance of Robert. The whole of the Place was given over to the fair, its *pavé* covered with stalls and roundabouts, and overflowing from the square it stretched away down one of the principal streets in a long perspective of lights and sideshows. The air was full of clashing music and the cries of men and women.

Before they plunged into the delights before them they surrendered themselves to the gingerbread stall and had their names written in sugar across the back of a gingerbread pig and then, each with a pig in hand, chewing the sweetmeat, they advanced on the fair.

Mr. Finchley knew something about fairs, but he had never encountered one of such size and variety. Robert and Mr. Hammerton soon showed that they were not daunted by variety. They tried the shooting gallery, the scenic railway, the snake-charmer's tent, the Wild West show, the animal oddities, the dwarf circus and the glittering swing-boats. They stood entranced before the stalls of nougat and scent, where silver-haired elegant young men in evening dress stood on little platforms and moved and blinked their eyes so that it was impossible to tell whether they were mechanical dummies or really alive.

Mr. Finchley could not be tempted on the scenic railway. He had far too much respect for his internal organs, and while he waited for the others he watched the circling, dipping pageant of a roundabout whose proprietor had enlisted cocks, cows, ostriches, motors and dirigibles to carry his passengers. Then, in the carriages swinging by, two faces appeared from he interior of a streamlined motor. At first Mr. Finchley was too surprised to be certain, but the motor swung round again, and this time he was certain he was looking at Marie and Hume. They were laughing and had no eyes for the crowd, and when the roundabout stopped they must have got down on the far side, for Mr. Finchley did not see them. He was glad that they had not seen him—it might have embarrassed them, especially as he had understood Hume was attending a lecture that evening.

He said nothing of what he had seen to Robert and Mr. Hammerton when they arrived, dizzy from their swoopings.

Leaving the scenic railway they found themselves standing before a booth whose banner proclaimed that within was enshrined the glamour, mystery and amusement of that marvellous presentation known in five continents as the "South Sea Follies". On the platform outside the booth a group of girls in reed skirts pirouetted and contorted themselves to the sound of music which was so weird that Mr. Finchley presumed that it must be peculiar to the Pacific. The girls, tired and unattractive, leered provocatively at the crowd.

Mr. Hammerton looked at Mr. Finchley and then, with a nod towards Robert, said: "I think we'll give this one a miss."

"But, m'sieur," cried Robert, "there is the magician."

And there was the magician, a short, chubby-faced man who beamed widely at the crowd as he pulled young chicken from his mouth, streamers from his ears, and kept up a cheerful patter. Robert stared at him, entranced.

"We'll find another magician for you," said Mr. Finchley firmly, and he pulled Robert away. But Robert was not to be led so easily away. After they had gone a few yards, Mr. Finchley let go of him, and it was not long before Robert took advantage of a press in the crowd to turn tail and go back to the "South Sea Follies".

The platform show had finished and a barker was now urging the crowd to take tickets and see the show. Robert stood, eyeing the painted canvas and wishing he had the price of admission. As he stood there a man who had been watching him closely came up to his side and nodded casually towards the show, saying: "Would you care to see the show, son?"

He was a Frenchman, and Robert, without turning to him, said "Very much, but I have no money."

"That's all right," said the man cheerfully. "I'll take you in. Come on—it's a fine show." He began to lead Robert towards the pay-box. Before he could take the tickets, however, Mr. Finchley and Mr. Hammerton arrived. They had missed Robert and guessed his whereabouts.

"Where are you going?" asked Mr. Hammerton, taking Robert's arm.

"This gentleman has kindly offered to take me into the show," said Robert, and added doubtfully, "that is all right?"

"No, it isn't all right," said Mr. Finchley.

"Mais, m'sieur—" began the Frenchman.

Mr. Hammerton interrupted him with a burst of French that made the man go red with anger, then white with shame, and finally turn away muttering to himself.

"Whatever did you say to him?" asked Mr. Finchley as they moved away.

Mr. Hammerton laughed. "I told him what I thought of a man who would take a young boy into a show like that, hinted that he was probably a kidnapper, and suggested he went away before I punched him on the nose and called the police to him for creating a public disturbance. So he went. Come on—let's forget him. I'm enjoying myself too much to worry about touts like that."

And Mr. Hammerton was enjoying himself. He seemed to have lost his sophistication and found as much delight in the joys of the fair as did Robert. They went from one end to the other and when they were through it was late. They emerged, three satiated pleasure-makers, their heads still in a whirl from the lights and the frolic, their hands full of trophies from stalls and galleries, their pockets bulging with nougat, sweets and cough cures.

Robert stopped and breathed freely of the fresh night air; his dark hair was banded by a paper streamer, his eyes bright and happy, and his face flushed with enjoyment.

"Oh, messieurs," he sighed happily. "What a night! Never in the whole of my life could I expect to be so happy again, and never shall I forget." There was something in his simple, enthusiastic declaration of happiness and gratitude that touched the two men, reminding them of their own boyhood when such pleasures had been the entrance to a wonderland that took no thought of the future or the past, when one resigned oneself to the deity of the booths and merry-go-rounds and found happiness. Mr. Finchley was suddenly chastened with sadness at the thought that tomorrow he would be gone from this boy, back to his known life, engaged again in the selfish mechanics of his everyday world. Robert would still be in Paris, carrying his small body through the round of disappointments, hopes and fears of youth, with only the vague Pépé to counsel him, and his real country no more than a colourful mystery to him. When he spoke it was gently, his voice full of the affection he was feeling for Robert:

"Well, Robert, it's growing late. I think I'd better see you home. You might get robbed of all your prizes unless you have a protector."

He was a little worried about the boy, for he fancied he had seen the Frenchman from the South Sea Show following them once or twice. But he had not been sure, so he said nothing.

"But I couldn't trouble m'sieur—" Robert began.

"Nonsense," interrupted Mr. Hammerton. "We'll both go and look after you."

He called a taxi.

"It is to the Boulevard de la Bastille we go," Robert said, and he was silent for the rest of the journey, and Mr. Finchley saw that he was tired and with difficulty keeping his eyes open.

Half-way down the Boulevard de la Bastille Robert sat up and called to the driver to stop. "This is the place, messieurs."

They got out and Mr. Finchley saw that the boulevard was one which ran down to the Seine from the Place de la Bastille. On the left-hand side were tall, rather dingy houses and a few cafés and warehouses. On the right-hand side, running the whole length of the road, was a coal and merchandise wharf, a long, dark-watered dock that disappeared under a bridge at the far end of the boulevard to join the Seine from whence came and went the barges that visited the wharf.

"This is the way," cried Robert, and he ran before them, crossing the road and passing down a narrow slip on to the wharf. At the dockside were two or three long barges, tarpaulins over their decks and small cabins at their sterns, very much like the barges Mr. Finchley knew on English canals. Robert waited on the dockside for them to come up to him, and then, pointing to the barges, said eagerly:

"That is the one, messieurs—the *Swan of Paris*—that is where I live with Pépé while we are in Paris. And now, messieurs, I wish you both good night. I am so tired, but I will never forget this evening. I shall see you, shall I not m'sieur, at the station tomorrow?" He looked at Mr. Finchley before hurrying off.

In their amazement the two men could do no more than give him good night and watch him cross the planks to where the *Swan of Paris* was wedged between two barges. He stood for a moment outside the cabin, waved to them, and then disappeared through the low doorway.

"Good gracious me!" cried Mr. Finchley, recovering from his shock. "I never dreamt of such a thing. Pépé must be a bargeman and Robert lives with him."

He and Robert had always had so much else to talk about that he had never questioned the boy about his home life.

"Do you mean you never suspected that he lived here?" asked Mr. Hammerton, frowning.

"Never—he told me he lived by the river. I don't mean he was trying to conceal it. Obviously he doesn't think it at all strange."

"Well, there it is—you can't do anything about these things. He's happy enough, I suppose." The old, weary look returned to Hammerton's face.

"So he may be, but for all that I'd like to know something about Pépé. Who is this Pépé, I wonder?" Mr. Finchley asked the question almost indignantly and his voice echoed between the piled heaps of coal and wood.

"I am Pépé, m'sieur," said a thick, not unpleasant voice close behind him. The words were spoken in French. "Did I hear someone speak my name?"

Mr. Finchley turned to find a short, thick-set man behind him. He wore an old felt hat, round his neck a twisted red scarf, and his hands were deep in the pockets of a pair of rust-coloured working trousers. As Mr. Finchley looked at him, the man took one hand leisurely from his pocket and stroked the long hairs of a straggling moustache which gave his round, innocent face a touch of incongruous severity.

"Are you Pépé?" Mr. Finchley asked.

"I am, m'sieur. And who are you?"

"I am Mr. Finchley—and this is Mr. Hammerton," said Mr. Finchley, picking his way carefully through the French phrases. "We have just brought Robert back from the fair."

"You have been to the fair? Robert likes such things. He has told me much about you. You are his friend from England?"

"That's right. And you, I understand, are his guardian."

"He lives with me, m'sieur, since his father is dead. M'sieur does not know about his father?"

Mr. Finchley admitted that he did not, hoping that Pépé would tell him something about Mr. Gillespie.

Pépé understood the unspoken curiosity and went on: "His father was my friend. He was an artist. He and his wife they lived in my house in Paris, and when his wife left him—then my wife and I looked after the little boy for him. But he always hoped that his wife would return, and then one day he learned that she had been drowned and after that, alas, he did not work at his painting. Ha, m'sieur, it was a sad thing to watch, especially for his friend, as I was. Often my wife has said to me: 'Pépé, there is one who does not want to live.' He died when Robert was a very little boy, and my wife looked after him, for he had no friends or relations in England to come for him. We have no children of our own, so we take him as our son, but always I make him remember his English, for some day, I say, he may want to go back to his country. And then my wife she die, too, and I am no good with our little café and I have to sell it, and Robert and me, we come to live on the barge. Is she not splendid out there!" He pointed proudly to the barge. "We travel much on the barge, but always our hearts are of Paris. It is a good living for a single man. I teach Robert what I can. He is a clever boy, but there are many things he misses. I hope he has not worried you, messieurs, but he is so proud of his English friends."

"You are quite sure that he has no relations living in England?" asked Mr. Hammerton.

"Absolutely, m'sieur. His father has told me so many times before he died, and has charged me to look after the boy. But, messieurs, I am rude to keep you standing here. Would you not come to my cabin and drink with me …"

They thanked him for his kindness. Neither of them felt they wanted to go aboard the barge. They wished Pépé good night and left the wharf.

"The great thing to remember," said Mr. Hammerton, sensing Mr. Finchley's feelings, "is that the boy is very happy. Think of the life he must lead aboard that barge. What boy wouldn't be happy there?"

"That may be so," replied Mr. Finchley after a while; "but most children can manage to be happy wherever they are. It isn't enough for a child to think merely of its happiness. There's the question of opportunity. What opportunities will Robert have later on from such a start in life?"

Mr. Hammerton did not answer that question. Instead he said: "We can't do anything about it, anyhow. Pépé's the one who should do the worrying."

XI
In which Mr. Finchley and Robert are taken for a ride

WHEN Mr. Finchley awoke the next morning his first thoughts were of the papers that Mr. Hammerton was to have signed and returned to him. In the excitement of the previous evening they had not even been discussed.

Mr. Finchley was catching the boat-train after lunch and he hurried his scanty breakfast and left the house to go to the Marivaux for the papers. As he walked up towards the Etoile to get a taxi he was not surprised to see Robert coming towards him over the lawns. It seemed to Mr. Finchley that there never had been a morning in his life when he had not gone out to meet that figure advancing towards him. But, somehow, this morning Robert's young face and eager little body had a new significance. He was not just an amusing, occasionally disturbing companion, but a personality that held the potentialities of much disappointment and sadness.

Robert was quite unaware of the gravity with which Mr. Finchley regarded him.

"You are on the way to the station, m'sieur?"

Mr. Finchley told him what he was going to do and gave way to Robert's plea that he should be allowed to travel to the Marivaux with him and wait until he had collected the papers.

Mr. Finchley left him sitting quietly in the lounge while he went up to Mr. Hammerton. He discovered that Mr. Hammerton, too, was awake and thinking of the papers, and he had dispatched them by a messenger to Mr. Finchley's lodgings where they were probably waiting for him now.

"I'm sorry you had the trouble. I should have telephoned you, but I didn't know your number. And anyhow I thought you'd be there. Well, I wish you a pleasant crossing. I shall be following you in a few days—when I've cleared up some affairs here. Don't forget you're engaged as a haymaker for my first harvest!"

Mr. Finchley smiled and left him. He collected Robert from the lounge, and as they stood on the hotel steps he said: "Would you like to come back with me and help me pack?" He had already packed, but he felt that the boy would perhaps like to have some lunch with him before he went to the station.

"I wish you were not going," said Robert quietly. "Paris will seem so different without you."

"Cheer up," said Mr. Finchley. "Come on, we'll take a taxi."

He stood on the pavement, and before he could lift his hand a long yellow and red taxi slid up to the pavement and the driver enquired eagerly, "Taxi, m'sieur?"

Mr. Finchley nodded.

"Could you not make some excuse for staying another day, m'sieur?" insisted Robert. "Pépé says that there is always a good excuse to be found for doing the thing you want to do."

Mr. Finchley shook his head—"It can't be done, Robert. I'd like to stay, but there's nothing to keep me here now." Which, as he was to discover very soon, was a rash statement to make in a city like Paris.

The taxi had not travelled far from the hotel when it suddenly slowed down and pulled in to the curb. It stopped alongside of a small café—the Silver Moon—and the driver leaned across the door of his cab and honked his horn three times vigorously. At the sound a man sitting at one of the outside tables rose to his feet and hurried across the pavement to the car. Rapid conversation passed between the two, and then, as the taxi began to move off, the man from the café opened the door and slid gracefully into the car, taking the small drop-down seat so that his back was to the driver and he faced Mr. Finchley and Robert.

"You will pardon me for taking this liberty, but I am compelled to it by a necessity which makes her own laws," he said in a low, strong voice.

"What does he say?" Mr. Finchley asked Robert. He had been too surprised to be able to follow the man's words. Robert repeated the man's speech and as he finished the stranger added politely:

"I had not realised that m'sieur was an Englishman, and that the boy spoke English. I speak very good English and perhaps it is better if I talk only in that language." He spoke in English, and with very little accent.

"Do you mind telling me why you have forced yourself upon us in this way?" said Mr. Finchley severely. "I have hired this taxi to take me to my lodgings."

The man laughed pleasantly, indulgently, as though he relished the joke. He was about thirty; his eyes rather large and bright, his head a great dome surmounting a long, pale, intelligent face which was forcefully marked with the clear lines of a firm mouth and hooked nose. He wore a light raincoat and was hatless, his fair hair straggling untidily over his forehead. "You may have hired this taxi," he said gently; "but it belongs to me. I gave exactly fifteen thousand francs for it a month ago, and the gentleman who is driving it is my secretary." As he said this his great eyes gleamed and his mouth twisted into a mocking grin so that his face assumed a fanatical, almost cruel aspect. "It is necessary," he went on unhurriedly, "sometimes to spend money in order to get much more money. In England I believe they call it capital outlay—though I do not like the word capital."

Mr. Finchley decided to take action. He ignored the man and, leaning forward, tapped the glass for the driver. The man pushed back the sliding glass panel and half turned towards him. "M'sieur?" he questioned respectfully.

"Please stop by the next gendarme and ask him to remove this person from the taxi which I have hired," said Mr. Finchley curtly. His only answer was a low chuckle from the driver and the panel slid back.

"Jacques is polite always, but he will not obey you," explained the stranger. "You do not recognise him today? That is because he is wearing his false moustache."

"Will you please explain what all this means?" demanded Mr. Finchley, forcing himself to control his alarm.

"Certainly," replied the stranger, "in very good time. But at the moment I am not in the mood for explanations.

Which is understandable. For a number of days now I have spent much time at the Silver Moon, waiting for Jacques to arrive with his taxi, and for the same number of days Jacques has played at being a taxi-driver outside the Marivaux. Now we have both succeeded and we are both enjoying our triumph. But we must enjoy it alone for a while. There is plenty of time for explanation. You must wait."

"He is a bandit, I'm sure. He wants our money," cried Robert suddenly.

The stranger stiffened at these words and replied angrily. "I do not care to be called a bandit by such as you. You had better be silent than so inappropriately talkative. Jacques"—he called through the panel—"stop at the next post-box and post these." He handed a bundle of letters to the driver and then closed the panel. At the end of the street the car stopped by a blue post-box and Jacques got out to post the letters.

"Come along, Robert," said Mr. Finchley. "We'll get out as well." He made a movement to the door, but was stopped by Robert tugging at his arm.

"M'sieur, we cannot. Look!"

Mr. Finchley saw that the stranger had drawn his hand from his pocket and was holding, pointing at them, a revolver with a curious swollen barrel.

"It will be better if you both sit very still and make no nuisance of yourselves," said the man, his words making his sincerity evident by their very tone. "I would not feel guilty if I were to kill you. It would be a pleasure, and I may mention that the revolver is a silent one."

Mr. Finchley sat back, one arm going round Robert's shoulder, convinced of the seriousness of their position.

He sat there until Jacques was back and the taxi on its way once more, his mind trying to find some explanation for this outrage. Jacques's face seemed familiar. Why should anyone, he asked himself, want to kidnap Robert and himself?

"I am glad that you have decided to be sensible," the stranger commended him. "You will notice, m'sieur, that we are not going to your lodgings as you put it so cleverly, but we are on the road to Versailles. It is not a lovely road, nor indeed is Versailles so lovely as the guide books would make out. There is a vulgarity about the Palace and the grounds which offends a man of simple tastes. Its associations are also unpleasant and offend. After Versailles I shall pull down the curtains so you cannot see the road, for that would not be wise. And now I must beg you both to be silent, for I have many things to think about."

"I know," said Robert suddenly, ignoring the command for silence, his face brightening with hope—"he is Arsène Lupin—"

"Arsène Lupin?" Mr. Finchley was puzzled.

"The boy refers to a famous fictional French character, much like your English Raffles or Robin Hood," explained the man. Then, as though regretting any show of interest, he snapped viciously, "I am not Lupin—and be silent or I'll silence you."

"I am sure it is he," Robert whispered to Mr. Finchley. "We are safe, m'sieur, Arsène does not harm the innocent."

The man leaned back against the partition, his eyes on Robert, his thoughts sliding away into a meditation which must have been pleasant if the happy composure of his features was any indication of them. The car rolled and bumped along the road and, as they entered Versailles,

Jacques pulled a cord which released the curtains and the three were in a semi-gloom which was broken now and then as the car lurched and a curtain flopped. Mr. Finchley soon gave up trying to see the road at these moments and he sat with Robert watching their capturer. He could tell that the boy was excited, but he showed no fear. Once or twice he smiled at Mr. Finchley as though to say he had nothing to worry about; everything would turn out well. And Mr. Finchley began to think after a time that everything would turn out well. There seemed to be no logic in the affair, and he gradually convinced himself that they must be the victims of some mistake on the part of this stranger with the silent revolver.

They sat silently for about an hour, and then the stranger came from his meditation and remarked pleasantly:

"We must almost be there now." A short while after this there came three sharp honks on the horn from Jacques, and at the signal the curtains went up and Mr. Finchley saw that the car was sweeping into the large curve of a gravelled courtyard fronting a low white house that stretched before them in a long façade. He had a glimpse of gardens and shrubberies and a distant line of woods, and then he and Robert were bidden to leave the car and enter the house.

They were conducted through a large hallway into a long room with wide windows which looked over a terrace that dropped by balustraded steps to a small lake on which moved swans and ducks. The lake merged into a swampy morass at the far side where a belt of beech and birch came to meet it from the neighbouring woods. The room was full of elegant china, graceful chairs and a long highly polished walnut table that would have seated fifty people. At one end of the table a meal was laid.

"I do not wish you to be hungry," the man said, "so you will make a good lunch. Jacques will wait on you. I must apologise for that, but there are no other servants. It would not be wise of you to try and escape. Of course you realise that." He left the room, leaving them with Jacques, who smiled at them without the slightest hint of animosity.

Smiling, Jacques put his hand to his moustache and pulled it off.

"That is better," he said pleasantly. "It tickles so much."

Robert and Mr. Finchley found themselves looking at the man who had wanted to take the boy into the "South Sea Follies".

"Do not be alarmed," said Jacques reassuringly, and he began to serve them.

Mr. Finchley gave up the riddle. He could not understand.

Despite the strangeness of their position, they both made a good meal, which consisted chiefly of salad and cold meat and tinned fruit. As Jacques was serving their coffee his master returned.

"You will take the boy to his room and serve his coffee there," he said, and, seeing Mr. Finchley's alarm, added reassuringly, "The boy will be quite safe, I assure you. I want to talk to you alone. It is important."

"It's all right, Robert," Mr. Finchley said, looking across at the boy. "I'll see you're all right. There's a mistake been made somewhere."

The boy accepted Mr. Finchley's word and allowed himself to be escorted from the room by Jacques.

"Good," said the other man as the boy left. "Now we can talk." He took his cup of coffee and offered Mr. Finchley a cigarette, which Mr. Finchley refused.

"How much longer is this farce to go on?" he demanded angrily as he pushed the cigarettes away.

"This is not a farce," came the reply. "I do not like the word."

"I don't care what you like!"

"So I have remarked. I did not expect to find so much spirit in you. It is interesting. However, that is all beside the point. I wish to talk, and I wish to talk because later on you may tell other people what I have said. Listen to me. In this house there once lived a very happy family. There was a father, a mother and six children, all boys, all beautiful boys who were the pride of their parents and well-loved by everyone."

Despite his anger and confusion, Mr. Finchley listened attentively and after a while with growing interest, for as the man spoke his manner lost most of its quiet theatrical affectations and revealed the real personality, a gentle, curious, questioning spirit which was finding itself isolated and out of harmony with the world around it.

"The war came, m'sieur," the man went on; "and the boys went as soldiers. All of them were killed, and at their death the father became a soldier too, and he was killed and the mother died of grief at home, for it was not possible for her to live when so much that she had loved was gone.

"After the war, m'sieur, the house was sold to a young man, a most peculiar young man. You would have laughed had you known him then. He believed that the war would give us peace, lasting peace. He believed in a new world. But he did not think so for long. Soon he saw with bitterness that there would be other wars, that the sacrifice of this family in whose house he lived was a mockery, that wars were made because of the greed of men, of wealthy men, and the stupidity of politicians and those who supply the materials of war. His bitterness, m'sieur, was terrible and gave him no rest. He lost his faith in ideals, m'sieur, but from his bitterness was born a new resolution. He would fight evil with evil and bring good from it. He became an altruist who was prepared to use the methods of men less noble. Now you understand everything, do you not?"

Mr. Finchley shook his head. "I don't see what I have to do with all this, or what the boy has to do with it."

The man smiled faintly. "M'sieur, my name is Jerome Giraud, I am the disillusioned man. I can appreciate such loyalty as you show, but it does not deceive me. What you are, or your name, I do not care, but for a tutor and a valet you show courage and fidelity—those virtues endear you to me, but they cannot deceive me. On our way here you saw Jacques post those letters? They were to the Paris newspapers to inform the editors that unless certain sums—very large sums—were paid at once into named charities by the guardian of Alphonse Reims, whom I have kidnapped, he would be found dead within four days. If the sums are paid he will be let free and you with him. This is the beginning of my work. I have waited and planned for a long time towards this moment of fulfilment. It has come."

He spoke these last words with a savage elation and an abandon of gesture which showed Mr. Finchley plainly how obsessed he had become with his idea.

"Alphonse Reims." Mr. Finchley mouthed the name, it was vaguely familiar.

"You do not know him? The child millionaire, the child of war, of death and destruction!" Jerome spat the words, revealing his disbelief of Mr. Finchley's ignorance, and then there came back to Mr. Finchley the memory of a newsreel and he recalled how, at his first dinner at Madame Mignard's, there had been a discussion of the child millionaire who was staying with his guardian at the Marivaux. At once it became clear that this purposeful, but not too efficient, Jerome Giraud had picked up himself and Robert in mistake for Alphonse and his tutor, and it was clear that his assumption of ignorance had been interpreted by Jerome as a bluff to convince him that he had kidnapped the wrong persons. In his present mood, Mr. Finchley thought there was little hope of convincing him of his mistake, but he decided that he must make the attempt.

Mr. Finchley coughed to get the other's attention and then said: "Monsieur Giraud, while I can very largely sympathise with your motives in this matter, I must inform you that you have made a very grievous mistake. Never in my life have I seen Alphonse Reims, and the boy who is with me is called Robert and is no more than a friend I have made while staying in Paris."

Jerome laughed and threw his cigarette stub through the window. "You act very well, m'sieur. But I do not believe you. It is, as I have said, natural that you should do your best to protect your charge, but you cannot explain so many things. You were both coming from the Marivaux where the boy stays. The boy is like the pictures of himself which appear in the papers. And there was your anxiety about him at the fair which you visited from the Marivaux last night. Jacques was too eager that night. No, m'sieur, it will not go."

"Very well then," said Mr. Finchley, seeing the futility of pursuing his explanation, "will you give me your word on one point?"

"What is that?"

"If you have made a mistake, as I assert—the papers will disregard your letters as the work of an eccentric and there will be no mention of the kidnapping. If Alphonse has been kidnapped the news will be on the wireless and in the papers. If this evening's papers and wireless report prove that Alphonse is safe at the Marivaux, will you promise to let the boy and myself return safely to Paris? I should have returned to England this afternoon and it is a great inconvenience to me to be held up in this way."

Jerome ran his finger through his hair, wrinkled his face into a grin of appreciation and replied: "Oh, m'sieur, what an actor you are! You almost convince me that I am mistaken. But no—you are bluffing. I cannot be wrong. However, I promise that if I have made a mistake you shall be returned to Paris unharmed and I shall never be able to make my apologies to you for so unjust a treatment."

"Thank you." Mr. Finchley felt happier at once. The only ill consequences of this episode would be his missing the boat train and the excuses he would have to make to Mr. Sprake for not returning when he was expected.

"But there is one thing, m'sieur, for I cannot take chances with you who are so clever that you have probably thought of this. My letters will not be delivered in time for the evening editions, and it is possible that the police may forbid any disclosure of the kidnapping today to give them some time to try and catch me. But I have said in my letters that the terms of the release of the boy must be made public by tomorrow, so I will only release you if there is no mention in the morning papers. I am sorry to disappoint m'sieur."

Mr. Finchley said no more. He resigned himself to wait, and it must be said in Jerome's favour that he made their imprisonment as pleasant as he could. Mr. Finchley and Robert were locked into a large playroom on the second floor which gave them a view of the surrounding wood and marsh.

Jerome showed them into the place, saying, "There is plenty to amuse you here."

When the man had left them, Mr. Finchley explained to Robert what had happened.

"He has mistaken you for this Alphonse, but in the morning, when he gets the newspapers, he will find that out. Until then he refuses to believe me, but he has promised to let us go if it should be so. So you see there's nothing to worry about. Come on, what about a game of table-tennis?"

"I am sure he is Arsène Lupin!" declared Robert vigorously as he picked up his bat. "Believe me, m'sieur, he would not make such a mistake. It is a trick."

They began to play and after a while they were laughing and enjoying themselves as though they had no care in the world. There was plenty to amuse them in the room and by the time evening came they were ready for bed. Jacques brought them their supper and conducted them to their rooms. Jerome made no appearance and Mr. Finchley was sure that the evening papers and the wireless had made no mention of the kidnapping of Alphonse Reims.

As Robert left him—for they were given separate rooms—the boy whispered to him: "Courage, m'sieur, it is going to be all right."

Mr. Finchley went to sleep cheered by the boy's manly disposition.

At half-past eight the next morning Jerome Giraud entered Mr. Finchley's room.

"There is nothing about the kidnapping in the papers," he said, after he had given Mr. Finchley good morning.

"I told you there wouldn't be," said Mr. Finchley, scarcely hiding his satisfaction.

"Do not look so satisfied," Jerome spoke harshly. "I do not intend to let you go on such flimsy evidence—"

"But you promised!"

"I know, but I did wrong. I shall make sure first that Alphonse Reims is still in Paris. I shall go to Paris today to see for myself. If he is there—then you are free. I regret this necessity, but it cannot be helped. Jacques will look after you."

Mr. Finchley stood up, his face reddening with annoyance. What did this fool think he was playing at?

"Now, you listen to me, young man," he began.

"I cannot wait," said Jerome shortly. "I must go." And go he did, leaving Mr. Finchley fuming and helpless.

XII
Where a photograph is found and a job is lost

AND that morning, at almost the same time as Jacques with the aid of a revolver was ushering Mr. Finchley and Robert into the playroom for the day, Jean came into Marie's tiny room and announced that Madame was asking for her.

"What have you done?" he asked with some concern, for he liked Marie.

"Done?" Marie looked up from the dress she was altering. "I haven't done anything—"

"But you must have," insisted Jean. "They are in full council in the small saloon."

"You've got me," said Marie. "I haven't done anything which would make them go into council."

"There is something," said Jean unconvinced, and he followed Marie towards the saloon, a private room undefiled by the pensionnaires. Marie knocked and a deep voice from within bade her enter. She pushed open the door and went in, leaving the keyhole to Jean.

Inside sat the Mignard family, in a half-circle at the end of the room, Madame Mignard in a chair at the centre of the group and slightly forward to give her prominence. On either side sat her husband, her daughter and her granddaughter, a freckled-faced child of seven.

They were in full council, all right, thought Marie. This was how the family acted when they had important news to deliver, or severe reprimands to hand out to their staff, and no servant ever received a discharge without this impressive preliminary.

"Mademoiselle—approach," said Madame Mignard, her voice icy and forbidding, every line of her face indicating that she would tolerate no nonsense.

"What is it, Madame?" Marie asked politely as she came forward.

"It is not for you to ask questions," answered Madame. "I wish to ask you questions. I have that right as your employer—if an employer has any rights these days, which it seems not." She accompanied this aside on present-day labour troubles with a roll of her eyes to heaven and a spreading of her hands in horror.

"My dear, perhaps—"

"Silence, Baptiste," commanded Madame, quietening the old man at once, and he leaned back in his chair murmuring to himself and shaking his head.

"Mademoiselle Peters, it is true, is it not, that I engaged you as the governess for my daughter's child?" Both daughter and daughter's child acknowledged this reference by a slight inclination of the head.

"That is so," answered Marie, knowing that Madame would take her own time to come to her revelation.

"And you have told me that you were for many years a governess, and have furnished me with the most excellent references?"

"Yes, Madame."

"And among those references there was one from Madame Hourticq, of the Avenue Wagram, whose service you left last July?"

"That is so, Madame," answered Marie, with less assurance. She did not like all this talk about references. Nothing could have gone wrong there. Louise Hourticq was a friend of hers in cabaret and had answered Madame's check on the reference. Marie, herself, had composed the letter.

"And while you were with Madame Hourticq you did nothing else but act as governess to her little girl?"

"Yes," said Marie doubtfully.

"And in this costume, I suppose!" Madame Mignard's irony was devastating, as she thrust her hand out to Marie.

Marie found herself holding a postcard photograph of herself in sequined trunks, brassière and feathered shako. On the card was the inscription—*Chez Martin, June, 19—*.

"Where on earth did you get this?" Marie asked, forgetting the relationship which existed between herself and Madame.

"Is it not right," said Monsieur Mignard suddenly, taking hope at the informal note introduced by Marie, "that I should not be allowed to see the card—"

"Baptiste!" The old lady poured her scorn on the poor man.

"I have seen it, grandpa," whispered the small girl loudly; "she has nothing on save—"

"Silence!" cried Madame in horror. "See, how the child is become disrespectful, and from whose influence?"

"But Madame," Marie began, only to find her plea swept aside.

"That card which flaunts your shame, Mademoiselle, was found on the floor of a bedroom in this house. Do I have to tell you whose bedroom? Do you wish your sins to be proclaimed before the innocence of the child and the respectability of her mother?"

"No, you don't have to say," said Marie unthinkingly. "I can guess." She had missed the card ever since she had shown her photographs to Mr. Finchley and Laurence Hume in the café. Hume must have kept it and then carelessly left it lying about his room. He would, she thought, her anger rising suddenly. It was just the sort of careless, untidy act that was characteristic of him, and because of it she was going to get the sack. Oh, that was obvious! Well, it was a good thing she'd got enough money saved to take her back to England and keep herself for a while. She'd had enough of France.

"She admits her shame!" Madame turned to the family, stricken with amazement, and they registered an appropriate stupefaction, though Monsieur regarded Marie with more interest than had formerly been his wont.

The sight of their faces, the shrill sound of their exclamations, brought Marie to herself.

"Oh, shut up!" she cried in English, and the force of her words stilled them. She went on in French, "I'm sorry I deceived you, Madame. It was wrong of me, but I had to live and I was desperate. What does it matter that I used to get my living from the stage?—it's not right to believe the silly stories people tell. I've been a good governess to the child, I've taught her a lot of English and looked after her and you have never complained, but now, because of this stupid bit of card—which came quite innocently in

Mr. Hume's room—you begin to think all sorts of horrible things—"

"Mademoiselle, we do not wish to discuss your motives. You have admitted, your deceit. That is enough. This house has no place for you." Madame's words were final and Marie realised that it was no good pleading. They were right, of course, and had every cause to dismiss her, and because of that she felt the more furious.

"All right," she said quietly. "I'll leave today." She left the room.

Outside, without the accusing faces of the family to force her confession of wrong upon her, she grew angry. All this might not have happened if it had not been for Hume. Suddenly she hated him for his carelessness, and all the anger she could not logically direct at the family went to him. She slammed the door of her room behind her and began to pack quickly. She wouldn't stay a moment longer in this country than she could help.

When she was packed she reached to the top of her wardrobe and lifted down the cigar box which contained her savings. She had her fare to London and enough over to keep her for a month in cheap lodgings. It could be worse. She went out, carrying her case, and in the passageway she met Hume.

"Hullo, where are you going with that case?" he asked.

Marie stopped, took a deep breath, and then said passionately: "I'm going home to England, and I'm glad I met you before I went. The next time you steal photographs from a lady's handbag don't go leaving them round your bedroom floor for any Tom, Dick or Harry to pick up. It's a habit that may get you into trouble some day. No, you can't help me with the case, if that's what you're going to say. Good-bye!"

She left him, dazed, uncomprehending, to watch her trim figure going swinging angrily up the passage. "But . . ." The slam of the apartment door was his only answer.

"She has gone." Monsieur Mignard had come down the passage to him. "It is a pity, but you will do no good to run after her, Monsieur Hume. It is not wise to show a woman that you care for her so much. They take advantage of you later on. By the way, I come to return your photograph. It was found on the floor of your room this morning. But maybe you do not wish to keep it now?"

Hume looked at him, then snatched the photograph from him and hurried into his room.

And while Hume stood at his window, frowning through his glasses at the blank wall opposite, Mr. Finchley stood at the window of the playroom frowning at the distant woods and marsh lands. He was convinced that Jerome would have to admit his mistake; but in the meantime, the hours were passing and he would have to apologise to Mr. Sprake for extending his stay in Paris. Not that Sprake would be angry at him. Oh, no; he would be amused, and it was just that which worried Mr. Finchley. It would be most embarrassing explaining why he had overstayed his time, since no one would be inclined to believe the truth.

At four o'clock Jerome had not returned, and Mr. Finchley could guess why. What with his suspicions of a trap and his general incompetence it would take him a long time to establish to his own satisfaction that Alphonse Reims was still in Paris. But when nine o'clock came even Mr. Finchley began to get irritated and angry.

There was no reason on earth for all this delay. How long, he demanded of Jacques when that individual came to placate him at supper-time, did they think he could be kept hanging about in France? He was a working man, he had a living to earn. As Jacques did not understand Mr. Finchley's English, he could do no more than look embarrassed, as though he wished to apologise for the unfair advantage his revolver gave him, and inform Robert that he should persuade Monsieur to go to bed.

Mr. Finchley went to bed, and to sleep, and he slept until three o'clock in the morning, when he was awakened by someone shaking his shoulder roughly. He sat up, rubbing the sleep from his eyes.

"I am sorry to wake you, m'sieur; but I thought it necessary."

Mr. Finchley dropped his hands and stared at Jerome Giraud.

"Where on earth have you been?" he asked, in not at all the tone a captive should use towards his kidnapper.

"I was a long time in Paris, and then my car broke down outside Versailles. It was hours before I could get it fixed."

"And so," said Mr. Finchley, glancing at his watch, "after keeping me here all day, when you do get back at three o'clock you wake me. Very considerate—" He stopped suddenly, his dream-laden head clearing. "Good Lord, what are we gossiping about? Did you find out in Paris—"

"Yes, m'sieur, I found out," said Jerome quickly. "It is a common failing among men and women that they will not admit their mistakes with good grace. Jerome Giraud, whatever his faults, is endowed with a nobleness of mind which forces him to acknowledge his mistakes."

"Alphonse Reims is in Paris!"

"Oui, m'sieur. Alphonse Reims is in Paris. I have seen him with my own eyes. M'sieur"—he stood upright, clicking his heels together and inclining his head—"m'sieur, I owe you an apology. I have been very foolish. I ask your forgiveness, m'sieur; but I also ask you to regard what I have said to you as a confidence. My work is still to be done."

Privately, Mr. Finchley considered that Alphonse was in no danger from Jerome. The boy was not likely to be kidnapped by such a muddler.

"I forgive you," said Mr. Finchley, "but in future you should exercise more care." His tone became severe as he felt himself in a strong position to rebuke this young man. His impetuosity needed some curb. "If you are determined to become a kidnapper," he went on, "then it is absolutely necessary that you should master the elementary principles of your craft, and surely the first principle is not to kidnap the wrong person?"

"I deserve your anger," Jerome murmured dejectedly.

"But I am not angry. I am censuring your methods. Had I, now, been determined to kidnap Alphonse I should have gone to work quite differently. You should, for instance, never carry a loaded revolver. A loaded revolver one day or other will go off. Carry an empty one—it will be enough, for few men will call your bluff, and you will never become a murderer. And it is no good waiting in a taxi for the boy. There are many better ways of reaching him—"

"And they are, m'sieur?" demanded Jerome eagerly.

Mr. Finchley paused. Exactly he didn't know what they were, but had he not been interrupted he might have found himself making rash suggestions. He hesitated, not wishing to have the kidnapping of Alphonse Reims to his discredit, and said firmly:

"That is for you to discover yourself, m'sieur. You are a man of intelligence and it should not be difficult."

"You are right, m'sieur," replied Jerome with a stiff bow. "And now, m'sieur, although it is so early, if you would care to return immediately to Paris, I will arrange for the car and—if you will still accept my hospitality—some breakfast."

"A very good idea. The less time we lose the better." As he spoke Mr. Finchley began to dress. "What about Robert?" he asked. "We must wake him. It's a pity to disturb the child's sleep, but—"

"I have sent Jacques to wake him," replied Jerome. As he said this the door of the room was pushed open and Jacques came rushing in.

"Master!" he cried in agitation, "the boy has gone. He is not in his room."

"Gone! What do you mean?" Mr. Finchley was the first to find words. He jumped to his feet and faced Jacques.

"Come and see," was all Jacques would say, and he led the way from the room.

When they reached Robert's bedroom it was very clear how the boy had escaped. The window was open and from it trailed a rope made of knotted sheets from the bed. The rope had been fixed to the leg of the bed and ended about four feet short of the ground.

Mr. Finchley stared out of the window, forgetting the others. He was aware only of the soft patter of rain in the darkness, and far off the retreating growl of thunder. Only now did he realise that while he was sleeping there had been a storm, the night dripped and sang with rain still, and in that storm Robert had ventured on some romantic dash for help. All around the house stretched dark, bare woods, sedgy stretches of swamp and pools, and somewhere out there was Robert.

For the first time since he had known the boy, he felt himself grow anxious about him, not with the dutiful anxiety of an onlooker, but with the anxiety that follows affection, preying upon its tenderness and stampeding its fears into horror.

"I did not think he could escape from the window or I should have locked it," said Jerome. "Why did I not think of those sheets—"

"I'll tell you why!" cried Mr. Finchley suddenly, his anger, as he thought of Robert, rising swiftly within him. "Because you're a pair of inefficient bunglers! Because you are not fit to be at large in the world, upsetting other people's lives and doing no good with your own. That's why!" His round face grew red and gleaming with his emotion and he found himself shaking his fist in front of Jerome's nose and crying passionately, "If anything happens to that boy I'll see that you get punished for it. I'll punish you myself. Goodness knows how long the boy has been gone. He may have been wandering through these woods and marshes for hours—and all because of your carelessness. Haven't you any sense of responsibility?"

The thought of Robert stumbling through the darkness made him aware of his fondness for the boy. If anything happened to him he felt that he, too, was to blame, and the thought that harm might have come to the boy through association with him filled Mr. Finchley with a royal anger at Jerome and Jacques.

"Well, don't stand there doing nothing. We've got to find him."

The pair of them looked at Mr. Finchley, their faces offering evidence of the contrition which they felt. Suddenly they were no more than a pair of repentant, chastened schoolboys.

"We must look for him," said Jerome. "We must take lanterns and look for him. He cannot be far away."

They got lanterns and set out. Mr. Finchley, in a borrowed raincoat, kept with Jerome, and Jacques left them to search in another direction. It was so dark Mr. Finchley had no idea of the direction they took. He followed Jerome, who knew the country, and at intervals he cupped his hands and called Robert's name. There was no answer but the steady drizzle of the rain, the creak of their raincoats and the splash of their feet in puddles. Now and again the lantern threw its light over the dark face of a pool or a ditch, and once, as they crossed a small stream by a trestle bridge, Jerome said warningly: "Keep to the side, behind me!" And his lantern showed a great hole broken through the rotten planks of the bridge. The black hole, its lips ragged with moss and slippery leaves, yawned at Mr. Finchley, leering in the dim light as though it mocked him. He tried to shut from his mind the fantasy which his imagination worked.

How long he followed Jerome, calling and flashing his lantern, Mr. Finchley could not tell. They slipped and slithered along muddy paths, between tall hedges of sedge and reed, and always around them fell the soft rain, its noise beating gently upon his ear-drums until the subdued murmur had risen in his anxious mind to a rolling, continuous thunder that began to make patterns with its own noise and shift its cadences into mocking calls and refrains, and when he answered some question of Jerome's he found himself shouting at the man.

Then through the darkness stole a grey pallor, and gradually against the light the straight swathes of rain began to show and trees shook their branches clean of the clinging night.

It was light, a cold, drear morning, when they got back to the house. Jacques was still out.

"We will wait until he comes," said Jerome quietly, sensing the turbulence and strain that fought in Mr. Finchley's mind and acknowledging the part he had played in bringing them there. "If he has no news I will ring up the police station at Villet-sur-Seine and we will get search parties organised."

Mr. Finchley nodded dismally.

"He will be all right, m'sieur," Jerome tried to comfort him, but when within the hour Jacques came back and had nothing to report, Jerome was not so confident.

"I will telephone to Villet." Jerome turned and made his way back to the breakfast room and the others followed him. The telephone stood on a small table near the window.

"Hurry up," urged Mr. Finchley. "Perhaps he's with the police. We've got to find him." He could not clear his mind of the thought that Robert might be in trouble. He remembered the gaping hole in the footbridge.

Jerome picked up the telephone receiver reluctantly. He had to get into touch with the police. That was his duty, but he saw that the moment the police were brought into the affair, it was unlikely that the whole explanation of the boy's presence in the house could be withheld. It was ironical, but it was necessary. He lifted the receiver with a shrug.

As he did so the room darkened, and turning to the window he saw that three men had advanced across the terrace and were standing watching him and the others. They were three rough, unshaven men, dressed in rust-coloured trousers and little navy-blue jackets.

"Who are you?" Jerome frowned and demanded. The men took no notice of him. Their heads went together in conclave, bobbed with the excitement of some decision and then broke apart like corks swirled by a stream. One of them spat over his shoulder, another rubbed his hands and the last pulled his nose, habits dictated by crisis, and then at a command from the middle man they launched themselves into the room with eager, excited cries that betokened battle, and the result of their conclave became clear. They each had selected a victim.

One threw himself at Jerome, bringing him and the telephone table to the ground with a crash; the other sprang at Jacques, hurling him backwards to the floor and fastening himself upon his chest with a vicious roar and flailing of arms, and the third lowered his head and charged at Mr. Finchley, who found himself overthrown and engaged in a strenuous tussle.

At one moment the room had been charged with the anxiety of the three men over the loss of Robert. Now they were struggling and kicking about the floor to the accompaniment of crashing furniture and the raucous battle-cries of these unknown assailants. Mr. Finchley joined forces with his erstwhile capturers and allowed himself to become part of the general pandemonium. Yet fight and twist as he would, he was helpless against the superior strength of his man, who smelt strongly of garlic. In a very little while the room was wrecked, lovely china littered the ground in pathetic shards, elegant chairs were maimed and foundered, and greasy smears from the breakfast sullied the floor and carpets. Mr. Finchley was overcome and jerked to his feet, his arms pinioned tightly to his side by a victorious and jubilant enemy. He found Jerome and Jacques in the same unhappy position.

"Voilà!" cried the leader of the three, an enormous man with bushy eyebrows and a thick beard, who held Jerome. "I have often longed for a tussle with bandits." He turned towards the window and whistled shrilly. There was a silence after the whistle and then across the terrace the noise of someone approaching, and Mr. Finchley, wriggling with the pain of his assailant's grip, saw Robert suddenly framed in the wide window.

"Robert!" he shouted happily, forgetting his position.

"Ha, m'sieur!" Robert rushed excitedly across to him, pulling away the man who held Mr. Finchley.

"Let go, Anton! He is my friend!" He threw himself upon Mr. Finchley, embracing him and patting him as though he would assure himself that Mr. Finchley was still sound in body.

"Ha, my friends," he cried to the three men. "Thank you so much. You are very brave. But this one—" he indicated Mr. Finchley—"he is my friend I told you about. He is no bandit."

"Robert," said Mr. Finchley, adjusting his clothes, and shaking himself into some composure, "what is all this?"

Robert laughed and the three men laughed with him. "M'sieur, it is as Pépé says—there is always a way to do what you want to do. M'sieur was brave to say there was no danger so that I should not be worried. But I could tell that it was not true. So early this morning I escaped from the house. It was easy, I did it as Arsène Lupin himself has done so many times. I was going to fetch the police to rescue you, but on the way I discovered the river and on the river there were the barges of my three friends. So I remembered what Pépé so often says—When you have trouble go to a friend, not the police. They have come to rescue you from these bandits. I hope they did not hurt you. It was not possible otherwise."

The three bargemen stood grinning at this recountal, their ugly faces happy with the expression of a duty well done. For a moment Mr. Finchley felt the situation beyond his control. Then he pulled himself together and speaking English explained the situation to Robert. He was amused by the disappointment that gradually came into the boy's face.

"So you see, Robert," he finished, "it was all a mistake, and Monsieur Jerome and his friend Jacques have apologised and are going to send us back to Paris this morning. It would not be right of us to bear any malice against them for such an accident."

Robert was silent for a moment and then he said anxiously: "But m'sieur, it is not so easy as that. You see, I have promised my friends that as a reward they shall have the pleasure of throwing the two bandits in the river. Anton particularly wants to do it because he was himself thrown into a river by a thief who once stole his watch and then so insulted him. They have made up their minds, m'sieur."

"Then they must unmake them, Robert. I cannot allow that. It is not a proper way to treat defeated opponents.

No Englishman would do that." He fished in his pocket for his wallet and handed some notes to Robert. "Give these to your friends for their help instead."

Robert took the notes and Mr. Finchley stood by while there was an excited colloquy in French, during which the bargemen grumbled and shook their heads and then finally took the notes.

Jerome and Jacques were released; the money made the bargemen forget the fray and in a few moments everyone was at work tidying up the room and clearing away the wreckage.

"There is much damage, m'sieur," said Jerome sadly as he worked. "But I accept it as the price of my folly. It is not easy to be a kidnapper in these days."

Their good work done, the bargemen took their leave and Robert and Mr. Finchley sat down to have their breakfast, while Jerome, chastened by his experiences, sat by and made consolatory remarks whenever the conversation gave him an opportunity.

After breakfast they took their leave of Jerome and got into the car which Jacques was to drive to Paris. Mr. Finchley enjoyed the drive back more than he had enjoyed the journey down, and they arrived in Paris before midday.

Mr. Finchley knew that there was a boat train he could catch late in the afternoon, and when Jacques dropped him at the rue Chalgrin he told him to take Robert on to the wharf by the river.

"I must go this afternoon, Robert. This is the third time I've said I'm going—and now it really is good-bye," he said, his voice not covering his sorrow at this parting. "But if you wish you can come up here at five o'clock and go to the station with me."

"I will be here, m'sieur," said Robert gravely, and Mr. Finchley fancied he saw his under-lip quiver a little. But the boy smiled, and as the taxi drove away he leaned out and waved his hand. Mr. Finchley watched it out of sight and then turned into his lodgings, walking slowly, and deep in thought.

XIII
Of a desertion and a decision

MADAME Mignard had not been unduly worried by Mr. Finchley's absence and accepted without comment his explanation that he had, unexpectedly, been required to accompany his client out of town.

On his way out to send a telegram to Mrs. Patten, who, he knew, would be worried because of his non-arrival, he met Hume in the passage.

"Hullo, I thought you'd gone back?"

"Not yet," said Mr. Finchley, preparing to explain. "You see—"

But Hume, his face gloomy, moved off to his room. "I've got to go out. In a hurry," he said, and his words lacked colour or life.

Mr. Finchley left him, wondering what had upset him. He sent his telegram.

When he came back from the post office it was to find Robert sitting on the bed in his room, staring at the fireplace and swinging his legs moodily.

"Hullo," said Mr. Finchley, surprised to see the boy back so soon. "How did you get in?"

"Jean let me in," explained Robert, and as he spoke Mr. Finchley knew at once that the boy was troubled.

"What's the matter, Robert? You don't sound very happy," he enquired, sitting on the bed by the boy.

It was some moments before Robert replied. He sat very still, staring before him, his dark eyes troubled and puzzled, and as he waited for the boy to speak Mr. Finchley experienced a moment of great tenderness for him. This slight-figured, dark-haired youngster with his not too clean knees and the open-necked blue shirt was become a very familiar part of his life in the last few days. He had given Mr. Finchley an entirely new aspect of children.

"How can I be happy, m'sieur?" Robert said at last. "I have been deserted. It is few children can be happy when they are deserted."

"Deserted! What are you talking about?" For a second or two Mr. Finchley wondered whether Robert's English had failed him and he was misusing a word.

"I have been deserted, m'sieur," repeated Robert simply. "I have never been deserted before and it is not a pleasant thing to happen. When I got back to the wharf I found the *Swan of Paris* there and I hurried to tell Pépé of our adventure. He would have been very interested. But there was no Pépé there. Only another man who told me to go away. So I went to the wharf-keeper to ask him what it all means and he tells me that Pépé has left his job with the boats and gone away to another, he doesn't know where. But there was a note from Pépé for me which he had given to the keeper. It was to say good-bye to me, m'sieur, and to tell me to bring this letter to you."

Robert handed Mr. Finchley a crumpled blue envelope. Pépé's spelling was bad, but Mr. Finchley soon translated his message.

> *MONSIEUR,*
> *I send Robert to you because it is not right that a Frenchman should be the guardian of an English boy. Robert has told me that your friend, Mr. Hammerton, is very rich and I know he is kind, as you are, monsieur. I go for the boy to be happy with you. It is useless to look for me, and better so. He is a good boy.*
> *PÉPÉ.*

Mr. Finchley was unprepared. He sat on the edge of the bed, his thoughts repeating Pépé's words. Pépé had left the boy, and not—that much was clear—because he did not love the boy, but from a sense of necessary sacrifice in order to bring to Robert the advantages he lacked. And Pépé did not mean to be found, that too was clear.

"What does it mean, m'sieur?" Robert asked anxiously.

"It means, I'm afraid, Robert, that Pépé has left you for good," said Mr. Finchley gently, taking the boy's arm.

"Mon dieu, m'sieur, what shall I do? I have no home. It is the first time I have found myself in such an embarrassment. I do not know what one does. Do you think we could find Pépé? Perhaps if m'sieur wrote an advertisement for me he would see it and come back?"

Mr. Finchley shook his head. In the face of the boy's helplessness he forgot his own confusion and set himself to right this tangle. "No, that would be no good. Pépé has gone for good. But don't worry, we'll see you are all right." As he spoke he had an idea. "Wait here," he said. "I'll be back in a moment." He left the room and hurried to the lounge. He must tell Mr. Hammerton the story and ask his advice. He would know what to do and the appropriate French authorities for … Suddenly the thought of Robert handed over to a home chilled him. But what could one do? Left to himself the boy might starve and eventually he would come to the notice of the authorities. He picked up the receiver and got through to the Hôtel Marivaux. He was soon speaking to a very surprised Mr. Hammerton.

"I thought you were in England?"

"No, I got detained here for another day. Yes, on some other business." Mr. Finchley told the lie in order to avoid an explanation. Very quickly he told Mr. Hammerton of Pépé's desertion. From the other end of the wire he heard the man whistle.

"What am I to do? I've got the boy here now, and obviously he doesn't know where to go or what to do? I feel absolutely bound to help him. Do you think there's any chance of tracing that Pépé?"

"None at all," came Mr. Hammerton's reply. "He's obviously slipped away and doesn't mean to be found. It's pretty clear what his idea was, too. Well, well, here's a pretty kettle of fish."

"It's made more awkward by the fact that I've got to catch the boat train in a few hours," said Mr. Finchley. "I simply can't spend any more time in Paris. But what am I to do with the boy?" He frankly confessed his anxiety.

At the other end of the wire Mr. Hammerton was silent. What did Mr. Finchley imagine he could do? Boys, children were always being deserted; it was only a question of informing the appropriate authorities. Something within him recoiled from this cold logic. But what else could he do? Then into his mind slipped a suggestion, born of this rhetorical questioning. He rejected it at once. But it came back, strengthened by the rebuff. Could he? Should he? Then with a swift enthusiasm he decided he would. It was fate trying him. It was his chance. No one could do it better than he.

"What shall we do?" Mr. Finchley's voice came to him, anxious, questioning.

"Listen, Mr. Finchley," Hammerton said. "I believe all this may have been the working of a benign providence on my behalf. It's a chance for me to show I'm still of some use in the world—and I believe it's the chance that wily old Pépé was banking on. I'll adopt the boy. Yes, that's what I'll do—"

"You'll what?" cried Mr. Finchley, startled.

"I'll adopt him. Why shouldn't I? I've got enough money to look after him and make up for his rotten start, and he's always talking about living on a farm, isn't he? Then he can come and live on my farm in England when I've got it ready. Why, the solution's simple—I wonder I never thought of adopting him that night after the fair. What do you think of that?"

"Think of it!" Mr. Finchley cried. "Why—" he hesitated. Was it a good idea? He did not altogether trust Mr. Hammerton's enthusiasms. There was so much against him in his past. Then he discarded the thought. It was unfair to discredit the man, and the boy would give his life perhaps the balance it had so long needed. "Why, I think it's an excellent idea," he said. "I'm sure Robert will think so, too. He'll be happy—shall I send him down to you at the hotel?"

"No, that's the point. He can't come with me just yet. I've got to go South again for a week to clear up some affairs down there, and I shan't want to take the boy. I wonder …" Mr. Hammerton paused.

"You wonder what?" enquired Mr. Finchley, his mistrust returning.

"I wonder if you would help me? Could you take the boy back to England with you today? The sooner he gets there the better. Of course I'm not asking you to look after him when you get there. You could make some suitable arrangement for him to lodge with an English family. But, perhaps, you'd see him settled near you where you could keep an eye on him until I come?"

Mr. Finchley was relieved. "There's no need for him to be lodged anywhere," he said at once. "He could stay with me. My housekeeper will see to him, and the boy would be glad of the company of someone he knows, especially during the first week. I should look upon it as a duty, Mr. Hammerton, a pleasant duty and a recognition of your great kindness to the boy. But how can he come with me today? I'm going in a few hours and he hasn't got a passport and there are sure to be all sorts of formalities about his leaving the country."

Mr. Hammerton chuckled. "You don't know France," he said pleasantly. "With friends and with money you can get most things done in a hurry. And I have both. You get him to the station with you in time for that train and I'll have my valet there with all the permits you'll need. I promise that."

Their conversation ended, leaving Mr. Finchley to take the good news to Robert, and Mr. Hammerton to employ friends and money for the necessary permits.

"Robert," said Mr. Finchley when he returned to the room, "how would you like to come back to England with me, to live there for always?"

Robert did not reply at once. He eyed Mr. Finchley as though he suspected a joke. "Do you mean that, m'sieur?" he asked at last.

"Of course. Mr. Hammerton—you remember him—is going to buy a farm in England and live there, and if you are willing he would like to adopt you and take you to live with him. But he will not come to England for a week or two yet, and you would have to come back with me today and live with me until he arrives. How does that sound to you?"

"Oh, m'sieur!" cried Robert suddenly, his voice soaring, his face brightening; "it is not true! Oh, what happiness! I cannot believe it! I am to go and live in England! Will I come? I could not refuse such a kindness! Oh, m'sieur, I shall be living with you ..." And the next moment he had jumped on the bed and was turning somersaults to express his joy, so that the bed creaked and winced and Mr. Finchley stood smiling by, the boy's happiness warming him and turning his thoughts gratefully to Mr. Hammerton.

XIV
In which Mr. Finchley has an uncomfortable homecoming

MR. HAMMERTON was as good as his word, for when Mr. Finchley and Robert arrived at the Gare du Nord there was the valet armed with the necessary papers for Robert to leave the country. The man recognised Mr. Finchley from his visits to the hotel.

During the train journey Robert was quiet, sitting in his corner smiling across at Mr. Finchley occasionally as though his friend's presence reassured him. For him this was the beginning of a new experience, a new life, and Mr. Finchley guessed a little of the tumult which must be agitating the boy's mind. He, too, was not in a normal state of mind. When he had come to Paris he had never expected to contract such a friendship and far less to return to England with the boy as a companion who was to spend some time in his house. A week ago and the prospect of a boy living in his house would have made Mr. Finchley wince; he appreciated his quiet comforts and the even movement of habit and procedure which made up his existence too much to want to disturb them. But now they seemed unimportant alongside the important excitement of having Robert to stay with him.

The train clacked along through the flat countryside, its hedgeless fields and low peasants' dwellings contrasting strangely with the picture of the English countryside which Mr. Finchley carried always with him. To him, this landscape was strange, and a little improper. It was salutary to consider that to Robert, sitting opposite, there was nothing remarkable about the country, and that the English fields and hedges and thatched cottages would seem queer to him. That topsy-turvy exchange of outlook, more than anything else he knew, convinced Mr. Finchley that it was high time for Robert to find his native land.

As the train drew near Boulogne and the sea, Robert began to grow restless and his eyes spoke his mounting excitement.

"The ship we go on, m'sieur, will it be large? As grand as the *Normandie*?"

"Hardly," said Mr. Finchley; "but it is big enough to carry us safely across the Channel. Far bigger than the *Swan of Paris*, for instance—"

Mr. Finchley said no more, for he could see that the boy had remembered Pépé. His meditation did not last long and soon he was lost to his excitement, his brain a process of questions.

Then the grey hill of Boulogne came into sight and the train ran slowly into the docks; porters shouted and invaded the corridors, snatching at bags and cases, the whole train broke into a turbulent eruption of hurry and nervous movement. Mr. Finchley surrendered their cases to a porter, and taking Robert's hand piloted him through the crowd on to the ship. It was growing dusk and already one or two lights shone from the town.

When the boat began to draw away from the docks Robert could contain himself no longer. He watched the darkening shores of France recede, saw the harbour lights and the bright windows of the town dying to faint stars and felt beneath his feet the steady rhythm of the engines.

"We are off, m'sieur! I am leaving France and we are going to England!"

Nothing could keep him in one spot, and, after promising to return to Mr. Finchley very soon, he went off to inspect the boat. Mr. Finchley watched him go and then settled himself comfortably into the corner of his seat and shut his eyes. He was feeling tired and felt the need of sleep. After a time he woke up, conscious of an accentuated motion to the boat. Robert was back at his side. For a second or two Mr. Finchley stared around him. They were well out into the Channel now and the seas were running high before a strong breeze. Through the thick glass nothing could be seen. Mr. Finchley could feel the swaying of the ship and sense the conflict of wind and water around him.

He looked down at Robert to find an anxious expression on the boy's face.

"It looks as though we are not going to have an entirely smooth crossing," he said cheerfully.

"Oh, m'sieur," said Robert gravely. "I do not like this rolling and the wind. It was never like this on the *Swan of Paris*. I have a feeling down here"—he patted his belt—"as though something did not belong there. Do you think I shall be seasick? It will be a new and unpleasant experience for me."

Mr. Finchley chuckled and laughed the boy's fears away. "You mustn't let Pépé down by being sick. You are used to the water, and besides sickness has nothing to do with rough weather—"

"Is that so?" Robert brightened up at this news.

"Yes, seasickness is entirely a malady of the mind. Most people say to themselves: I am going on a boat, I shall be sick—and they are sick because they expect to be. But if you say to yourself: this sickness is all nonsense—and forget about it, then nothing happens. Look at me. I am not an experienced sailor, yet I have never been sick in my life, merely because I always say firmly to myself before I go aboard: I shall not be sick! And I never am." Mr. Finchley delivered this credo with the confidence of one who has accepted and proven it beyond doubt, and he could see that Robert had been impressed, convinced almost, for he was smiling now and his hands had left the region of his belt.

"That is a very sensible thing," said Robert. "I have been sick before, through eating, and I did not like it. I am very glad that I shall be spared the malady."

Mr. Finchley was glad to have this evidence of the strength of Robert's mind, and to help him forget seasickness more he took him down to the restaurant and they had tea and cakes.

Once or twice while they were eating Mr. Finchley fancied he felt the ship pitching badly and he began to congratulate himself that he was to be given a taste of rougher weather than usually accompanied his sea trips. So far, they had proved altogether too mild. He was looking forward to going on deck, to get face to face with the elements, when a strange thing happened to him. Across the table he caught sight of Robert, smiling happily and lifting to his mouth a particularly jammy and creamy cake.

The sight of the extravagant confection produced a most peculiar effect on Mr. Finchley. His optic nerves flashed a message of revolt and disgust to the brain, and the brain obediently translated the message into sensory terms and handed it on to that department which usually concerned itself with cakes and other comestibles. The attitude of this department was at once definite and deplorable. Instead of passing the message on to some other department in the honourable way, marking it For your attention, please, and so shelving the responsibility, it considered the message slowly, read it again with mounting feelings and finally thrust it into its files, reeling away with faint and appalled look, forgetful of all its duties and customs.

Mr. Finchley felt this dereliction within him, decided to ignore it as a temporary lapse which might be forgiven a department which had served him long and honestly, and then found he could not ignore it because the department was now in open revolution from the effect of the message, all its members opposing one another, tugging and straining towards different procedures. Mr. Finchley himself began to reflect this dissension. His face paled, his eyes watered slightly, his body tilted to the roll of the boat, a roll that started low down and went swooping upwards as though it would never stop, and stopped suddenly, leaving him with the feeling that most of his members had been somehow stranded in mid-air, sustained by some mysterious force of levitation.

Then the egregious movement would finish and Mr. Finchley found himself leaning weakly back against his seat, attempting a normal expression so that Robert might not take alarm. He knew now what was about to happen. All his life he had been smiling about this, in the jokes of humorous papers and the antics of comic actors. It had been a rich, human misfortune; and with the arrogance of a few hours' voyaging he had imagined himself immune.

"M'sieur—you look very queer," said Robert as he finished his tea.

Mr. Finchley ignored the solicitation and said hurriedly:

"Wait for me here, Robert. I shall be back soon." He got up, and with rapid but dignified steps sought sanctuary.

There followed for Mr. Finchley a period of intense misery and, when he was able to frame coherent thoughts other than a concern for his own well-being, he reviled the sea, the English seafaring tradition, all creamy cakes and small boys who ate them, the indecent rocking of the ship and the quiet insistence of the steward who was ministering to him.

When at last he returned to Robert, he was pale but better, and already beginning to assume some of the lost cheerfulness of his normal personality.

"You have been a long time, m'sieur," Robert said, and added innocently, "and you look pale. Are you ill, m'sieur?"

"No, no," said Mr. Finchley quickly, "I am not ill. Not at all, but the sea always affects my complexion in this way. It is most curious."

"She is very curious, the sea," said Robert slowly. "Pépé always would say that she was uncertain, like a woman. But I do not mind the sea. I have not been sick, thanks to you, m'sieur, and soon we shall be in England."

Mr. Finchley's spirits gradually revived, and by the time the lights of Folkestone Harbour showed up across the night he was almost forgetful of his disgraceful weakness.

He wished that it were still light so that Robert might see the cliffs rise from the water to greet them, and as they stood watching the lights he tried to explain what it would have looked like. Robert listened gravely, but his eyes shone with excitement, and it was in this manner that he greeted his country, taking in every new impression. When the ship drew alongside the dock and they were through the Customs he walked along the platform to the London train, his lips silently reading the English notices and advertisements, and in the railway carriage he considerably embarrassed Mr. Finchley by circling round reading the titles from under the photographs of show places.

There were two other people in the compartment: a stout elderly clergyman with small eyes and a well-fed, irritable face, and a middle-aged man with tired eyes and travel-rumpled clothes who went to sleep the moment the train started.

As the train rolled out into the night Robert looked around with pleasure. There was nothing to be seen through the windows, and he was forced to a comparatively introspective examination of this new world. Mr. Finchley, who faithfully observed the formula of never speaking in a carriage unless he was addressed, and so perpetuated the silence which is characteristic of most travellers, was horrified to see Robert turn gaily to the clergyman and say happily:

"M'sieur le curé, today I am in England for the first time."

There was a pause during which the clergyman shook himself free from the review he was reading, and finally rumbled a non-committal:

"Indeed."

"Yes, sir," said Robert, for Mr. Finchley had told him that in England he must not use 'm'sieur'. "I am English, too, but I have never been to my country before."

"Indeed," said the clergyman dully, and he went back to his review with the obvious air of one who has no desire to converse.

Mr. Finchley, uncomfortable, put out a hand to prevent Robert from talking further, but he was too late. The boy, puzzled by the clergyman's lack of response, went on unperturbed by any consideration of embarrassment or shyness:

"You are not very interested, sir? That is curious, because in France the curé he was always pleased to know what one was doing."

Mr. Finchley said severely: "Robert, you must not say things like that. It is not polite." He glanced apologetically at the clergyman.

"It's a pity we arrived in the dark," he went on hurriedly, to engage Robert, "otherwise we could have seen some of the country. The train is going right across Kent, which is famous for its hops and fruit, Robert."

He began to tell Robert about Kent, but before long the boy, who had passed through a tiring day, started to yawn, and very soon, with the ease of an animal, snuggled against Mr. Finchley and went to sleep. The unspoken confidence of the boy's pressure against his side sent a proud thrill through him.

The boy woke as the train neared Victoria, and as they entered the station the clergyman stood up. "Here we are in London," he said benevolently. "I hope you have a very happy time, my boy," and he departed with the satisfied air of one who has disposed of a most-needed blessing.

"Well," said Mr. Finchley, on the platform, "here we are in London. Now for home and a good supper provided by Mrs. Patten. Come along."

It was late, yet despite that, Mr. Finchley could not refrain from ordering the taxi-driver to take them by Trafalgar Square and Piccadilly, so that Robert might see those places at night, and hence it was that Robert's first impression of London was one of gay lights, flashing advertisement signs and a busy stream of traffic. He said little, remaining with his nose pressed tightly against the cab glass, his eyes taking everything in, his face reflecting his pleasure. But by the time they reached Nassington Avenue, he was stifling an occasional yawn.

"You've had a long day," said Mr. Finchley. "Bed's the place for you."

The taxi-driver carried their cases to the door and then departed with his tip. Mr. Finchley rang the bell, saying to Robert: "She wouldn't dream of going to bed until we were home." The bell jingled within the house and he stood waiting for the welcoming footsteps of Mrs. Patten. At least, he hoped they would be welcoming, for he was not sure how Mrs. Patten would react towards Robert. His telegram to her had mentioned only that he was bringing a visitor.

The echoes of the bell died away and the house was silent. Robert looked up at him enquiringly. Mr. Finchley rang again. There was no response to the bell.

"Surely she can't be in bed already?" Puzzled at Mrs. Patten's unusual tardiness he fished for his key and finding it unlocked the door. "In you go," he said, feeling for the light switch. The lights came on and the door closed behind them.

"Hullo!" called Mr. Finchley.

"There is no one here?" asked Robert.

"Of course there is. She must be asleep. Wait here a moment." Mr. Finchley dropped his case and went upstairs to Mrs. Patten's room. The door was wide open and he could see that the bed was undisturbed. He stood there for a moment, perplexed by the mystery and growing conscious of a faint, stale smell about the house. He went down to Robert.

"She's not here," he said, his voice distressed. "What can have happened to her?"

"Perhaps these will explain," said Robert. "They were lying behind the door." He handed a letter and a red envelope to Mr. Finchley. The letter was addressed to him in Mrs. Patten's handwriting and the red envelope to Mrs. Patten. He opened the letter and read. It was short and apologetic. Mrs. Patten had received his letter telling her that he was coming back, but her sister had suddenly taken a turn for the worse and she could not leave her. She had written to him at Paris and to London in case her Paris letter did not reach him in time. Could he manage by himself for a few days until she could leave her sister? The red envelope, he guessed as he read the letter, was from the post office, informing Mrs. Patten of the telegram they had been unable to deliver.

Mr. Finchley dropped his hands to his side in a gesture of impatience.

"She's gone," he murmured, and turning to Robert he said: "Robert, we're all alone."

Mr. Finchley found solace in the commiseration on Robert's face. The boy took his arm sympathetically, and said: "Never mind, m'sieur. You must be brave. Pépé always said that it was better for the wife who could no longer love her husband to go away. I am sure she could not have been a good woman to want to leave you. But you have me, m'sieur, I will look after you."

Mr. Finchley came out of his trouble with a frown. "What on earth are you talking about, Robert?"

"About your wife, m'sieur. It is a great blow to find her gone, but you must be brave, m'sieur. Besides—you can now marry another wife. I will find one for you. There must be many who would want to share your life, you are so good. I will find such a good one; she will be beautiful, she will cook like Pépé, she will sing and we shall all be happy together."

Mr. Finchley smiled to hide his embarrassment and then shook his head.

"You don't understand, Robert. I am not married. It is not my wife who has run away, but my housekeeper, who has to stay with her sister who is very ill. She cannot come back yet to look after us."

"Then that is easy! We will look after ourselves. I am a good cook and you shall not suffer. And also I will still find you a wife. I had promised it for Pépé, to find him a wife. But he was most difficult to please. She must not be like this, she must be like that. This one does not know how to prepare the sauce for crayfish, and that one does not walk properly. Many a time going along the river I have pointed one out to him, but always there was something wrong. M'sieur would not be so difficult. With Pépé it was that he did not wish to get married again really."

Mr. Finchley stopped this scheming by propelling Robert into the kitchen.

"We'd better content ourselves tonight with a hot drink and biscuits and cheese," he said. "You must try to find them while I go upstairs and see about a bed for you."

The spare bedroom, as he expected, was ready except for the making of a bed, a process with which Mr. Finchley was not very conversant. From the airing cupboard at the head of the stairs he fetched sheets, blankets and pillows, and very soon was struggling to spread them evenly. At his efforts the bedding seemed to take life and resentment. The sheets twitched and rumpled themselves, draped folds around his legs, smothered his eyes and subsided gracefully over his bald head, so that he looked like an Arab sheik. And as he struggled with the bed he was wondering what he should do until Mrs. Patten came back. He could not leave Robert alone in the house all day, and there was the very important problem of meals. Even if they went to a hotel to escape the meal problem it still left Robert unattended, and Mr. Finchley found himself strangely reluctant to place the boy in lodgings away from himself where he would be left to the attentions of strangers. With Mrs. Patten the boy would have been well looked after.

"*M'sieur—c'est servi*!" came a shout up the stairs. "The supper's ready."

Mr. Finchley left the bed and went downstairs. On the kitchen table was supper and at its head, within reach of the cooker, stood Robert, his small body enveloped in an apron intended for Mrs. Patten's amplitude, and on the table two hot plates holding omelettes.

"There was no cheese, so I made omelettes. They are good, and you must excuse the coffee for it is made with tinned milk. Oh, m'sieur," said Robert unexpectedly, "this is a wonderful house. The things you have in this kitchen.

I could not be unhappy here, and the rooms—I can well understand that you only use some of them on feast days."

Mr. Finchley ate and enjoyed his omelette. Robert could cook. Once the supper was over it was not easy, although he was tired, to get the boy to bed. He had to be shown the house and have explained a great many things. Of all the rooms the bathroom held his enthusiasm longest; the hot and cold taps, the long gleaming bath and the shower were luxuries he had never expected, and the little light behind Mr. Finchley's shaving mirror was a refinement that suddenly lifted Mr. Finchley into an aweful station. With difficulty he explained that they must be content without a bath that night, for the hot water came from a domestic boiler in the kitchen which was without fire.

"This," said Mr. Finchley, leading Robert from the bathroom to the spare room, "is where you sleep, and you'd better have a pair of my pyjamas for tonight. Tomorrow we'll get some for you." He left Robert flapping around the room in pyjamas that held him like sails, and went weary but happy to his own room. It was good to be back, even without a welcome from Mrs. Patten, and it was pleasant to know that Robert was sleeping close to him and not tucked away in some corner of the *Swan of Paris*. Satisfied, Mr. Finchley fell quickly to sleep, while Robert still lay awake, his eyes fixed on the patch of light that came through the window from the street lamp, while he repeated quietly to himself: "Very soon now, I shall be going to sleep in England, in London." He lay, waiting for sleep, not wanting to miss the experience.

XV
The promotion of neighbourly feelings

AT seven o'clock the next morning Mr. Finchley was awakened by sounds that had never before disturbed his rest at Nassington Avenue. Dimly, then growing louder in his consciousness, came the noise of running water, splashing, bubbling water, and mixed with it the unrecognisable words of a French dance tune. He frowned, looked at his watch, and frowned harder. Then as a gurgle, followed by a shrill cry of fright, wafted into the room, he got out of bed and pulled on his dressing-gown. He went on to the landing to be met by a cloud of billowing steam that swept towards him from the open bathroom door. Wiping the steam from his face he went into the bathroom to be greeted with a cry of "Good morning, sir." Robert was lying in a bath well filled with water, where he was twisting and ducking himself like a young otter, the water glistening over his fresh skin and puddling the floor as he splashed. He came to the surface, blew away a soapy lather from his face and grinned at Mr. Finchley.

"I've been up for hours," he cried. "And I lit the boiler for the hot water. We had a stove in the barge, but it wouldn't light so well as yours. Oh, this is lovely, I could stay here all day. Already I have been here an hour. At first I was quite red, it was so hot. Pépé used to say that the English were mad about bathing. Now I know why—it is a lovely thing to do. If you will give me permission, sir, I will bath every day."

Mr. Finchley, his first surprise over, grinned and blinked his eyes free of steam. "All right, but on condition you come out of there at once. You must never stay so long in a bath. Come on!" He held out a bath towel and wrapped it about the boy. "Now get dry and dress yourself. I hope you've left some hot water for me."

"Hot water—it is boiling. Downstairs I could hear it going bubble-bubble in the tank ..."

Mr. Finchley did not wait to hear more of Robert's realistic imitation of a hot-water tank at bursting point. He dashed out of the room and made for the kitchen. He found the stove crammed with anthracite, all the dampers open and the top plate beginning to take on that dullness which preludes red heat. A wave of hot air struck him and the tank bubbled a mad good morning. Quickly he shut the dampers down and began to run off some of the boiling water through the kitchen tap.

After breakfast he decided he would have a chat with Robert about boilers. He went back to the bathroom to find Robert gone to his room where he could hear him singing. Slowly he began the luxury of a shave. This was Saturday morning and he had to go to the office.

As there was neither fresh milk nor bread in the house, they breakfasted from omelettes, drank coffee, and then discussed their plans.

"I have to go to the office," explained Mr. Finchley, "and you must stay here. If you can manage to tidy things up, so much the better, but don't worry over that. If you go out, don't go far. I'll show you around this afternoon. We can get some lunch in a restaurant when I come back—"

"But I could make the lunch, sir," protested Robert. "It would be something for me to do. I am a good cook, and if you gave me some English money I could go and buy food. Please let me do that. It would be such good practice for me. And I will be careful. I cannot lose myself."

Mr. Finchley considered this and then decided that there might not be any harm in it. Before he gave way, he treated Robert to a lecture, with demonstrations, on the electric cooker, the domestic boiler and English coinage. As for the boy losing himself, he knew that Robert was too quick-witted to let that happen. Robert walked with him to the bus stop, and there Mr. Finchley left him. As he sat back and shook out his paper and the bus rumbled along the street, the old life rose around him and welcomed him back. He was home again, going to the office, the breath and call of Paris a long way behind him. He felt a mounting eagerness to be in the office, to watch and hear the greetings of the staff, to assume the Olympian kindness of one who has returned from abroad. He even felt capable of telling his typist why he had been unable to buy her scent or stockings.

He took his chorus of good mornings when he went into the office as an emperor would have taken the joyous exclamations of his troops. Sprake was less enthusiastic.

"If you ask me, Finchley, you went off on a spree and spent more time in Paris than you need have done."

Mr. Finchley, although he had expected it, privately resented this aspersion. Where business was concerned he was rectitude itself, and he had no intention of allowing Sprake to believe that he had been an unworthy servant.

"Mr. Hammerton was not the kind of man to be hurried, Mr. Sprake, and as you instructed me to try to get his business I thought it advisable to humour him. Actually I am two days later than I should have been, and I must admit that the delay was entirely unconcerned with business. I had a rather unfortunate accident which kept me from travelling as I had arranged—"

"You slid?" Sprake shook off his office manner and became friendly at once. Mr. Finchley considered that this sudden interest in his misfortunes was scarcely polite or decent, and he thought he detected a waiting, anticipatory note in Sprake's voice, as though he had imagined Mr. Finchley was going to regale him with details of some characteristically human failing which might beset a man in Paris.

Mr. Finchley decided that it would be wise to tell him the whole story, and, although it was rather a different story from what Sprake expected, by the time Mr. Finchley was finished his employer was in an indulgent and amused mood.

While Mr. Finchley was explaining to Mr. Sprake, Robert had returned to the house and wandered into the little garden behind it to explore. Mr. Finchley was a gardener of moderate enthusiasm. He had a man in to cut the grass and dig the beds and he let Mrs. Patten amuse herself by weeding, while he occupied himself with the more interesting business of choosing and setting the plants. It was the end of May and the plane tree at the bottom of the garden was in full leaf and the small cherry tree white with deceptive blossom, for Mr. Finchley had never picked one cherry from it in all the years it had bloomed. In the beds that skirted the walls were dark tulips, neat edges of daisies and primula, while reaching up towards the creeper-topped wall were the green promises of hollyhock stems.

Robert walked slowly round the garden, enjoying the seclusion and the sensation of being contained within a house and garden. It was a new sensation for him and made him feel very important. On a barge one had a sense of freedom and movement which was delicious, but there was never this important knowledge of being surrounded by permanent, personal things that need not be widely shared. After a time he grew tired of strutting about the garden and, pulling out his penknife, he started to make himself useful by going round the beds cutting off the straggly tops of the dead daffodils. It was nothing to him that Mr. Finchley always most religiously allowed the stalk and leaves to die right away so that the bulbs should not be disturbed before he lifted them and stored them for the next season's planting. Robert approached his work with an eye for tidiness.

He had finished one bed and was standing in the corner of the garden, eyeing the little rockery, wondering if there might not be work for him there, when a voice said scornfully

"You'll cop it from old Father Finchley." The, sentence was ended by a quick gurgle, a rich aquatic sound.

Robert looked up to find a boy sitting on the wall above him, his legs dangling against the creeper. He was about two years older than Robert, his head bare to reveal the splendour of a carroty crop of hair, and his face snub-nosed and freckled where it was not hidden by an orange which he was eating noisily, and in true juvenile fashion.

"You didn't ought to cut those leaves off. I did that once with my old man's, and he was as mad as a hatter until Ma told him to shut up. He always shuts up when she tells him to."

"What's 'cop it'?" asked Robert, ignoring the bulbaceous question.

"Cop it?" The boy looked down enquiringly. "Why, cop it's cop it. You'll get it. You're for it. You trying to be funny?"

"Oh, no, not at all," Robert assured him quickly. "You see, I've only just come to England and I don't know the slang."

The other boy was silent for a moment. Then he withdrew his face from the orange and spat a pip expertly at Robert, following it with the question: "Are you trying to make out that I talk slang? My Ma says—" He stopped and then went on, "Where do you come from?" The question was emphasised by another pip which hit Robert on the cheek.

"I come from France," said Robert shortly.

The boy savoured this information and then grinned in an unpleasant way. "I should have guessed it," he said with the help of a volley of pips that rattled off Robert's clothing. "You're too skinny and girlish to be anything but a Froggy. I'll bet you wear a sailor suit on Sundays, don't you?"

"I am not French and I do not wear sailor suits!" replied Robert indignantly, dodging another pip.

"What are you, then? An Eskimo?" This brilliant piece of wit so convulsed its creator that for a moment he was in danger of falling from the wall in his mirth.

"I am English, the same as you," declared Robert, his dark eyes troubled and his lips trembling with anger. "And please stop spitting those pips at me."

"I like doing it, so why shouldn't I do it?"

"Because I don't like it. It is very unmannerly to annoy people without cause."

"Oh, I'm very unmannerly am I, Froggy?" The boy stopped sucking to frown at Robert. "Well, you listen to me. I don't like Frenchies and I don't like you, and I shall go on popping pips at you as long as I want to—and you'll like it." To show that he meant no bluff he scored a hit on Robert's face with a pip.

Robert stood very straight and his face went white with the contraction of his muscles. "I give you warning," he said severely, "that if you spit another pip at me I shall pick up a piece of earth and throw it at you."

The boy laughed, rolled his eyes and answered mockingly: "Oh, aren't we getting brave? So you'll throw a lump of earth at me, eh? If you do, I'll come down there and give you a good licking. I could beat you with one hand behind my back—Froggy."

"I am not very interested in what you think you can do," replied Robert stoutly. "I am telling you what I shall do."

The boy considered this challenge for a moment, sucking gently at the orange skin. The two stared at one another, each trying to assess the ability of the other. With a sudden movement the boy flicked his sucked orange from him so that it struck Robert on the face.

"Take a bite of that, Froggy!" he cried, and before Robert could bend for the earth, he jumped down and hurled himself upon the boy. The impact of the orange on Robert's face and the following attack found him unready, and before he could throw up his hands to protect himself he was struck under the eye and sent rolling backwards on to the turf.

The boy stood over him and said victoriously "Well, Froggy, had enough?"

His victory was brief. Almost before he had finished speaking Robert was on his feet, his face flushed and his lips mouthing a torrent of words which Pépé would have appreciated. The few seconds that followed contained so much that was surprising to the boy from next door that he never fully worked out afterwards what had happened. One moment Robert was on the floor, and the next he was on his feet, and there followed three stunning blows on the boy's nose and a vicious jab in the stomach which laid the red-haired lad on the grass groaning. But he was to find no peace there, for Robert dashed to the border, took up a handful of earth and proceeded to rub the mould hard into his opponent's hair and face. Ten seconds later the boy fled, groaning and earthy, over the wall to the safety of his own terrain and Robert hastened his retreat with handfuls of soil.

He made sure that the enemy had withdrawn for good and then he went back to the house. It was time he thought about the lunch. He spent a quarter of an hour with Mrs. Patten's cookery book, for he was determined to prepare an English meal, and then he sallied out to buy provisions, feeling that his morning had begun well.

Two hours later Mr. Finchley came into the house and opened the kitchen door to be greeted by an appetising smell. Robert half-turned to him in greeting and called happily:

"We shall be ready in two minutes, sir. It is a real English dinner."

While he was waiting for lunch to be served he telephoned Mrs. Crantell. He told her about Robert and

Mrs. Patten, and heard her chuckle from the other end of the wire.

For a time they talked and when they had finished it was arranged that he should bring Robert to supper on Sunday evening.

"Who is Mrs. Crantell?" asked Robert, who could not help listening to the conversation.

"She is a friend of mine," answered Mr. Finchley.

"She is beautiful, this Mrs. Crantell?"

The question, surprisingly, did not embarrass Mr. Finchley. This morning he felt equal to anything. "Mrs. Crantell," he said soberly, "is past that stage where it is permissible to describe a woman as beautiful or plain. The comparative terms are dull or distinguished. Mrs. Crantell is distinguished, a most interesting personality. I think you will like her."

Mr. Finchley withdrew, washed his hands in the bathroom and came down to find the table laid in the dining-room. Apparently, he mused, Robert had overcome his feeling of awe of the room.

"Here we are." Robert entered the room bearing a tray. "Sausages, potatoes and cabbage!"

He took his place and they began lunch. Mr. Finchley was hungry and for a while he engaged himself with the sausages.

"Well, Robert," he said, after he had taken the first brightness off his hunger. "I must congratulate you on your cooking. Pépé must have been a good master."

"Oh, Pépé was wonderful, sir. There was one dish of his which I will prepare for you one day. Stuffed carp. Some people do not çonsider that carp is good eating. But river carp cooked properly during the months of April, May and June … Ha, the good dishes of *carpe farcie* which Pépé and I have—"

"Robert!" Mr. Finchley dropped his fork and looked at the boy intently. "What's the matter with your eye?"

"My eye, sir? Nothing, oh, nothing at all." And Robert went on quickly. "And this is how it is cooked. Many times I have heard Pépé repeat so—First, pick yourself a fine carp, one with soft roe. Boil it quickly for three-quarters of an hour, then scale it and cut off the head and the tail. The middle part you fillet and with the flesh make balls of meat—"

"Don't tell me there's nothing wrong with it. It looks like a black eye to me. How did you get it?"

"I did not get it. It just came like that. It often happens with me that way. But surely you want to know about the carp? Then you place the head and tail of the carp on a long plate, but in the middle where the body was you put cold calf's sweetbreads and arrange the stuffing around the fish. Then you pour a beaten egg over it all, sprinkle bread crumbs and then bake it until it is a beautiful colour and serve it with a sauce made from the soft roe. Ha, how Pépé loved to do that—"

"Robert, stop talking about carps and Pépé and tell me how you came by that black eye?" Mr. Finchley spoke sternly and Robert saw that there was no escape. He was not sure how Mr. Finchley would regard fighting, even defensive fighting.

"It was given to me," he said simply.

"That is how one usually comes by a black eye," answered Mr. Finchley. "What I want are the details. Who gave it to you?"

"Have you never had a black eye?" Robert asked.

Mr. Finchley hesitated before this change of question, and very vividly there came into his mind an occasion when he had been given a black eye, and the memory was surprisingly pleasant. He was silent as he let his mind wander in the past, and Robert, seeing the look on his face, said shrewdly:

"I see that you have had a black eye, sir. Cannot you understand then, that I would rather not talk about my black eye? It is not a beautiful thing."

Mr. Finchley came back to earth quickly and coughed.

"Nonsense, Robert. I want to know what mischief you've been up to. Remember that I am responsible for you until Mr. Hammerton comes to England."

Robert sighed and chased a piece of sausage round his plate with his fork. There was no escape for him. In a subdued voice he told his story, omitting some of the shameful details and considerably cleaning up the end of the fight by making no reference to soil.

Mr. Finchley listened, his face imperturbable, showing no emotion, but in his heart relishing the story. He knew the boy next door, and had suffered his rudeness and uncouth behaviour more than once. He still had clear recollections of flowers broken off and the sobs of Mrs. Patten over the body of her cat slain by a pebble from a catapult. How true it was, he thought, that justice overtakes every wrongdoer sooner or later, and often at the moment of triumph. For every Goliath there lurked somewhere a David. Then his gladness passed to surprise as he considered that it was Robert who had conquered the boy; Robert who was smaller, thinner and less brawny than the other.

As Robert came to an end of his story, Mr. Finchley fished out his pipe and maintained a judicial silence for a moment as he filled it. This was an important moment and he wanted Robert to catch every shade of meaning.

"Robert," he said at last, "I don't want you to misunderstand me. But you must realise this. You are no longer in Paris, living a carefree life with Pépé. You are in England now, and about to begin a very different life, a life which brings you responsibilities, and you must begin to act in a way befitting those responsibilities."

"But I did act. I did very well."

"In some ways, yes. I admit that you had justice on your side. That you were provoked and that you had every right to defend yourself. But that is not all. The proper conduct would have been to have withdrawn before affairs reached a state which made fighting unavoidable. Fighting is vulgar and it is much better to withdraw than to brawl—"

"But he would have thought me afraid, sir!" protested Robert.

"What your opponent thinks is of no importance. You know that you are not afraid and that is all that matters—"

"But my honour, sir. Think of my honour!"

"You are mistaking honour for pride. When you must fight—then fight. But if there is any other alternative, you should take it. That is the true Christian spirit."

"And do you act like that, sir? Did you when you got your black eye?"

Mr. Finchley puffed a smoke screen to hide his features and from his cloud he said: "We all of us fail at times, Robert. You must try to do as I say, not as I may do. The thing I can't understand is how you managed to lick that snub-nosed ruffian ..." He broke off quickly as he found his most insistent thought breaking out.

Robert chuckled, taking the question as forgiveness, and he got up and came round to Mr. Finchley.

"If you will stand up, sir, I will show you. It is most simple. Pépé taught me. Pépé always said that when one is attacked one is permitted to use any method of defence. He taught me the four-in-one."

"The four-in-one?" Mr. Finchley stood up.

"Yes, it is like this. You take a swinging blow at the nose, so"—Robert brought his fist round in a right swing to Mr. Finchley's nose. "Let the fist pass on and strike the nose with the elbow, so"—Robert let his fist curve away from Mr. Finchley's face so that his elbow was brought into contact with Mr. Finchley's nose. "And then you bring your arm back again and deliver a backhand blow to the face, so, and at the same time you jerk your knee upwards into the stomach—*et voilà*, where is he?"

"Good gracious me!" exclaimed Mr. Finchley. "What a villainous trick. Show me again."

Robert demonstrated the operation once more.

"See; it is easy when you know."

"I should say it was. And very useful too in a rough house. Stand still and let me see if I've got it." And Mr. Finchley, quite carried away by the novelty of the trick, experimented on Robert.

"It is the jab in the stomach with the knee which does most harm, Pépé always said. It makes a man sick very often for a long time. But I did not do it very hard to our friend—"

"Ha! Hum! Yes, of course!" Mr. Finchley recovered himself. "Well, no more of it in future. Remember that. You'll be getting me a bad name in the district otherwise."

The morning which had been bright had turned dull and now there was a gentle rain falling, and after they had cleared away the lunch Mr. Finchley found himself faced with the problem of entertaining Robert. For the first time in his life he found himself saddled with the problem of arranging the life of a young boy, and the additional complication of a rainy afternoon did not make the task easy. What, he wondered, did people with children do when it rained?

"If it were fine, we could go out and see some of London," he said.

"What do you usually do on a Saturday afternoon when it rains?" asked Robert, turning from the window where he had been watching the rain fall on the empty street.

"I ... ugh ... well ..." Mr. Finchley decided that he had better let that question pass. Usually he retired to his room and enjoyed a nap. To suggest that course would have sounded impolite. "Well, I usually read or write letters. I know—" his face brightened. "We'll begin your education. You don't have to go to school until Mr. Hammerton arranges about that. But there's no reason why you shouldn't start to get in some groundwork. For instance—how much English history do you know?"

"Oh, a lot, sir. Pépé had the most wonderful book of famous English ladies. It was in French, of course. But I know all about Boadicea, and Lady Godiva—what a woman she was! She was Pépé's favourite. For myself I like Mary Queen of Scots, and I hate Elizabeth. Pépé called her a painted—"

"Quite!" interposed Mr. Finchley. "Well, let's do some history. I've got a school history book upstairs and I'll read to you from it."

Mr. Finchley fetched his copy of Green's *Short History of the English People*, and began to read to Robert. He began at the beginning and read slowly, stopping frequently at first to let the various points be assimilated by Robert, and later on in order to light his pipe which he found it was difficult to keep going while reading aloud. For half an hour he read, informing Robert of the Germanic origin of the English people, and then he felt his eyes growing heavy as the desire for sleep spread about him. He jerked himself to freshness and read on, and for a while the sleepiness was gone. Then he felt it coming back again. Invariably on a Saturday afternoon he allowed himself a nap and the old habit was not to be easily pushed aside.

'Of the character of their life in this early world, however, we know little save what may be gathered from the indications of a later …' Every muscle within him tensed with the sudden need to yawn. Mr. Finchley fought the instinct and with a great effort conquered it. He looked across at Robert to see whether the boy had noticed his momentary embarrassment. Robert was curled up in his armchair, sleeping quietly.

Mr. Finchley was outraged. "Well," he declared to himself, "there's gratitude for you. But how like the young!" He found a certain satisfaction in recognising in his own experience the truth of a popular opinion about children. He read on, in a louder voice to give Robert a chance to wake and resume his attention without being aware that his dereliction had been noticed—"Each little farmer commonwealth was girt by its own border or 'mark', a belt of forest or waste or fen which parted it from its fellow villages."

The recitation had no effect on Robert. He slept on quietly, smiling gently in his dreams. Mr. Finchley put down the book, gave the sleeping boy a reproachful look and then settled happily down into his chair and shut his eyes. Although he could have kept awake, if necessary, he told himself, it would have been cruel to have wakened Robert. The change of air was very likely making him sleepy. In five minutes Mr. Finchley was away in a dark German forest, winding his horn as he strode the paths to give news that he came as a friend and no foe, and as the faint reboant sounds of sleep began to mark his oblivion, Robert opened one eye warily from his chair and then uncurled himself stealthily and tiptoed across the room. He shut the door carefully behind him and with a satisfied grin made his way to the kitchen, thinking to himself that all men were much alike. Pépé, too, had enjoyed an after-lunch nap.

In the kitchen he sprawled himself across the table with the Saturday supplement of Mr. Finchley's paper and began to interest himself in the puzzles. Outside the rain dripped across the window pane and the garden seemed to have lost its colour to the greyness which had followed the rain.

An hour later the ringing of the doorbell interrupted Robert from his industry of making wooden dolls with Mrs. Patten's clothes pegs and his penknife. That the pegs could never serve a functional purpose again, and that the dolls were not really a success, could not destroy Robert's creative joy. Reluctantly he went to the front door and opened it. Standing on the doorstep, just closing an umbrella, was a thick-set, round-faced man, dressed in rough tweed plus-fours.

He looked like a prosperous pugilist, but wore on his nose a pair of pince-nez which would not have gone well with that profession. He was a tall man, and he stared through his glasses at Robert as though he were registering a protest that for one of his size it was unfair to be confronted by microcosms which strained his sight.

"I want to see Mr. Finchley," he said firmly. "My name's Barker."

Robert motioned him into the hall and then went into the sitting-room and woke Mr. Finchley.

"There is a gentleman, a Mr. Barker, wishes to see you," he explained.

"Barker? Don't know the name," said Mr. Finchley, running his hand over his bald head and then putting his tie right. "Anyway, ask him to come in, Robert."

Robert showed Mr. Barker into the room and then left the two men. The moment they were alone, and before Mr. Finchley could ask the other to take a chair, Mr. Barker said almost truculently, as though he wished to have no mistake about his attitude: "Mr. Finchley, I am your next-door neighbour!"

"Indeed," answered Mr. Finchley, a little surprised at this opening. "I'm very glad to know you," and he really was glad, for he had frequently deplored the London habit of living for years next door to a person and never getting to know him. "Are you," he added, "left or right?"

"Facing the street," explained Mr. Barker, with a sudden lapse into a mood of mathematical accuracy, "I am to the right." Then recalling his first mood he went on sternly: "Mr. Finchley, I have called upon you to make a protest. This morning my son, Henry, was set upon and brutally assaulted by a member of your household, with the result that his face is considerably cut and bruised, and a very good shirt ruined. In addition we have had to call the doctor to him for the pains in his stomach. He has experienced considerable vomiting, I'm told, too. Now, sir,

I do not wish to create unneighbourly feelings, but you will surely appreciate that it is my duty as a father and a householder to protect the interests of my family. My son has been injured and I have been put to some expense."

"What do you want me to do about it?" asked Mr. Finchley.

"I expect an apology from the person who assaulted my son and I shall send you the doctor's bill."

"And supposing you get neither?"

Mr. Barker was plainly unready for this. He coughed, twiddled his cap and then said, rather lamely, "I had not expected to have to meet that contingency."

"Then you had better begin to face it now," said Mr. Finchley sternly, "for I certainly do not mean to meet your other demands. And while we are on the subject of your son, I should like to mention—without in any way wishing to promote bad feeling—that I consider he got exactly what he deserved, and I hope it is a cause of humiliation to him that he was beaten by a boy little more than half his size—"

"Oh! That's the first I've heard about that—"

"That is understandable. Nevertheless it is true. Your son met his Waterloo in the boy who opened the door to you just now—"

"You mean that slim little ..." Mr. Barker sat down suddenly and to Mr. Finchley's surprise there spread over his face a broad, contented smile and through his pince-nez shone a warm, friendly gaze. "Well, I never! So that's what happened." He chuckled to himself and then said to Mr. Finchley: "Mr. Finchley, I want you to understand something. Between ourselves I think my son got all he deserved. It was about time someone took the cockiness out of him. But you know what women are. I shouldn't have come here today if it hadn't been for my wife. You know how they feel about children. Let a boy learn in the school of hard knocks, I say. But a mother can never understand that. So, please forget all I said previously."

"That's all right, Mr. Barker," beamed Mr. Finchley. "I understand perfectly. And as a matter of fact I shall be glad to pay the doctor's bill—"

"I wouldn't dream of it! Not another word! If I may be so vulgar, I think a little vomiting will do my son good. But how"—he frowned suddenly—"how could that little chap have beaten my son? It doesn't seem possible. Is he your son?" He asked this with a sudden quickening of interest, a swift mounting of reverence for a man like Mr. Finchley, who could endow his progeny with such superlative arts of self-defence.

Mr. Finchley took the compliment gratefully. "No, I'm his sort of guardian. Actually your son fell a victim to a trick that is common enough in the Parisian underworld. The four-in-one we call it. If you like I'll show you how it's done. It's a useful thing to know if ever you get into a rough crowd. Not strictly Queensberry, of course, but, uh ... very effective."

Mr. Finchley stood up and demonstrated the punch on Mr. Barker. The other's interest was encouraging. "Once more," he urged, "and I think I shall have it. Let's see—fist, elbow, backhand and then the knee. Excellent! And you taught the boy that?"

Mr. Finchley did not deny the implication. "One picks these things up, you know," he said.

"Not in the sedentary life of an accountant," insisted Mr. Barker regretfully. "A man must have lived and travelled to become so adept."

Mr. Finchley let him out finally, feeling like an adventurer, an explorer magnanimously ushering out the leader of a deputation of adoring admirers. He felt so good that he went back to Robert and informed him that they were going out to tea in a café and then on to the pictures. They went and enjoyed themselves and never once did either of them remember that the next day was Sunday and they had no provision of food made for the morrow.

XVI
In which Mrs. Crantell is left thinking

MR. FINCHLEY laid down his knife and fork, wiped his lips with his napkin and then smacked his hands together, as though he wished to convey that that was the end of that: which was exactly what he did wish to convey. The two sausages which he had eaten for breakfast represented the end of the food left in the house.

"The last shot is gone from the locker, Robert," he said merrily, for the sun shone outside and it was impossible to be depressed. "Our water is nearly spent and we've been twelve days in this open boat without food. What do we do now?"

"In the film last night, they sighted a sail," said Robert. "Would that help us?"

"It might if it were a provision ship."

"Something will turn up," said Robert, not worried by the future since the immediate past had been so satisfying.

And something did turn up. The telephone bell rang. Mr. Finchley answered it.

"Is that Mr. Finchley?" asked a woman's voice.

"It is. Who is it?"

"Mr. Finchley of Bardwell & Sprake?"

"Yes, that's right. Who are you?"

The voice, assured, went on pleasantly: "Can't you guess?"

Mr. Finchley was sure he'd never heard the voice before, but the telephone so changed voices it was hard to be sure.

"I'm sorry, but I can't."

"It's Marie—"

"Marie!"

"Yes, I thought you'd be surprised. I got your name from the telephone book. I got the wrong one at first."

"But Marie, I mean Miss Peters—what are you doing in England?"

"I'm back here for good. Didn't you know?"

"No, I didn't. You see ..." Mr. Finchley wanted to explain that he had left Paris in such confusion that he had quite forgotten about her, but he found it difficult to be informative and polite.

"I suppose," the voice went on, assuming a casualness which deceived Mr. Finchley for a moment, "that you travelled back with Mr. Hume."

"No, I didn't. He's still over there. Where are you speaking from?"

"Camden Town—I've got rooms here. Why?"

"I was just wondering—"

"Wondering what?"

"Well, I suppose there'd be all sorts of shops open down there, even on a Sunday?"

"You can get most anything you want if you know where to go. But—"

"That's what I thought." And before another minute had passed Mr. Finchley had invited Marie to lunch and tea on condition that she did some shopping for them first in Camden Town. He had no doubt that she would accept the invitation. He remembered how preoccupied Hume had been when he had said good-bye in Paris, and now here was Marie in England and taking the trouble, apparently, to ring him up merely to enquire whether he had travelled back with Hume. Something had happened, and Mr. Finchley was curious enough to make some effort to find out what it was. So Marie had lunch with them and after lunch they went for a walk across the Heath. Robert walked ahead of them, leaving them free to talk, and if Marie had been surprised to find Robert in England, Mr. Finchley was surprised as she told her story.

Marie made no hesitancies. She told what had happened frankly.

"And now," she said, when she had explained, "I'm sorry that I spoke so rudely to Mr. Hume. I don't like people to have the wrong impression of me. I suppose you don't know his address in England."

"No, I don't," said Mr. Finchley. "What would you want it for?"

"I should like to write and apologise—"

"But you could write to the Paris address—"

"He was leaving there yesterday, I know, and I doubt whether he's left any forwarding address. He wouldn't—"

"No, he wouldn't," said Mr. Finchley.

"Well," Marie threw off her cares, "what does it matter, anyway? Here I am back in England again, making the rounds of the agents, hunting for a job."

"Well, I wish you luck," said Mr. Finchley. "And whenever you feel lonely you must come up and see Robert and myself. You said most of your afternoons were free?"

"Yes, you call on agents in the morning generally, and if you haven't got anything by lunch time you can go home."

While she was speaking an idea had occurred to Mr. Finchley. Marie was almost certainly living in London on her savings, and when they were gone she would have to go home or find a job other than on the stage. Mr. Finchley had a quick sympathy for her ambition; so many girls, he told himself, were too easy-going and devoid of interests other than their faces and clothes. Here was a girl who knew what she wanted, and he felt he wanted to help her. It was convenient, too, that in helping her he could solve some of his own troubles.

When she had finished he began to put his proposition to her. Would she, if she really was free most afternoons, care to earn a little money then? It wouldn't be much, but enough to cover her bus fares and stocking bill. He told her about Robert—who was walking happily ahead working out a vow to make friends with every dog he met—and impressed her with the relief it would be to him to know that someone could come and take the boy out in the afternoon, show him London and keep an eye on him. He would pay all their expenses, of course, and add something more for her trouble.

"I know it's asking you to be a governess again, but you like Robert, and it's only in your spare time."

"But I don't want to be paid for that," Marie declared. "I shall be as glad as Robert for company in the afternoon. I am lonely, too." Her face filled with a passing longing as she said this, and her eyes, darkening, followed the flight of a butterfly which zigzagged over the path. "I wonder what kind of a butterfly that is," she asked. "Isn't it pretty?"

"I don't know," replied Mr. Finchley, and he added quietly, watching her face as he did so: "We ought to have Mr. Hume here, he would know."

Mr. Finchley decided that she should be a good actress.

As Mr. Finchley stood with Robert on Mrs. Crantell's doorstep that evening and rang the bell, he was nervous. It seemed years since that evening when he had arrived, eager to make himself known to her, and had gone away feeling that there was little in life that could interest him after her clear indication of how she might feel constrained to reply to the question that trembled within him. His time in Paris had dulled the sadness and disappointment.

The maid answered the door and showed them in. Mrs. Crantell was waiting for them in her sitting-room. The May evenings were chilly and there was a small fire burning brightly, throwing gentle movements of light over the furniture and curtains. She shook hands with Robert, put them both into chairs, and then sitting down herself turned to Mr. Finchley and gave him a long look:

"So you're back, and you look all the better for your trip." She smiled at him and he fancied he detected in her look a pleasure which was more than normal. She was glad he was back because … he wondered … because she had missed him.

"And this is Robert. Mr. Finchley told me all about you over the telephone. And how do you like England?"

This was a question which Robert found easy to answer; that his reply was lengthy, involved and enthusiastic worried no one.

They passed a very pleasant evening, and Mr. Finchley and Robert did justice to an excellent supper, and as she watched them eating, taking a joy in their appetites and her ability to satisfy them, Mrs. Crantell said:

"And you don't have to go on living like a couple of bachelors until Mrs. Patten gets back. Goodness knows how long she'll be away, if her sister really is ill. I've arranged for my Mrs. Mohun to come and see to you. She'll come every morning, except Wednesday and Saturday—she has other duties then, I'm afraid—and she'll see to your breakfasts, tidy up the house and cook Robert's lunch for him before she goes—"

"But Mrs. Crantell, I can't let you—"

"It's all arranged, Mr. Finchley. I wouldn't dare to tell Mrs. Mohun she isn't wanted now. She's a most independent woman and might take offence. You'll like her and she's very good."

"Mrs. Mohun—that is a good name, I think I shall like her," said Robert. "In fact I like everybody so far in England—"

"You've got a long time to live yet, young man," Mrs. Crantell cautioned him. "You won't find everyone as you expect them."

"You were as I expected," countered Robert illogically.

"Was I?" Even Mrs. Crantell could not resist the swift pride which comes from being approved.

"Oh, yes. You were just as Mr. Finchley said."

"Oh"—she glanced sideways at Mr. Finchley—"and what did he say about me? Nothing unpleasant, I hope?"

"Oh, no, madame." Robert ignored Mr. Finchley's warning cough. "He said the most pleasant things about you. I think he is very fond of you. What I cannot understand is, if he is so fond—"

"Surely, Robert, you're going to taste some of Mrs. Crantell's junket and cream?" Mr. Finchley cut into the conversation quickly. He did not trust Robert on the subject of women. Pépé had definitely warped the boy's attitude towards the relationship of men and women, reducing emotions to a simplicity which could be embarrassing.

Robert looked at the junket and then at Mr. Finchley, and realising that in all innocence he might be embarrassing his friend, he nodded, "I should like some."

Before they went, while the maid was helping Robert with his coat, Mrs. Crantell had a moment with Mr. Finchley.

"I like your Robert," she said. "He's a nice, frank boy." Then she added more slowly and with a quick, bird-like glance at him, her dark eyes bright with amusement: "I hope you didn't give him too high an opinion of me. You know I'm very human and I shouldn't like to disappoint him or you one day ..."

Mr. Finchley rubbed his chin nervously, felt himself suddenly in need of fresh air, and for a rash moment, despite the fact that he knew he would be refused, contemplated declaring himself, and there came into his mind fragments of his proposal speech, rising like ghosts to taunt and haunt him with reproaches. He thought he had done with all that.

He coughed, recovering himself, and passed his hand slowly over his bald head, the movement giving him assurance: "He's all right, just a little unused to civilisation as yet. Um, well, we must be going. Thank you again for getting Mrs. Mohun."

After they had gone Mrs. Crantell went back to her fire. What a change, she thought. Finchley with a boy—and a pleasant boy. Was it her imagination, or had she detected a new liveliness in his manner, a freshness of spirit which he had not possessed before he went to Paris. From the way he looked at the boy—even the way he prevented him from making embarrassing remarks—one might have taken him for a proud father.

She shook her head, a thought had come to her which hurt.

XVII
How Mr. Finchley changes his habits

MRS. MOHUN arrived the next morning at half-past seven. Mr. Finchley was shaving, so Robert went down in his pyjamas to let her in. He found a small, elfish woman, wearing a hat like a coal scuttle and a raincoat with a draggled fur collar. Her figure gave little indication of her vitality and good humour. She was a woman whose body had long given up the effort to cavort in double harness with her exuberant optimism and had resigned itself to the colourless part of jogging wearily behind the verbal gallop which had so quickly tired it.

"Mrs. Mohun, me dear, as you've, no doubt, heard about," she announced before Robert could speak. Coming into the hall, she carried on gaily: "This is Mr. Finchley's house, ain't it? But, Good Lord, look at you there, standing shivering in your pyjamas and staring at me as though I was a choir of angels! Now then, you get along upstairs and dress yourself, I can find me way about any house!" She accompanied this command with a smartish smack on Robert's rear, and he, chuckling at this delightful creature who had come into his life, bounded away upstairs to dress hurriedly so that he might join her as soon as possible.

"It's nothing but toast and marmalade, sir," she informed Mr. Finchley when she brought in the breakfast. "There's not a thing else in the house until I put on me hat and go and get some stuff for you. But still, with the summer coming on you don't need much to your breakfast, I always say. I can see you're the accommodatin' kind—a skimpy breakfast for once won't hurt you. Not like my hubby that was. Lor' bless you, if he had to go without …"

An ominous rustle of Mr. Finchley's newspaper made her pause. She went out for fresh coffee, saying: "He was a one, too, for reading at breakfast. The racing page, of course …"

When she was gone, Mr. Finchley said aloud: "I believe she's a talker."

"Isn't that good?" Robert asked.

"It depends," answered Mr. Finchley. "Some of them work as well as they talk, others just talk, and a very few, like Mrs. Patten for instance, whom you have not yet met, just work. Now, you won't forget, will you?"—Mr. Finchley swung into another subject—"you'll spend the morning in the sitting-room studying and then this afternoon Miss Peters will come along for you. You want to surprise Mr. Hammerton by the amount you will have learnt when he comes for you …"

"Most certainly I do. How long do you think it will be before he comes?" Robert asked the question quietly.

"Well"—Mr. Finchley paused, wondering what was in the boy's mind—"it takes a long time to arrange these things. You can't buy a farm like a pound of butter. Mr. Hammerton had affairs to finish in France. But it won't be long. You're not getting tired of living here?"

"Oh, sir, how could I? I am very happy here." There was no doubt of Robert's sincerity.

Mr. Finchley gave some instructions to Mrs. Mohun about ordering and then he left for the office, feeling contented that Robert would be in good hands until he returned.

When he was gone Robert dutifully went into the sitting-room and sat down with his books. Mrs. Mohun clattered about her work. After a while the door slammed on her as she went out to do her shopping. She was back before long and there was the sound of activity in the kitchen. Robert listened with only half his mind on his books. He would have liked to have gone out to her, but his promise to Mr. Finchley could not be broken. He was rewarded for his constancy by Mrs. Mohun's coming to him. She knocked on the door and slipped inside, saying:

"Don't bother about me, me dear. I'm just going to run round this room with a duster and I'll be so shadow-like you won't 'ardly know I'm 'ere. My!"—she uttered a small cry of surprise at the sight of the books on the table—"you have got a dollop of learnin' there, to be sure. Never was one for learning meself—but the late Mohun! He was—and it was 'is own way of puttin' it—relatively educated compared with others. Towards the end of an evening he was as full of long words as a professor. Many a time from the bedroom I've 'eard him standing on the doorstep thankin' some gent for seein' 'im home, and his langwidge was beautiful."

"Did Mr. Mohun read Shakespeare?" asked Robert. "Mr. Finchley says every English person should know Shakespeare."

"Shakespeare ... that would be poetry, wouldn't it?" She moved around the room working as she talked.

"That's it. He wrote plays."

"Well, I dunno whether he was up to Shakespeare, but he was good at poetry. Maybe it ain't decent for a widow to say it of one who's gone beyond, but he was as poetical a man as ever I wished to meet. Why, the things he used to say to me—even after we was married! Used to call me his little moon, his little silver moon and such things."

"I think I should have liked Mr. Mohun," said Robert pensively.

"You would—he had magnetism. Nobody could resist him, and if you're aimin' to be a poet, he could have given you some help. There was no end to the limericks he knew. Why, up at Mr. Burton's the other day I heard 'im and another gent laughin' fit to burst over a limerick my hubby used to tell before the war. Not that I was listening to what don't concern me, but Mr. Burton 'as a strong voice and sometimes you can't help hearin' things."

"Who's Mr. Burton?"

"Mr. Burton! Ain't you never heard of him? Why, he's my Saturday-morning gentleman. Been going there regular for years, I have, and many a time when I've been down the West End and seen the queue waiting outside some theatre to go in and see Wayland Burton, I've said to myself: 'Ha, you wouldn't be so keen to wait there if you'd seen 'im in his pyjamas as many times as I have.' He lives close to here. Only got one servant, a man, and I goes in for the rough work on Saturday. I could tell you some things about him, but in my profession you 'as to learn to keep a closed mouth. Ettikwet, that's what it is."

She babbled on about Mr. Burton and her other clients until the room was done. When she was gone, Robert turned to his book with a dull sense of returning to the land of the dead after a brief glimpse of a lively arcady. He stuck at his books until his lunch was ready, though he found it essential once or twice to move to the window and stare into the street while he thought over some of the things he had read. It helped him to remember if he could look into the street.

Despite Mrs. Mohun's protests, he had his lunch with her in the kitchen, and not long after she was gone Marie called for him.

That afternoon began a strong friendship. Robert, under Marie's care during the next few days, came to know a lot of London. Almost every afternoon Marie called for him and, with bus and tram and underground for galleons, they sailed through oceans and strange waters, crowded with discoveries and surprises. Often they walked, scorning any conveyance, obeying a deep instinct within Robert which drove him to this exertion and rewarded him with a widening knowledge of the city, for London only reveals its true self to those who have the courage and energy to tread its pavements and pass meekly in the shadow of its buildings and monuments. One of the most thrilling moments for Robert was when he discovered the canal wharves at Camden Town. Once, on an afternoon when Marie could not accompany him, he went alone to the wharf. He made friends with the gatekeeper. Then, wandering and nosing his way about the boats, he soon discarded the friendship of the gateman for that of Lanky Harris, a tall, gloomy-faced, tobacco-chewing bargeman, who knew every bit of canal between London and the Manchester ship canal.

"If you've lived on the boats," he said as he poured dark, long-brewed tea into Robert's tin mug, "even though they was French boats—you'll get tired of a bed in a room. I know you will. I tried it myself, after the war; got a job as a lorry driver. But I didn't stick it long."

Robert shook his head in happy denial. He was far from wanting to leave the pleasures of a house. Lanky began to share a place with Pépé in Robert's affections and there were times when Robert fancied that the *Milly Brown* was a prettier boat than the *Swan of Paris*. But wherever Robert went in the afternoons, he was always home before Mr. Finchley; and when that gentleman opened the door of the house, he had come to look out for the cry of greeting and Robert's sudden irruption from kitchen or sitting-room, his tongue ready with the tale of his day's doings.

There were times, of course, when Mr. Finchley found Robert's presence trying. He would not have been human otherwise, for the boy enforced a definite change in his habits. He was seldom allowed to sit quietly during the evening listening to the radio or reading. Robert had little use for broadcasting beyond the variety turns. He enlisted Mr. Finchley's help in the solving of cross-word puzzles or took him for a walk across the Heath where he embarrassed Mr. Finchley by making a friend of every dog that came along. There were several occasions when Mr. Finchley had to forgo attendance at concerts because he knew Robert would be bored by them and he could not leave him alone, or did not like to leave him alone.

On the other hand, Mrs. Crantell was glad of these changes. Mr. Finchley's set routine of taking her to concerts and plays now became disorganised, and she found herself accompanying him and the boy to the cinema and once to a revue.

Mr. Finchley need not have been worried at this interruption of his habits. Mrs. Crantell assured him of her pleasure in the new regime. Nevertheless, when these things happened Mr. Finchley momentarily sighed for his lost days of freedom, though within a few minutes his regret was gone. The boy possessed unmistakably the quality of making other people interested in what he was doing, and for Mr. Finchley, who had lived alone so long, his life complete in himself, it was a new and exhilarating adventure to find himself responding to the moods and demands of another person and to discover that he really liked to have Robert insisting that they did things together. Mrs. Mohun, too, felt what Mr. Finchley knew to be true.

"He's a spark, that boy," she confided to him one day. "Not, mind you, that I don't think 'es got funny little grown-up ways what I don't altogether care to see in a boy; but there ain't nothin' escapes 'im. He's like a puppy, all eyes and action. 'Minds me of the late Mohun sometimes …"

XVIII
How Mr. Finchley seeks sanctuary on a table

IT WAS Friday evening and the day had been hot, a wicked, scorching summer day strayed into May to hint at coming glories. Arriving so unexpectedly it was not so welcome, its promise not so pleasing, as it would have been if warning had been given. Mr. Finchley was hot, he had been hot all day, partly because of the breakdown of the electric fan in his room and chiefly because he was—owing to the absence of Mrs. Patten's wise supervision—still wearing his winter underclothes when he should have been wearing what Mrs. Patten always referred to as his 'in-betweens', neither thick nor thin, but suitable for the vagaries of an English May.

He walked up Nassington Avenue, wondering whether he should take a cold bath and thinking longingly of iced drinks and of swimming at the sea. He fanned his face with his hat as he walked, and his eyes were dreamy with the various problems and thoughts that revolved within his mind. He wondered what Robert had done that afternoon and hoped, with a paternal solicitude which was becoming almost habitual, that Marie had kept the boy out of the streets and gone for a walk over the Heath. He knew that it was unlikely, Robert loved the streets so much in any weather.

He pushed open the front door and entered the hall, calling "Robert!" He stood waiting for the tumult of Robert's greeting to sweep upon him and was surprised when nothing happened.

"Robert, are you in?" he called once more. Puzzled, he dropped his hat on to the table which stood against the wall of the hall and went to the kitchen. The boy was probably in the garden. He pushed open the kitchen door and called "Robert". This time he got an answer, but not from Robert. From the cushion of Mrs. Patten's much-loved armchair by the window a dog looked up and growled, and two things became very evident to Mr. Finchley: the dog was a bulldog, and the growl was a growl of resentment, voicing clearly an irritation with this disturbance of its sleep.

"Where the devil did you come from?" Mr. Finchley put the question in order to give a start to his own enquiry, but the dog seemed to take his words literally. It growled a fierce "Get to hell out of here," and then as Mr. Finchley made no move it rose, stretched insolently and jumped down, lurching towards Mr. Finchley with very much the expression and mood of a bandy-legged pugilist who has invested his savings in an unpopular public-house and has decided to throw out a traveller who has innocently said: "Bit quiet in here, ain't it?"

The moment the dog began to move towards him Mr. Finchley realised that his home was no longer his castle. The skin along his spine became extraordinarily sensitive.

"Now then, good dog, good dog!" He made an appeal to the bulldog's better nature, but he might have been an Abyssinian entreating Mussolini. In fact the dog had a distinct facial resemblance to Mussolini, but Mr. Finchley had little time to indulge in political fancies. The dog came on with a slow, deliberate lurch and Mr. Finchley backed into the hall as one who retreats at the point of a gun, and his mind was probing his chances. It was too late to shut the kitchen door and keep the animal there, and he dared not make a dash for dining- or sitting-room, because he was sure that the animal could show a pretty turn of speed. There was only one escape for him, to back along the hall until he reached the long table and then take refuge on top of it. He would be safe there unless the bulldog showed any ability as a jumper, which he hoped it would not.

Very carefully he backed along the hall, making soothing noises at the animal, and the bulldog followed him, growling continuously, its voice holding tones that left no doubt of its opinion of Mr. Finchley.

Mr. Finchley put a hand behind him and felt the rim of the table; the balm of that moment was that which is known by drowning persons who, about to go under for the third and final instalment of their life's review, find the last instalment denied them and a lifebelt for necklace. Mr. Finchley let his joy shine from his eyes, and the bulldog realised that his prey was slipping from him, that he was not going to rip the seat off those pin-striped pants and slash to ribbons the tail of that black jacket. Its white hairs bristled, its red-rimmed eyes widened with ferocity and it hurled itself at Mr. Finchley as that gentleman turned adroitly and vaulted neatly to the top of the table. For a moment the dog raved and growled around the table, but it made no move to jump up and Mr. Finchley understood that the dog knew to an inch the limit of its powers.

"And now what do I do?" Mr. Finchley thought as he watched the dog take up guard on the mat outside the sitting-room. "And how did the beast get into my house?"

He decided that there was nothing he could do for himself and that the beast's entry into the house was probably connected with Robert, so he squatted himself cross-legged on top of the table and eyed the dog with a frown which was far short of revealing his true feelings about that animal. They sat for some minutes watching one another, Mr. Finchley Buddha-like, the dog, yawning occasionally, possessed of the reassuring knowledge that at some time the demands of hunger would drive Mr. Finchley from his perch. They settled themselves to a siege.

Time went slowly. Mr. Finchley's legs got cramped and for a while he felt shy of standing up and pacing the four-foot length of the table to relieve the cramp. Even before a belligerent bulldog he felt he had to retain his dignity. But in the end the cramp won, and he paced solemnly up and down the table, ducking to avoid the lamp bracket. The dog stretched itself on the mat and watched him through one eye, giving the impression that it was good of Mr. Finchley to amuse him with this exhibition, but it would in no way soften his ire nor turn aside his just revenge.

Mr. Finchley was at the point of working out whether he could make a rope from his tie, braces and suspenders to lasso the telephone from its stand on the far side of the hall and so call for assistance (How would one frame such an S.O.S. he wondered? Is that the police station? I am marooned by a bulldog on my hall table. Will you send a man along? Or should he get into touch with the fire brigade? Or was it simpler to dial 999 and risk a crowd forming outside the house as the flying squad roared up?) when his distress was forgotten in the sound of footsteps coming up the front garden. Through the frosted panels of the door he made out the dark patch of someone standing outside. The dog heard the noise and looked up. The bell rang and Mr. Finchley found himself undecided what to do. If he called out, whoever it was might come inside and receive the same treatment from the dog. The best thing to do was to let them ring and go away without an answer and with them his hope of being rescued.

The bell rang three times and then, before Mr. Finchley could call out, the person at the door twisted the handle and stepped into the hallway. It was Mrs. Crantell and she saw Mr. Finchley at once.

"What on earth are you doing there?" she asked, prepared to laugh at his explanation.

Mr. Finchley became a man of action. "Quickly, get outside! You're in danger. Can't you see?" He pointed to the dog, which had risen silently to face this newcomer, but Mrs. Crantell merely looked at Mr. Finchley, her brows knit into pretty lines of perplexity.

"Are you all right, Mr. Finchley? Shall I—"

"The dog!" Mr. Finchley roared, interrupting her. "He'll bite you!"

Mrs. Crantell followed his pointing hand and saw the dog. What followed might have filled Mr. Finchley with admiration for Mrs. Crantell's powers of swift decision and action in an emergency had he not been almost frantic with anxiety for her safety. She saw the dog, she realised its inimical nature and she calculated that there was no time for her to back out and shut the door, but a sporting chance for her to reach the table. The dog had as far to go as she. She ran and the dog bounded, and as she ran she proved what Atalanta had done long ago, that the race is not always to the swift. She used Atalanta's device. As the dog came towards her she threw her handbag towards it and by good fortune hit it on the muzzle, so that for a second the dog wavered, undecided whether to rend the handbag or leave that task until later. Its indecision saved her, and Mr. Finchley hauled her to safety alongside of him as the dog came growling to her heels.

She flopped down on the table, showing more leg than Mr. Finchley cared to think he had seen, and then said: "Well, you've put me in a funny position, Mr. Finchley. I think I'm entitled to an explanation. I didn't know you had a dog."

"I haven't." Mr. Finchley's voice was pathetic with a desire to be understood. "I'm terribly sorry about this. That was very clever of you to throw the handbag."

"Very," observed Mrs. Crantell, settling herself comfortably on the table as though Mr. Finchley always entertained his guests so. "I shall have to get another bag though."

The dog was giving them a vicious demonstration of its prowess by tearing up the bag. The silk lining seemed particularly to infuriate it.

Mr. Finchley explained what had happened to him and she listened without interrupting him. "I suspect Robert," he finished.

"Well, here we are and here we stay until we are rescued," Mrs. Crantell summarised their position, and added, "Have you any suggestions?"

Mr. Finchley shook his head. He was certainly not going to mention his lasso idea. The thought of taking off braces and suspenders on a hall table with Mrs. Crantell sitting beside him was impossible.

"Then we'd better make ourselves comfortable. I've often wanted to squat on a table like a tailor, and now I've got my chance."

Mr. Finchley was grateful to her that she did not blame him for her trouble. He congratulated himself for having for a friend a woman of such good sense and steady equanimity.

If two strangers are suddenly by some capricious twist of Fate thrown together into a common danger or isolation, their first impulses lead them to a mutual solidarity which quite obliterates any radical differences of race or creed—such differences only develop under the prolonged forcing of isolation. To Mr. Finchley, five minutes after he had been marooned with Mrs. Crantell, there came an awareness of the strengthening of all those moments of affection and friendship which had existed between them. It seemed almost prophetic that they should be so exposed to ridicule and danger in order that they might reveal to the full the hidden qualities of each other and so attain a higher assurance of their fundamental virtues. Mr. Finchley thought Mrs. Crantell was displaying superb calmness where other women might have grown hysterical, and Mrs. Crantell respected Mr. Finchley for not embarrassing her by a plenitude of excuses for the plight he had to share with her.

"When Robert goes to live with this Mr. Hammerton you'll miss him, won't you?" she asked suddenly. Mr. Finchley nodded. “Yes, I shall. I didn’t think it was so easy to grow fond of a boy.”

“But you’ll be glad to get back to your old way of living—free of little accidents like this?” She nodded towards the dog.

“How could I object to an accident like this,” said Mr. Finchley, conscious that he was reddening a little, “when it brings me such pleasant company?”

“Why, Mr. Finchley, you amaze me!” Mrs. Crantell smiled merrily at him and Mr. Finchley knew that there was no sweeter smile in the world.

“Do I?” he asked, feeling foolish and yet liking the sensation.

“I had no idea you could be such a cavalier!”

“Well, I suppose there’s a streak of the cavalier in all of us—”

“But it takes a perch on a hall table to bring it out, eh?” Mrs. Crantell laughed, the dog growled disapprovingly and Mr: Finchley wondered whether he should not pursue the topic further. He might even … No, all that was settled long ago. But still, there was always the chance that a woman might change her mind. As he was debating this he was interrupted by the sound of footsteps running up the garden, and before he could call out the door was thrown open and Robert came panting into the hall, holding a small parcel to his breast.

“Robert, mind the dog!” The cry came simultaneously from Mrs. Crantell and Mr. Finchley. Robert looked from them to the dog and then without alarm said:

“But what are you doing up there?”

“Quickly, Robert, get out of the way of that dog—it’s dangerous!” cried Mr. Finchley, and his voice took on a quick note of alarm as the bulldog rose and began to move towards Robert.

"But he is all right. He will not hurt me," replied Robert. "I know him. His name is Boxer and he will not touch you if you call him by his name. Here, Boxer, come along!" He bent down and from the parcel took out a dog biscuit and held it to the dog.

Boxer, for there seemed to be no doubt about his name, approached Robert, his stump of a tail wagging amiably, and accepted the biscuit with great gentleness.

"There you are! He is all right."

"Robert," said Mr. Finchley sternly, "take that dog into the kitchen and lock him in."

Robert recognised the tone in Mr. Finchley's voice and he led Boxer into the kitchen and shut the door. The moment the door closed on the dog Mr. Finchley slid from the table and then helped Mrs. Crantell down. He turned to Robert.

"Now, young man," he began seriously. "Will you please explain how that dog got into this house? I may say that had it not been for our quickness we might both have been seriously injured by the beast."

"But, Mr. Finchley," pleaded Robert anxiously, "Boxer is not fierce. Only when you do not first call him by his name so that he knows you are a friend. I found that out on the Heath this afternoon when I went for a walk by myself. Miss Peters could not come today. He was lost, the dog was, and he was fierce towards me when I tried to make friends, but I happened to call him Boxer and at once he was friendly."

"Do you mean you found the dog on the Heath?" asked Mr. Finchley.

"Yes, sir. You are not angry with me for bringing him home? It would have been cruel to leave him. I left him in the kitchen while I went for some biscuits. I did not think you would go in there. Tomorrow morning I will take him to the police station."

"You will," said Mr. Finchley definitely, "and until then he can remain in the kitchen. I do not trust that dog."

"Wasn't there any name on his collar?" asked Mrs. Crantell. "The owner may be worried about him."

"He is not wearing a collar," answered Robert. "But I will see he goes back tomorrow."

"Very well. But he stops in the kitchen until then," insisted Mr. Finchley, and in the kitchen Boxer stopped, making himself very comfortable in Mrs. Patten's chair.

Over the ruins of Mrs. Crantell's bag Robert was doleful.

"I was saving for a razor like Mr. Finchley's," he said unhappily, "but now I will save first to buy you another bag. I am ashamed of Boxer. How much," he asked anxiously, "would a bag like that cost?"

Mrs. Crantell hid a smile and replied firmly, "For a pound I should think you would be able to replace it."

Robert sat down with his pencil and paper and worked out that in forty weeks he would be in a position to recompense Mrs. Crantell for her loss. "It is a long time," he announced heavily.

"It might have been longer if you had to buy me a new pair of trousers," added Mr. Finchley. "But cheer up, time passes very quickly."

Mrs. Crantell had called to see whether Mr. Finchley would accompany her that Sunday into the country. It had been their habit for the past two years during the summer to spend every other Sunday on some trip into the country. It was a staid, enjoyable pastime to which both of them looked forward. A train or coach ride took them from London, they wandered until they found a pleasant place for tea and then returned to spend the evening quietly at Mrs. Crantell's house listening to the radio or, if the evening was warm, sitting in the garden talking.

"There is Robert—what about him?" asked Mr. Finchley. Robert was in the kitchen feeding Boxer.

"That's all right. He can come with us, surely?" said Mrs. Crantell. "He won't make any difference."

"No, I suppose not," answered Mr. Finchley, though he was dubious about Robert's inability to make things different.

Mrs. Crantell left them with the promise to spend Sunday together and to take Robert to see the Thames above Henley. Robert, feeling he must do something to make up for her loss of the handbag, insisted upon accompanying her home. Mr. Finchley would have gone with them, only he had made an arrangement for his insurance agent to call that evening, to discuss the details of a policy of his which had just matured. Reluctantly he watched them go, resigning himself to the confines of the house. He took up his paper and began to read. He had not been reading long when there came a ring at the door. He got up, expecting to find his insurance agent.

When he opened the door two men were standing on the doorstep. One was in the uniform of a chauffeur, the other wore a soft black hat and was in evening dress, a white silk scarf trailing over his shoulders. The man with the scarf was tall, had a lean, intelligent face and a mouth that was long and expressive.

"We are looking," he said in a deep voice, a voice which was controlled and obviously the slave of his intellect, doing its bidding to perfection so that his words held a significance Mr. Finchley found refreshing, "for a Mr. Finchley who, according to the local directory of inhabitants, lives at this address. Have we come to the right house?"

"You have," said Mr. Finchley. "Won't you come inside?"

"Thank you." The man cast a look at his chauffeur, a look of satisfaction, and they both entered, following Mr. Finchley into the sitting-room.

"Please take a seat." Mr. Finchley waved them to chairs.

"Thank you, no," the man replied, and he looked around him with considerable interest; Mr. Finchley's sitting-room was very much the same as other sitting-rooms, though a little less crowded with ornaments. Both of the men seemed to find their survey of the room illuminating. The chauffeur coughed gently and addressing his master, said: "If I may venture the opinion, sir, there seems to be all the marks of a very comfortable and prosperous household. One might almost say, a nest well feathered—"

"And the bird at home, we hope," finished his master. "Might we," he went on, turning to the perplexed Mr. Finchley, "might we see Mr. Finchley?"

"You may indeed," he replied. "I am Mr. Finchley."

"You're Mr. Finchley!" The man gazed at him in amazement. Then he recovered himself quickly and frowned, a frown that expressed consternation and deep disapproval, and at the same time he struck an intimidating attitude and, pointing his finger at Mr. Finchley, uttered the single word "Fagan!" in tones that sent chills along Mr. Finchley's spine.

"Fagan!" he repeated, his voice warming to wrath and loathing. "Perverter of innocent minds! And from such villainy, from the proceeds of your despicable crimes, you furnish yourself a comfortable house and assume the guise of respectability. But tremble, monster, your hour has come, the moment of your judgment hangs over you like a sword to strike from you your deceitful trappings and reveal your naked iniquity. I thank God that it has been granted to me the blessed power to expose you and to rescue the innocent from your clutches. I pray only that I may be permitted to complete my task with the humility and … and …" he coughed awkwardly and his manservant prompted him gently—"May I suggest 'charity', sir?"

"With the humility and charity becoming a Christian confronted with the sin of another. Wretched man, what have you to say?"

Mr. Finchley sat down quickly, overcome by the power of the man's words, and he murmured confusedly: "What on earth are you talking about, and who are you, anyway, to come like this into my house and—"

"Silence, craven!" thundered the man. "Seek not to escape by subterfuge and wordy evasions. I demand the truth!"

"The truth about what?" So serious were the faces of the two men that Mr. Finchley had earnestly begun to search his soul for some sin which might fit their anonymous accusations.

They looked at him with the incredulous air of men who find themselves faced with a phenomenon unknown in their experience.

"He is hardened," said the chauffeur sadly. "If I might suggest it, sir, force would probably prevail where your words have failed. His kind are deaf to the sensitive beauty of speech, they understand only the tongue of the rod. Shall I slug him one, sir?"

"He is hardened, Perkins, hardened into his sin, but I do not despair. Force must be our last resource."

"Will you," said Mr. Finchley with a sudden asperity, "please tell me what all this nonsense is about?"

"It is not nonsense, it is a serious accusation," said the man sharply, and the chauffeur fidgeted impatiently.

"An accusation of what?"

The man sighed, a long-drawn sound that indicated how great was his patience, and then he said slowly: "Perhaps if I show you how much I know of your sins you will adopt a different attitude. My name is Wayland Burton—"

"The actor?" Mr. Finchley was interested.

Mr. Burton bowed slightly to show his pleasure and Perkins said severely: "The famous actor."

"Myself I make no claim to fame. It is for others to judge my art. But there is one pursuit in which I am capable of forgetting my profession, and where I willingly throw myself into the scramble for fame. I make no apology for that. Possibly"— he smiled sarcastically as he said this—"you may have heard of Belladonna Bilker, of Belladonna Blacksmith and Belladonna Boxer?"

"I have not," answered Mr. Finchley. "What are they?"

"What an actor is lost in this criminal," exclaimed Mr. Burton admiringly. "I will explain. The Belladonnas are dogs, my dogs, and they are all championship winners at Crufts and other shows. I breed them, I nurture them; I groom them, I slave for them, I carry them to championship fame, and then they are taken from me. First Bilker, then Blacksmith and now Boxer—"

"Do you mean ... Are you talking about a bulldog called Boxer?" Light began to seep into the darkness of Mr. Finchley's troubles.

The two men looked at each other.

"Let me slug him, sir," pleaded the chauffeur.

Mr. Burton raised his hand in denial. "No, we will tolerate his insolence. His hour is coming. Yes, sir," he turned to Mr. Finchley, "I am talking about a bulldog called Boxer. Perkins, here, has charge of my dogs' exercises and on three occasions within the last two years my championship dogs have disappeared from him whilst he was walking them on the Heath. But today you, or rather your emissary, your confederate, your young minion in crime, was not clever enough. My man saw him and followed him to this house and then came to me so that we might take joint action. Can you deny that you have my dog in your house?"

"Well"—Mr. Finchley hesitated. It was going to be difficult to explain to Mr. Burton. Damn that young Robert! "Well, as a matter of fact I have, but—"

"You see, Perkins"—Mr. Burton was triumphant—"he confesses."

"I confess nothing," snapped Mr. Finchley.

"You are making a very great mistake. It is true that I have a bulldog called Boxer in this house. But he was certainly not stolen from you, and as for Bilker and Blacksmith, I know nothing about them. I am no thief. I'm a respectable solicitor's clerk and I demand an apology from you for the outrageous way in which you have come here and insulted me. Do you think you have acted politely and decently to have carried on in this way merely because your man saw the dog brought into this house?"

Mr. Burton shook his head sadly and turned to Perkins
"You had better slug him, Perkins. Not only does he steal our dog, but he demands an apology from us because we resent it. You may slug him."

"Thank you, sir." Perkins beamed gratefully at his employer and then slowly began to roll up his sleeve, and from his manner Mr. Finchley knew that he was a man who must have had considerable experience of slugging.

"I do not like to witness scenes of brutality, though I am well aware that there are times when they become necessary," said Mr. Burton gravely to Mr. Finchley; "so you will excuse me if I look out of the window while Perkins interviews you. Carry on, Perkins."

"But, listen …" Mr. Finchley cried anxiously. Mr. Burton merely shook his head and turned away.

Perkins, with a brief disregard of niceties, spat accurately over his shoulder into Mr. Finchley's fire-grate and then approached menacingly.

Mr. Burton looked out into the street; Bilker, Blacksmith and Boxer were to be avenged. Their loss had grieved him, for he was a sensitive man and hated to lose those who held his affections. He shut his eyes and listened. From behind him the silence was broken by the swift, unmistakable sound of a fist striking flesh, a horrible, inhuman sound, then a gasp, and the thud of a body being resisted by floor carpet.

"Thank you, Perkins," he said quietly. "I am sorry that you should have to do this for me, but you know my hatred of violence." He turned to survey the scene of carnage and found himself facing a determined Mr. Finchley, untouched, unruffled, and an overthrown Perkins who was sitting on the floor, clasping his hands to his stomach and making wry faces while he sought for his breath. The chauffeur's nose let flow a reluctant stream of blood.

"And now, perhaps," said Mr. Finchley, endowed with a new courage after finding that Robert's four-in-one was as good in practice as it was in theory, "you'll listen to me and try to be sensible."

With his prompter windless, Mr. Burton found himself bereft of words. He just stared at Mr. Finchley, fascinated as a bird before a snake, and as he stood there the door opened and in came Robert.

He stopped as he saw the men, and then as the chauffeur looked up to him the boy's face changed its expression from surprise to alarm and he made a movement towards the door. Mr. Finchley, however, caught him by the arm and dragged him back. "Mr. Finchley—what has happened?"

"That," said Mr. Finchley, "is what I want to know. Will you please explain to me what you meant by stealing this gentleman's dog—"

XIX
Of irises

IT IS a profound, though quite common saying, that the innocent frequently suffer for the guilty acts of others, though it is not so generally admitted that the innocent very often enjoy the vicarious excitement which comes from their temporary association with sinners. It is good and satisfying to share the criminal's experiences without partaking of his load of nagging conscience. Mr. Finchley knew that and the knowledge made him less angry with Robert than he might and should have been. Robert, through his sin, had given him an opportunity of proving the efficiency of a strategy which had seemed too good theoretically to pass the test of practice. Now he knew it to be true. Moreover he rather liked the barbarous satisfaction of smacking a man on the nose, fist, elbow and backhand, and then kicking him in the stomach, all with a perfect legitimacy, since he was the injured, innocent party. He was in Robert's debt, but he still had his duty to perform.

"Robert," demanded Mr. Finchley, "did you steal this gentleman's dog?" He indicated Mr. Burton.

"I do not know the gentleman," said Robert, his poise recovered.

"I am Wayland Burton—please answer your father's question. I am beginning to feel that I may have perpetrated a grave injustice."

"You are Mr. Burton—the one Mrs. Mohun has seen in pyjamas so often, the actor? Oh, I have long wanted to meet you, sir. My name is Robert Gillespie, and Mr. Finchley is my friend, not my father."

"Robert, answer my question about the dog. You told Mrs. Crantell and me that you had found it wandering on the Heath. You said it had no collar—"

"That is true, sir. I told Mrs. Crantell when she asked that it was not wearing a collar, and it wasn't, not then—"

"That is the boy I followed from the Heath, sir." The chauffeur rose painfully from the ground, still holding his injured stomach. "And if I may mention so distressing a subject, sir, I feel that I shall very shortly be compelled to vomit, so if there is no further testimony you require, sir, from me I will ..." The rest of his words were lost as he rushed from the room out of the house.

"One has hit him?" asked Robert.

"One has," said Mr. Burton. "But we still await your story, young man."

Robert looked from him to Mr. Finchley: in neither face did he find any comfort. He sighed, looked around the room as though he imagined there might be some last-minute escape for him and then, realising his helplessness, said:

"It is true. I am a thief. I am sorry if I have caused trouble. I did not think anyone would know."

"But, Robert, I don't understand?" Mr. Finchley was distressed at this confession. For a moment he wondered whether there was more in Robert's character than he had imagined, hidden turmoils which the boy had been powerless to control. He remembered the stolen haddock … but there had been a reason then. "Why did you steal the dog? What did you want to do with it?"

"I meant to give it back."

"Give it back—what, to me?" asked Mr. Burton.

"Of course, sir. You see, I knew about you from Mrs. Mohun—the lady who looks after you on Saturday mornings. You know her?"

"I believe there is such a person," answered Mr. Burton distantly. "Though I repudiate here and now the suggestion that she has ever seen me in my pyjamas. But what of her?"

"Oh, it is not her," Robert went on, gaining some courage as he told his story. "You see, I wanted to know you. I wanted very much to meet you, and she told me about your dogs and Mr. Perkins taking them for a walk. So I decided to steal Boxer and then take him back to you tomorrow morning, so that I could meet you."

Mr. Burton was obviously impressed and pleased by this explanation. "You are very young to be such an admirer of my art," he said kindly.

"Oh, it is not that, sir. I do not admire your art. I know nothing of the theatre. It was not for myself. See—" Robert put his hand into his pocket and pulled out a postcard. He went to Mr. Burton and handed him the card.

"Is she not beautiful? She is lovely—do you not think so, Mr. Burton?"

Mr. Burton looked at the card, held it first away and then near to him, and finally said: "Yes, yes, a most interesting type. But whose photograph is it and what has it all to do with me? Do you know, sir?" He handed the card to Mr. Finchley, who recognised it at once.

"Why, that's Marie Peters," he said.

"Of course," cried Robert. "It is Marie and it was for her that I wanted to speak to Mr. Burton. He is so famous an actor and it would be easy for him to see her, and, maybe, give her a job, only a little one, but it would be a job. And she is a good actress. It touches my heart to hear her say she will soon go back to Gloucestershire if she does not get a job—"

"Robert!" Mr. Finchley spoke crossly. "That's enough." Then he turned to Mr. Burton. "I'm sorry that you have been put to all this trouble, Mr. Burton. Robert is rather an unusual boy and he does not fully understand things. I very freely forgive the suspicion which you held me in and I hope you will show the same spirit towards the boy's misdemeanour."

Mr. Burton coughed and hesitated, feeling the lack of a Perkins to start him, and then said:

"Let us forget the whole affair. I will take Boxer and you shall forgive the boy."

A few moments later Boxer followed his master to his car, where a pale Perkins leaned uncomfortably across the wheel.

When they were gone Mr. Finchley spoke to Robert. "I am not going to lecture you, Robert, for I understand that you were not consciously doing anything naughty. It was in fact very good of you to try and help your friend, but you must not try to help unless you can do it without getting into the wrong. I don't ask you to promise not to do any such thing again. I merely rely upon you not to."

"Oh, Mr. Finchley, I am so unhappy," was Robert's reply. "And if it had not been for that man seeing me I should have probably got her a job, he would have been so glad to get the dog back. It is as Pépé says, to help others it is not wise to injure oneself."

He was very silent until bedtime and Mr. Finchley left him alone, realising the extent of the boy's disappointment. But the next morning there was with the mail a letter addressed to Master Robert Gillespie. It ran, dispelling all Robert's disappointment:

> *MY DEAR ROBERT,*
> *If you will hand the enclosed card to Miss Peters and ask her to present it at the Majestic Theatre at ten-thirty next Monday morning, I will see what can be done. Boxer sends his compliments and Perkins is quite well, except for severe pains in the breadbasket.*
> *Yours affectionately,*
> *WAYLAND BURTON.*

And even Mr. Finchley had to admit that it was a very satisfactory end to a business which had not begun too well.

"He is a gentleman," cried Robert enthusiastically, "I shall always remember him."

"And I," thought Mr. Finchley pleasantly, cracking the top of his egg adroitly, "shall always remember Perkins."

The next morning saw them early at Mrs. Crantell's house. The weather, favouring the resumption of their Sunday habit of going into the country, was kind to them. The sun beamed down upon the trio as they made their way to the coaching point, and its warmth upon their backs made Mr. Finchley and Mrs. Crantell stir with contented gratitude. These excursions meant a lot in their lives. They looked forward to them and mused back over them, catching again the quiet, uneventful measure of the long hours spent away from the town. At heart neither of them was a town-dweller, each carried a firm love of country things, and it was on these days, once every other Sunday, that they took out their loves and fancies, handled them in the sun and let its rays burnish and glisten them.

Robert, as though he detected the spirit which moved them, was as unobtrusive as possible. He sat quietly in the coach as it ambled out of London. When they left the coach a short walk down the winding lane brought them to the towing path of the river and Robert was given his first sight of the young Thames, untouched by the sea, confident in its strippling strength and hastening, bright with hopes and colours, towards the waiting tide banks and the bulky traffic of the Pool.

They walked along the path and Robert kept Mr. Finchley and Mrs. Crantell busy with questions. What were the mayflies that danced so crazily up and down, up and down, beating the warm air with their black wings? And that bird—was that a woodpecker? What was a tormentil? And this, was this a colt's foot?

He showed more interest in the wild flowers, for he knew many of them by their French names and longed to have the English for them. So avid was his desire for this knowledge that they were both hard pressed to satisfy him.

The morning passed gently away to an accompaniment of river noises and Robert's happy talk, and Mr. Finchley was glad to think that Robert's presence made little difference to the old pleasure of these Sunday walks.

They stopped for lunch at a riverside café, where the lunch for three cost Mr. Finchley five shillings, and Robert's expenditure on slot machines amounted to two shillings in coppers. The slot machines worried Mr. Finchley. They were new, and, he thought, unnecessary, and he made a note to avoid the café in future. He could not easily reconcile himself to these mechanical reminders of the town. Robert—and indeed Mrs. Crantell—had no such qualms.

"It is a pity Pépé is not here," said Robert as their last copper was sucked into the maw of the fruit machine. "He has such a way with these. Once, I remember, in Rheims there was a fight because the proprietor insisted that Pépé should not be allowed to shake the machine—that was part of his system. Do you think—"

"Yes, I do," said Mr. Finchley hastily, foreseeing Robert's request. "In England it is absolutely forbidden to shake them. Come on, shall we have a boat out for the afternoon?"

This new suggestion made Robert forget the slot machines and soon they were pulling up-river in a skiff, Mr. Finchley at the oars, Robert in the bow, and Mrs. Crantell holding the ropes. Mr. Finchley pulled steadily. When you have been cooped up in an office all the week, he felt, it was good to stretch your arms and put an honest strain on your muscles. He drove the boat through the water, cutting against the current of the river, and with each dip of the oars the bow caressed the river, making soft, murmuring sounds as though it apologised for disregarding the current and knew, of course, that if the river really cared to exert itself nothing could force its way against the stream. In the shade of the pollarded willows, and under tall clumps of poplar and beech, other boats and punts were moored, their occupants stretched in flannelled oblivion.

"Being in a boat like this," said Robert, "reminds me of the lake in the Bois de Boulogne, and meeting Mr. Hume."

"Hume?" Mrs. Crantell looked at Mr. Finchley. "He's the young naturalist you told me about?"

"That's right," said Mr. Finchley, wondering what had happened to Hume. Marie never mentioned him now.

"What's that?" asked Robert, pointing to the bank. They looked and saw in a river field a dozen caravans, steam-engines, and men and women busy with tents and cages.

"Looks like a circus," said Mr. Finchley. "I expect they've just arrived and are getting things ready for next week."

And he was right, for as they came downstream the field had resolved itself to order and a large marquee was in the course of erection. They drifted by, watching the work, and when the field passed out of sight Mrs. Crantell said:

"We shall be back too early if we go straight on. Let's tie up for a while. If Robert's energetic he can go off hunting for wild flowers and we'll rest in the shade. It's very hot, isn't it?"

"It is," replied Mr. Finchley, who had wished to remove his jacket, but felt that to do so, or ask for permission, would have been disrespectful to Mrs. Crantell. They drew into the bank and made the boat fast.

"Don't go too far and don't be too long," cautioned Mr. Finchley as Robert sprang ashore.

"If you're very lucky, you may find some yellow irises around here, Robert," said Mrs. Crantell. "Mr. Finchley and I found some last year." Robert shot away.

"It's amazing what a restless thing a child is," said Mr. Finchley as he lay back on the bank and stared at the sky.

"You're very fond of Robert, aren't you?" Mrs. Crantell asked, as she sat by his side, her fingers busy with a daisy chain. "You'll miss him when Mr. Hammerton takes him."

"I suppose I shall," answered Mr. Finchley. "But he'll be happy with Mr. Hammerton and soon forget about me. Children soon adapt themselves. Anyway, Mrs. Patten is coming back next week, she hopes, and I don't think she's the kind to care much for children—"

"Do you mean you'll be glad to return to your old way of living?"

Mr. Finchley looked across at her before he answered. All he could see was her profile, neat and clear against the blue sky.

"I suppose so. He's a responsibility, and you don't feel the same about a boy who has no claim on you. I mean, if he were my own … Well, you see, it's rather different, isn't it? The circumstances—"

"You mean if he were your own boy you wouldn't mind the new responsibilities and changes you've had to make in your life?"

"In a way," Mr. Finchley confessed after a moment's thought. "But he isn't my boy—"

"He could be, couldn't he?"

Mr. Finchley sat up suddenly. "Of course not! Mr. Hammerton's going to adopt him. Besides, he can give him so much—he's very rich. And anyway, what do I know about children?"

"What does Mr. Hammerton know, what does anyone know until they have one and find out? Besides—" Mrs. Crantell paused a moment before continuing, a hesitancy that escaped Mr. Finchley: "you could get someone to help you with the child. That should be easy."

She looked to see if Mr. Finchley had understood her. He was staring across the river.

"But most people have children when they are fairly young."

"What about it? The older you are the more sense and experience you have and the better fitted for the task, and that is especially so with a boy like Robert who has such precocious, almost adult views—"

"Do you know," said Mr. Finchley, suddenly bold, "I almost believe you're trying to persuade me to adopt Robert."

Mrs. Crantell smiled and hung the daisy chain around her neck. "How could I be? Mr. Hammerton has the first claim, hasn't he? I was just wondering—that was all."

Mr. Finchley lay back, knitting his brows and inwardly despairing of ever understanding Mrs. Crantell. Once she had told him that elderly people being set in their ways were wrong to try to alter those ways, and now—he could swear—she was as good as trying to persuade him to adopt Robert.

He watched the clouds, his mind busy with thoughts while his eyes followed the convolutions of the sky masses. No, he could not adopt Robert. Mr. Hammerton was going to do that, and Robert was looking forward to living with Mr. Hammerton. To live on a farm ... He could remember Robert saying to him more than once:

"I shall wake in the morning and hear fowls and pigs and, maybe, I shall be allowed to milk the cows. Pépé has often said that there is much to be admired in cows that they allow themselves to be robbed so regularly and yet never turn upon those who steal."

What was it about him, he wondered, which had brought him well into middle age as a bachelor? All these problems of marriage and children should have been solved long ago.

A bachelor faced them in the twenties and made his decision. Mr. Finchley suddenly discovered that he had never faced them, that he had just drifted along, each day confirming him in his selfish mode of life. After all … he found himself swept into the turbulent whirlpool of racial duty, eugenics and the complete function of the individual, a whirlpool which threatened to suck him under. Did a man really have a duty to his race? Should a man, if he could afford it—and Mr. Finchley could easily have afforded it—welcome the responsibility of marriage and children?

Why did Mrs. Crantell have to start all these hares on a lovely Sunday afternoon? She was looking down at him, smiling as though she knew and enjoyed the conflict in his mind. Women, decided Mr. Finchley, could be very annoying creatures, even the best of them.

It was some time before Mrs. Crantell disturbed the silence. Then she said:

"Robert's been gone a long time. I wonder where he's got to?"

Mr. Finchley stood up and brushed the creases from his trousers. "He's probably gone back to that circus. I'll go and look for him."

"I'll come as well," said Mrs. Crantell.

They walked up the river path, in the shade of the pollarded willows. The river began to bend and they found themselves walking with water to one side and a dark fir plantation on the other. As they came out of the darkness of the plantation a man came running down the towing path towards them. He stopped when he saw them and stood panting.

"Have you," he gasped, "seen a small boy go this way within the last few minutes?"

He was a short, plump man, with a round face and white whiskers, the kind of man, Mr. Finchley settled, who should avoid violent exercise of any kind.

"Nobody has passed us in the last five minutes," said Mrs. Crantell, and she added kindly: "Don't you think you ought to sit down and rest? You look very hot."

"Of course I'm hot, madam," the man cried. "I've been running, and you would have run, too, if some scamp had stolen your irises. My beautiful irises!" he moaned softly through his handkerchief as he wiped his hot face.

"Did you say irises?" asked Mr. Finchley, suspicion creeping into his mind.

"I did. Japanese irises—not the ordinary kind, but a special lot that I've hybridised myself with some sent to me from India. I've got a gold cup for them. I'm the only man in England to grow them, and now the first half-dozen blooms I've had this year have been stolen from my garden—"

"And this boy," said Mr. Finchley, "was he about so high, dark haired, and wearing an open-necked blue shirt?"

"He was! You know him then?"

Mr. Finchley backed away from the explosive cries. "Now, now …" he began.

"You know him?" The man stepped forward angrily. "Is it your son?"

Mr. Finchley was saved from violence by an unexpected interruption. From the mass of foliage which crested the willow they were standing under, there came a sharp, anguished cry of despair and then the thin branches broke asunder and a small form fell backwards towards the river.

Mrs. Crantell had a glimpse of a blue shirt. Then the river rose into a spout of protesting foam. The agitation of the water died away and discovered Robert anxiously treading water, eyeing the group on the bank, while around him, moving slowly downstream, floated a handful of broken irises, their blue and gold a royal tribute on the waters.

"It is he!" cried the man and he began to dance and shout. Robert, knowing there was no forgiveness from him, turned and began to swim downstream, making for the further bank. The angry man followed him along the towpath.

"Come on," said Mr. Finchley.

"Wait," cautioned Mrs. Crantell. "Let him get ahead, otherwise there'll be trouble." She held Mr. Finchley back until the man was some way ahead of them. Then they followed until they reached their skiff.

"Quickly," cried Mrs. Crantell. "Before he realises we have a boat."

A few moments later they were rowing in pursuit of Robert, who had settled himself happily to outdistance his towing-path pursuer. But the iris lover gave up before the skiff reached Robert. He had already run a long way, his irises were ruined, and eventually he flopped down on to the grass staring dejectedly at the water, his lungs working like wheezy bellows.

The skiff soon overtook Robert, who seized the edge of the boat and hung on. In his other hand he held two irises.

Mr. Finchley leaned over the side to Robert.

He took his hand and heaved. Robert wriggled himself upwards and, as Mr. Finchley pulled, there rose from the water and confronted him a pink and shining backside, presenting itself unashamedly. For a moment he was in danger of letting Robert fall back to the water. Then he recovered himself and hauled the boy in quickly.

"Robert!" he demanded sternly, as the boy stood up and hastily pulled down the frill of his wet shirt to cover himself. "Where are your trousers?"

Robert looked regretfully upstream. "They are up there somewhere, Mr. Finchley. I could not help it. I lost my belt getting the flowers and while I was swimming they came off. I had no free hand to hold them, because of the flowers. And I did not steal the flowers, sir. I did not know I was in a garden until the man chased me. It was by a little stream, just like the river. When he chased me I got ahead and climbed the tree, hoping he would pass. In the tree it was difficult to hold on. You see, sir, there was my trousers to hold, the flowers and the branches to catch hold. I did not have enough hands and—"

"That's enough!" said Mr. Finchley stemming Robert's hurried vindication. Mr. Finchley's embarrassment was setting him an angry course. "What on earth are we to do with you?" he asked, and with a typical masculine helplessness he turned instinctively to Mrs. Crantell.

For a second that good lady looked at his embarrassed, reddened face and then at Robert, trouserless and grinning, and the next moment she flopped weakly back into the stern seat and began to laugh. Mrs. Crantell abandoned herself, vulgarly Mr. Finchley thought, to her laughter, shaking her head and patting her breast to relieve her mirth. Mr. Finchley did the only possible thing. He took off his jacket, handed it to Robert and then getting out the oars began to pull for the café from whence they had hired the boat. Mrs. Crantell, he thought, had disappointed him and Robert was a nuisance. He pulled viciously, digging his oars fiercely into the river.

Before he reached the café he was in a calmer mood and Mrs. Crantell had recovered herself.

"Forgive me, Mr. Finchley," she said, and said it so sweetly and contritely that Mr. Finchley had to pretend that he had never been angry, and that everything was his fault.

"I think," he said, "we'll pretend that we have had an accident. Robert can have fallen into the river whilst playing."

"Quite," agreed Mrs. Crantell. "But how are we to get him back to London without trousers? Could you row to Westminster Bridge? We could get a bus there."

Mr. Finchley ignored this suggestion. At the café they explained that they had had a boating accident.

Mr. Finchley telephoned for a car to fetch them, and while they waited they sat around, Robert wrapped in a blanket, in the proprietor's dining-room.

The car soon arrived. They passed out, Robert draped like a red Indian, and so intrigued was he by the likeness that he said stubbornly:

"Me sit by driver. Little Bull no like to sit behind in thunder-machine. Only squaws and children sit behind. Little Bull has spoken."

Mr. Finchley gave way, and it did not occur to him, so much had his spirits revived, to deplore the influence of the Wild West magazines Robert had purchased to "improve his English".

XX
In which a party is arranged

IN two days Mr. Finchley began to see that Sunday in its proper light. At the time he had been embarrassed. Now, he was realising that he alone had been the only person to feel like that. Robert had not been at all flustered, and, more surprisingly, Mrs. Cantrell—who had more reason than any of them to resent this spoiling of her pleasant Sunday walk—she had taken everything with a calmness that might have made it seem usual for her to meet such adventures every Sunday. Here was a side to her character that Mr. Finchley had not known, a cheerful evenness of temper in the face of embarrassments and ridiculous situations. She, who had once preached the maintenance of a quiet, habitual mode of living, had shown herself quite able to depart from her own gentle flux of habit to accommodate herself to the unusual.

Women, thought Mr. Finchley, as he walked towards the office, were very curious creatures. He wondered if they meant half they said. It was a thought which gave him hope, and his hope increased his good humour so that as he entered the office and overheard the office boy call to the junior clerk "Look out, here comes Father Finchley!" he could smile indulgently and pretend not to have heard.

And while Mr. Finchley was settling down to his work, Robert had taken his work into the garden. Stretched on a rug, he was reading, while behind him in the house Mrs. Mohun clattered about.

Now some people can take a book into the country with them and, reading, forget everything around them, and others lie down and forget the book. Robert had taken his book into the garden because it was pleasant to be in the sun and he was constantly chiding himself for allowing his attention to wander. He had to study in the morning and he would not allow himself to forget his duty. But there were so many things which seemed to attach no importance to his resolution. First a woodlouse came creeping across his page, a lumbering armour-plated monster that waved its antennae, in greeting and stretched itself along an exclamation mark to rest. Robert let it stay for a while, examining it with interest. Then—*flic*—a frog-hopper flirted to the page and he forgot the louse as he eyed this mechanical midget in bright green. He put out his finger gently and touched the hopper. *Flic*—it was off into blue space, and the woodlouse, annoyed by so much activity, strolled away to find another resting place, and Robert turned to his reading.

He did not read for long. The next interruption came from two sparrows quarrelling over a nest under the eaves of the house. Robert watched them, tails spread out and down and wings arched, making bullying advances at one another, and after a while he gathered that the argument was concerned chiefly with the hen bird sitting on the nest, both cocks claiming marital rights and the hen not at all disposed to settle the question by an indication of her choice. Their noisy voices drowned all other sound. Robert put his fingers in his ears and turned to his book to find that now his eyes betrayed him, catching any movement that came within their compass. Now it was the shake of a duster from a window, a yellow signal that left him speculating about the room that had been dusted; now the quick up and down of a hover fly causing him to forsake the print for this aeronautic wonder, and last a cat, black and white, which walked across the garden wall and reminded him of a cheetah, so that from cheetah he travelled to the Paris Zoo, and was soon miles away down the Seine with Pépé. Where was Pépé now, he wondered. In his speculation he rolled over on his back and surveyed the sky, his mind playing the sculptor with clouds, so that he fashioned idly for himself long frescoes of moving figures and carved familiar faces, watching their expressions change as the wind moved gently among the clouds.

And while he lay there he became conscious of a regular *pat, pat* coming from close by. For a while he disregarded it, then the noise, affronted by his disregard, forced itself upon him and he lay, listening to the sound that went so regularly for a time and then broke off, only to begin again. He tried to find an explanation for it, but none of his theories fitted. Finally he sat up and listened. The sound was coming from the next garden. He was sure of it.

He tried to ignore it, turning to his book. The noise would not be banished. He fought a losing battle with his curiosity, and, finally, he got up and walked to the bottom of the garden. Using the rockery as steps he climbed high enough to look into the next-door garden. On the lawn stood Henry Barker, the red-haired, and in his hand he held a tennis racket with which he was striking a ball that was attached to a cord hanging between two wooden posts. He struck the ball and, at the end of its tether, it was jerked back by the string to receive another stroke. Robert watched. Henry played with quickness and skill and, fancying himself unobserved, accompanied each stroke with some taunting remark at the ball:

"Take that, pie-face!"

"Ha, thought you'd dodge me, leather-belly!"

And then came a long rally of smashing strokes delivered with a—"That's for Ratty! That's for Stinks Harris! That's for Jumpin' Joe!"—references, it was not difficult to guess, to masters who had incurred his displeasure at school.

Robert watched this exhibition with admiration for a while. Henry stopped for a rest and saw him.

"Hullo," he said doubtfully.

"Hullo," replied Robert. "That's a good thing you've got."

Henry smiled pleasantly, taking his interest to indicate a peace settlement.

"Yes—pretty good. I'm going to be a champion tennis player one day, no kidding. Dad gave it to me for my birthday. Did you hear us last night?"

Robert shook his head.

"Gosh, I thought everybody round here would. It was a party for my birthday. We kicked up no end of a row. Dad got a bit worried, but mother told him not to be silly. He's always scared of annoying the neighbours."

"What did you do?"

"Oh, we played games and ate. Pretty good it was, too. And, of course, everyone that came brought me a present.

It's pretty good having a birthday." Robert nodded agreement. It was pretty good having a birthday, especially the birthday party. He wondered why Pépé, Pépé who usually thought of everything, had never marked his birthday with a party. For the last four years, Robert thought, he had been capable of enjoying a birthday party and no one had told him about it. How careless people could be.

"Do you want to have a smack at this?" asked Henry politely. He bore Robert no enmity now.

"No, thanks," answered Robert. "I'm supposed to be studying."

"So am I," grinned Henry. "I should be at school, but I always feel ill after a party so I stop at home. Mother says it's best to let your stomach get settled before you start again. Boy, what a party! I wish I'd thought of asking you."

"That's all right." Robert passed the omission away without a thought. He was not much interested in other people's parties.

While he was having his lunch with Mrs. Mohun, he asked her: "Do you have a party on your birthday, Mrs. Mohun?"

"A party, deary? Haven't got time for such nonsense at my age. Maybe, I'll have a drop of Scotch instead of stout that evening. Now Mr. Mohun—he was a one for parties, if ever there was. The life and soul of any party. It was a great loss when he went. But why do you ask?"

"Just that I think I may be going to have a party," said Robert quietly. "To make things right, I should really have about four parties."

"Lord, love us! What's the child talking about?"

Robert made no answer, and he was rather preoccupied that afternoon when Marie called for him, though he did manage to be jubilant when she told him that Mr. Burton had given her a small part in his new play.

When Mr. Finchley had settled down that evening, Robert allowed him a full hour with his paper. During that time he kept very quiet, apparently deep in his book, but his eye on the clock gave him away. He could scarcely wait until the hands should point to eight o'clock, which was the limit he had set. Mr. Finchley he knew would be in a receptive mood when his paper was finished.

"Did you ever," said Robert as the clock finished striking eight, "have a birthday party when you were young, sir?"

Mr. Finchley put down his paper and began to refill his pipe.

"Party? Party?" he said absently. "Oh, why, yes. Yes, I did. I remember very well. It used to be quite an event in my life—"

"Did it?"

"Yes, indeed, it was—quite an event. I think it is for all boys." Mr. Finchley fell gently, unsuspectingly into the trap, and Robert, his prey so easily taken, had a moment of remorse for his conduct. Then he shook the feeling aside as he thought of the four years' injustice he had suffered.

"Not for all boys" Robert said sadly.

"What do you mean? Every boy enjoys a birthday party—presents, games and good food—what more does a boy want to make him happy? I remember one birthday of mine when I was given an airgun. An uncle gave it to me—I know there was some opposition at the time because it was felt to be dangerous for a boy. I remember that present well—" Mr. Finchley smiled through a smoke wreath as the memory floated back to him. Good Lord, could it have been him, all those years ago, who had sat freezing at a bedroom window waiting with his gun for cats? He could hear now the soft *phutt!* of the gun and the astonished yelp of a marauding cat.

"No, they don't," said Robert obstinately. "Not all boys—because not all boys have birthday parties—"

"Nonsense," cried Mr. Finchley, waving aside this sociological incursion. "Even the humblest family manages to mark a boy's birthday with some celebration, no matter how small."

Robert shook his head and looked doleful, his large eyes heavy with unspeakable sorrow, his head drooping with the burden of his past neglect. "Not all—I have never had a birthday party. Not once that I can remember. All that happened was for Pépé to say—'Today you are a year older—let us hope you are a year wiser'—and he would kiss me and it was over."

"How like the French," thought Mr. Finchley, doing that race an injustice, and then aloud: "Dear, dear—well, it's no use crying over spilt milk. You'll have parties when you live with Mr. Hammerton. He's not the kind to forget anything like that. When is your birthday?"

"Very soon," replied Robert, "but I was wondering …" He hesitated.

"Wondering what?"

"Well, my birthday is coming soon, but I shall probably spend it with Mr. Hammerton and I shall very likely have new friends to my party. It is a pity that the friends I have made in London will not be there. I was wondering if I could have a party this week for last year?"

"This week for last year?" Mr. Finchley sat up, for the first time suspecting the disinterestedness of the conversation Robert had started.

"Yes, you see, I had no party for my last birthday, and I should like to have all my new friends at a party before I go away. It will not be long now before Mr. Hammerton comes for me. If I had a party I should always remember it, and it would be pleasant to have all my friends together. Do you think we could do that?"

Mr. Finchley did not answer immediately. He stroked his chin and stared at the smoke trails rising to the ceiling. After all, he mused, the boy had missed his birthdays—there were a lot of things which Robert had missed, and most of them could not be easily given to him. Here was one thing which could be restored to him. Although it sounded stupid to adult ears to have a birthday party a year late, it could—and Mr. Finchley had the wisdom to realise it—be an immensely important affair to a child. It was satisfying to know that here was something which he could give Robert. After all … he pondered. Then he gave a short laugh and, leaning forward, took Robert's nose in his fingers and gave it a friendly tweak.

"Robert—you're a villain. I don't know what's put this party idea into your head. But I do know that you've very skilfully put me into a position from which I cannot withdraw. Never mind—quite apart from all that, you shall have your party whenever you like. When shall it be?"

"The day after tomorrow," cried Robert happily. "Mrs. Mohun shall do the cooking for us, and I'll invite my friends. And you too, you have friends you would like to invite?"

"Perhaps," said Mr. Finchley.

And so it was arranged that Robert should have his birthday party.

"So that's why you were talking about parties," said Mrs. Mohun when she was informed the next day. "You're deep, Master Robert, deep. Just like the late Mohun."

And Robert lay that morning on the lawn, listening to the *pat, pat* of Henry's ball from next door, quite unperturbed by its sound, his only curiosity being the excuse that Henry had made for another day off from school. He felt grateful to Henry and wished he had not hit him so hard at their first meeting.

XXI
Of an evening of surprises

THE first guest to arrive at Robert's party was Mrs. Crantell. Robert met her in the hall, his face shiny and himself neat in a new suit which he and Mr. Finchley had bought the previous evening. Robert was rather proud of his suit. It was grey with a light line in it, and the trousers had a deep back pocket.

Mrs. Crantell kissed him, wished him many happy returns, and presented him with a copy of *Treasure Island*.

"You're the first," said Robert. "But the others won't be long."

Marie was the next to arrive.

"See," she said, as she took her coat off, "I've put my party frock on." She stood for a moment to let Robert admire her. She wore a green frock, puffed at the elbows and swinging low and free around her feet.

"You are very pretty, Marie," said Robert, "and that is as it should be at a party, for you never know who you will meet."

"That's why I wore my party frock," she cried gaily, "and now see what I have for you." She held out his present and watched him as he opened it.

"Oh!" Robert announced his surprise. It was a magnificent pocket knife with a full assortment of blades, corkscrew, nail file, and a peculiar instrument which Mr. Finchley swore was intended for taking stones from horses' hooves. No one else believed him, though Mrs. Mohun—who had come up to look after the supper—could make a better suggestion, and she insisted that it was a patent tin-opener.

"I've seen hundreds of them patent tin-openers," she declared, "and none of 'em's so good as the old-fashioned dog's-head kind that you jam in and jerk up and down."

"Perhaps it's a tin-opener and a stone-hoover," said Marie.

Robert said nothing, and Mr. Finchley, watching him as he looked around the room, had an uneasy feeling that the boy was hunting for something on which to try the qualities of his new present. If he found initials carved on any of his furniture he would never be able to regard his friendship with Marie as complete.

There was a ring at the door, and Mr. Finchley sprang up, stopping Mrs. Mohun from answering it. They heard him in the hall, and then the door was opened and he was ushering into the room a tall young man wearing horn-rimmed spectacles. The young man blinked, hesitant, as though he had been entrapped and was not yet convinced of his betrayal.

Hume turned quickly to Mr. Finchley. "But you told me—" he began.

Mr. Finchley interrupted him. "Of course I did, but I had forgotten."

The day before he had been surprised to receive a telephone call at the office from Hume. The young man had been vague about the reason for the call, but Mr. Finchley had guessed that he was wondering if he knew anything about Marie. Mr. Finchley had given no indication that he had met Marie and, without mentioning the party, had asked Hume to spend the evening with him. Robert had entered the conspiracy joyfully.

"This is Mr. Laurence Hume," Mr. Finchley said, introducing him, "and he is not a stranger to all of us, eh?"

"Mr. Hume!" Robert shot towards him with an excitement which Marie, who was watching closely, felt was not altogether genuine. Then she rose, too, her heart beating quickly, schooling herself to compose her features, and greeted him.

"Why, Miss Peters!" There was no doubt of Laurence's surprise, and as they stood together in the centre of the room, Mr. Finchley shot a quick glance at Mrs. Crantell which told her all she wanted to know.

"Didn't you expect to see me?" Marie asked.

"I certainly didn't expect to see you here." He turned to Mr. Finchley. "You didn't tell me that Miss Peters would be here."

"Didn't I?" said Mr. Finchley innocently. "I thought I did. Must have slipped my memory. Anyway, what does it matter now?"

"Are we all here?" asked Mrs. Crantell.

"No, there's another one," answered Robert.

"Who?" questioned Marie.

"You'll see," said Robert mysteriously, and at the end of ten minutes they did see, for Robert, returning from the door, led in a tall, thick-set, gloomy-faced man dressed in a thick serge suit, a hard white collar, heavy boots and a bowler hat which he carried as though it were an offertory box. This was Lanky Harris of the *Milly Brown*.

"Evenin', folks," said Lanky, not at all abashed by his projection from a Camden Town coal wharf to a respectable Hampstead sitting-room. He very soon made himself at home in Mr. Finchley's house, and it soon became apparent that his gloomy face was a false indication of his spirits. Lanky was one of those men which every party discovers. Without him the evening would have been pleasant, with him it became exciting and hilarious. He pretended to no delicacy of feeling, he let himself go, and with his example to encourage them the others threw off their reserve and reticence and enjoyed themselves as people should at parties.

They played games, they ate an enormous supper, they laughed, they joked, and in the midst, bright-eyed, flushed of face, moved Robert. He liked them all, and this was his birthday party—the first he had ever had. And Robert's happiness reflected itself around the room.

Laurence Hume began to be grateful to Mr. Finchley for finding Marie for him. Until he had met her he had imagined that the love he bore his work was a passion that demanded his whole heart. Now he was beginning to realise that a man had to make many compromises and that this compromise was not hard to make. He looked at Marie, her fair hair waved and picked with highlights, her face smiling, lips half-parted in laughter and her strong throat full of hidden, lithe movements, and he wondered that he had not noticed sooner the beauty she brought to every gesture, the music she spoke with each word.

And Mrs. Mohun, as she moved in and out of the room, found her eyes going continually to Lanky. What a man he was! full of quips and jokes—just like the late Mohun. The life and soul of the party. And he had a sauce with him, too. She could tell that by the way he had looked at her in the kitchen when he insisted on carrying the tray out for her.

He said: "You're a fine woman to be a widow, Mrs. Mohun."

"And who told you I was a widow?" She had her answer for him. It didn't do to let the men think they could flatter you into stupidness.

"Why, the boy, to be sure. Young Robert has told me a lot of things about you, so that I was achin' to meet you. And I've a great respect for your late husband, too. I've been told about him."

"Don't you malign the late Mohun. He was a man of character—"

"And if it comes to character, what about me?"

And there he was, now, sitting down in the room, telling some funny story of a ghost barge that was putting everyone's hair on end, just the way the late Mohun had told stories.

"And now," said Lanky, as he finished his story, "it's someone else's turn to amuse us. In a party everyone must do something. Come on, Robert—your turn next. What will you do?"

"I could throw my knife—Pépé taught me a little—"

"Not in here, Robert," cried Mr. Finchley. "I want to have some furniture left when the party's over."

"What about a song, Robert?" asked Mrs. Crantell, who had heard him sing before.

With a gramophone record for accompaniment Robert sang to them, and as he sang, Mr. Finchley was reminded of the time he had spent in the Quartier Latin with him. Mrs. Mohun, her work in the kitchen done, had been forced to join the party, and she sat, with tears in her eyes, listening. A good song always affected her. His words came pure and sweet, clearing away the heat and noise of the room, transporting them all to private places of imagination.

Then, after little persuasion, Mrs. Mohun obliged with *In Dublin's Fair City* and they joined in the choruses. Marie played the piano, Mrs. Crantell recited as much as she could remember of the *Spanish Armada*, and Laurence, after much hesitation, did card tricks, and to wind up the evening they rolled the carpet back and danced. Robert took charge of the gramophone and encouraged them with excited cries. Mr. Finchley, who had not danced for years, found himself clasped to the expansive bosom of Mrs. Mohun, being swung about the room, hitting his shins on chairs and growing steadily hotter. Lanky took Mrs. Crantell and Marie and Laurence wove their way between the others with a skill which brought admiring comments from Robert.

The evening passed, and it was with regret that Mr. Finchley closed the door on Mrs. Crantell, the last of the guests, and listened to the beat of the taxi engine dying away along the street. He stood for a moment in the hallway, holding the nine o'clock post in his hand. None of them had heard the postman's knock and it was now gone eleven.

Robert, who had been in the bathroom preparing for bed, came to the head of the stairs and looked down at him, his pyjama front open, his trousers flopping over his slippers.

"Good-night, Mr. Finchley," he called.

"Good-night, Robert," answered Mr. Finchley, his round face lifting towards the boy, the electric light smoothing his bald head into a white island midst the sombre colourings of the hall. "Did you enjoy your party?"

"More than I can say, sir. Thank you for letting me have it here. When I go to live with Mr. Hammerton I shall always remember this evening. Did you like Lanky? He said he would come and visit me in the country when I go to Mr. Hammerton."

"Lanky is a very nice fellow," said Mr. Finchley sincerely.

"I think," said Robert, pursuing another thought, "that perhaps Mr. Hume will marry Marie, no?"

"I should say," answered Mr. Finchley, fingering his letters, "that it would be very likely."

"And what about Mrs.—"

"You'd better get along to bed, it's late," said Mr. Finchley, stopping any further reflections about marriage from Robert.

He heard Robert pad away to his room and then, still warm from his exertions, he sat down on the hall chair where it was cool and began to look through his letters. There were three bills, the notice of a cricket club meeting, an invitation to a church concert, a letter from Mrs. Patten giving a full account of the stages of her sister's illness during the past week and making no mention of returning, and a letter with a French stamp which Mr. Finchley recognised as being from Mr. Hammerton. He opened it last, wondering if he was perhaps already on his way to England.

He read the letter slowly and when he had finished read it once more. It went:

DEAR MR. FINCHLEY,
I hope that you and Robert are well, and that the boy is not giving you any trouble. I have wound up all my affairs here, and for the last few days have been going through agents' details of farms for sale which have been sent me from England. None of them seem very attractive. In fact, the more I read the less inclined I became to buy a farm in England.
I might as well be frank with you. I know I shall disappoint you, but I must be wise and recognise my own failing. I can never settle down in England. I am rather like the person who said that he was ready enough to die for England, but preferred not to live there. Frankly, I don't want to return to England—especially as I have an attractive business proposition made to me which will leave me free to travel without settling anywhere. I have thought about this matter carefully, especially as far as it concerns Robert. I decided to adopt the boy in an enthusiastic moment and I have regretted that moment because the responsibility would have tied me down and I don't want that. Selfish, yes, but, at least, believe me to be honest. I have decided to set aside a substantial sum for Robert's education and to give him a small income for the rest of his life. This money will be administered by three guardians. I should like you to appoint these, yourself being one if you so choose. Would you do that?
I think I am doing the wisest thing. It is better to settle the affair now than to come to England for a

few years and find I should have to make just such a decision later on and cause more disappointment. Please don't mention this to Robert yet, but let me know if you will handle the guardianship business.

Yours sincerely,

J. HAMMERTON.

Mr. Finchley was not surprised somehow. He should have been, but he could not shake from his mind a doubt which had rested there ever since he had met Mr. Hammerton. The man had inspired himself with a momentary desire to settle down and consolidate his wasted life, and the moment had passed. Looking back now, Mr. Finchley felt that any shrewd judge of men would have known that this might happen. Then he thought of Robert. The boy was looking forward to living with Mr. Hammerton. To him had been held out the promise of a life he longed for. He was to live on a farm, and now … Suddenly Mr. Finchley was angry, bitterly angry with Mr. Hammerton.

This wealthy man, this thriftless idler, thought that he could make promises and break them at will, thought that it was enough if he made some monetary compensation for his lack of faith, for his cowardice in the face of resolutions. Did it mean nothing to him that Robert would be disappointed, that the boy's dreams were going to be swept away, even though his future was to be cared for? The boy was an individual, a personality, not an animal that could be driven and stabled from one place to another.

His anger rising, Mr. Finchley went to his room, and, aided by his bitterness, wrote to Mr. Hammerton. For an angry man it was a mild letter; for Mr. Finchley it was a bitter letter. He pointed out to Mr. Hammerton that it was not easy to break the promise which had been made, nor an adequate honouring of that promise to leave Robert to be looked after by guardians and possibly sent to live with an indifferent family, when the boy had been looking forward to the life Mr. Hammerton had promised him. Mr. Finchley, with all the sincerity his pen could command, asked him to reconsider his decision. He reminded him of the conversation they had in the Marivaux Hotel, and when he had finished the letter his impatience sent him out, late as it was, to post it so that it should get away by the early morning mail.

XXII
How Mr. Finchley demands a plain answer

MR. FINCHLEY said nothing to Robert about the letter. He ate his breakfast the next morning, returning cheerful replies to all Robert's enquiries, and not by one word giving away the distress which was clouding his spirits.

When he had gone off to the office, Robert settled down to his study, ignoring the repeated conversational overtures made by Mrs. Mohun as she tidied the room. At twelve o'clock, as Robert and Mrs. Mohun were finishing lunch, Marie came in. She had called early to take Robert to Richmond.

"I won't be a minute," he said, and dashed out of the room to get himself ready. A few minutes later, as he came from his bedroom to the landing, he heard Marie and Mrs. Mohun talking in the dining-room, and catching his name stopped to listen.

"But not while Robert's in the house," Mrs. Mohun said.

"What do you mean?" Marie asked, and the curiosity of her tones stilled Robert.

"Well, it's plain enough. In fact, I never see'd it plainer. Mr. Finchley wants to marry that Mrs. Crantell, as sure as the late Mohun is lying with a black marble curb full of gravel chippings placed square on top of him, but he won't ask her until Robert's gone. You know what we women are—that Mrs. Crantell don't want to be takin' a boy as well as a husband—"

"But Robert is going to live with a Mr. Hammerton, Mr. Finchley is only looking after him—"

"So it may be, my dear, but you never know what's going to happen, and if it did happen that Mr. Finchley kept the boy—then Mrs. Crantell would never marry him. And if there was ever a man that ought to be married now or never it's Mr. Finchley."

"You're letting your imagination carry you away, Mrs. Mohun. Mr. Hammerton will take Robert away soon, there's no doubt of that."

Robert came downstairs slowly, thinking. Mr. Finchley had been always kind to him, severely kind at times, and always fair. He had come to be so fond of him that Mr. Hammerton was a mythical figure representing the future, and there were times when he would, if it could have been arranged, have gladly given up the prospect of a life on a farm in exchange for life with Mr. Finchley. But now he knew that if Mr. Finchley were to be happy, he must go to Mr. Hammerton. The thought obsessed him for a time, but his child's mind soon forgot it in the glories of Kew.

But with Mr. Finchley that evening the thought came back to Robert.

"Will Mr. Hammerton soon be taking me to his farm?" he asked.

"Why—" Mr. Finchley was embarrassed by the question. "Why—are you getting anxious to go away?"

And Robert gave what he thought was the best answer.

"Oh, yes. I am longing to live on a farm. All my life—"

Mr. Finchley scarcely heard the rest. He was doubly hurt; hurt because Robert might never reach the farm, and hurt at the eagerness the boy showed to be away from him.

It was three days before Mr. Hammerton replied. The answer came unexpectedly. The office boy informed him that Mr. Sprake wished to see him.

"Thank you," said Mr. Finchley and he followed him.

"Hullo, Finchley." Sprake looked up cheerfully. "Letter here from Hammerton I should like you to read." He handed Mr. Finchley the letter. So, Mr. Hammerton had made an official matter of it, thought Mr. Finchley as he took the letter. He walked to the window holding the letter. Sprake's room had the same view as his.

It was a warm day and the vista of roofs and red chimney pots was not unpleasant with the sun spread over them. A few daws played around the chimney stack of a brewery. For many years, almost every day of his adult life, Mr. Finchley had looked out at that scene, a little corner of London which he knew well, noting the changes of curtains at windows, watching the drab decline of hoarding bills, the blossoming of window boxes and the courtship of sparrows. It was easy in dull, weary days to imagine the scene depressing. But with rain on the roofs it could be an enchanting stretch of country, full of rich colours and unexpected contours, and each day brought some new feature to prominence. It was over this that he exercised his cramped eyes, it was on this scene that he built a thousand fanciful hopes, and today it met his mood with the trained obedience of a servant. It waited, as he waited, ready to sympathise, to feed his anger, to depress him further to gloom.

Slowly he read the letter. It was short, it was curt, it was frank, and it revealed the mind of a man who could allow himself no retraction from a decision which pleased his desire. Mr. Hammerton would not change his mind. It was an official commission. He remarked that, if Mr. Finchley still did not want to look after the affair of guardians, he handed the whole affair over to Bardwell & Sprake.

"Well," said Sprake, taking back the letter, "that's the end of that. You can stop playing father now. Our Mr. Hammerton is a changeable fellow."

"He is," said Mr. Finchley with sudden fierceness. "And a thoughtless one. It doesn't matter to him, I suppose, that Robert is looking forward to living on a farm, to having a home! He treats the boy as though he were a bag of potatoes. A child needs more than Hammerton's provisions can give him—"

"Phew!" Sprake whistled. "You do feel strongly about it, don't you? Why don't you adopt him then? You can give him a home, if not a farm, and he likes you, I believe."

"Me! I know nothing about children!"

"We can all learn. Besides, you could get someone to help you with the child. That should be easy—"

As Sprake spoke, Mr. Finchley had a vision of a sunny river and he heard a woman using those same words. He repeated them to himself and a great understanding came to him, making him ashamed of his dullness. He looked at Sprake menacingly: "You're right; I will, and I can!"

Mr. Finchley's lips were set tightly, his face marked with determined lines. He felt himself strong and competent and resolved. There rose within him the spirit of a new Finchley, a man who could not hesitate, a man who saw his path and followed it quickly, undeterred or distracted by wayside fancies.

"Do you mean it?" asked Sprake gravely, sharpening a pencil.

"Of course! It's the only thing to do!"

"I think it is," said Sprake. "Do you know anyone who would help you with the boy?" There was a wrinkle around his eyes as he spoke.

"Mr. Sprake, I want the day off. I must have the day off." For a moment Mr. Finchley disregarded the fact that he was addressing his employer. He ordered the man to give him the day off. Sprake stopped sharpening his pencil, looked curiously at Finchley and then let forth a long, low whistle.

"You have got it bad! And suppose I say no?" Sprake asked the question from curiosity, his interest in this unusual apparition prompting him.

"Then I shall take it and … and bother the consequences," said Mr. Finchley.

Sprake laughed. He knew Mr. Finchley and he liked him, and he believed in him.

"Off you go then," he cried merrily, dismissing him as though he were a schoolboy impatient for his games. "But I shall expect to hear all about it!"

Mr. Finchley thanked him and was gone. He left the office, walked fifty yards up the road, and turned into a public-house.

"A large brandy-and-soda, please," he ordered, and he drank, not to gain courage, but to mark his liberation from reticence and hesitancy. When he left the public-house he stood on the kerb and called a taxi, and a few minutes later he was being borne towards Highgate, an emperor advancing to triumph.

He rang Mrs. Crantell's bell without a tremor. The maid answered him.

"Yes, Mrs. Crantell is in, sir. Will you wait in the hall a moment. I'll call her."

"Don't bother," said Mr. Finchley, sweeping her aside. "Is she upstairs?" He could hear the sound of movement from the landing. The girl nodded, surprised at this unexpected vigour and determination.

Mr. Finchley went up the stairs two at a time and arrived panting on the landing. An open bedroom door showed him Mrs. Crantell standing by a bed which she had been helping the maid to make.

"Mr. Finchley! What on earth are you doing here at this time of day?" She came forward, holding a pillow in her hand.

Mr. Finchley held up a hand. "Not on the landing, please," he requested and propelled her back to the bedroom and shut the door. With his back to the closed door he faced her.

"Mrs. Crantell," he said, "I want to speak to you."

"Mr. Finchley," countered Mrs. Crantell, sniffing, "you've been drinking."

"One brandy-and-soda at the Harrington Arms, but that has nothing to do with the matter," said Mr. Finchley impatiently. "Mrs. Crantell, that day on the river, did you mean what I now think you meant when you told me I should adopt Robert and it would be easy for me to get someone to help me look after him?"

"I don't know what—"

"Answer me. You know what I'm talking about all right. I won't be side-tracked!" Mr. Finchley spoke sternly.

"Well, I suppose—"

"I knew it. I was a fool not to have understood there and then! Well, Mr. Hammerton has decided not to adopt Robert after all. Don't interrupt, please. I am going to adopt the boy instead. I like the child and I think he'll be happy with me—"

"Why, that's splendid—"

"Maybe, but that's not the only thing at the moment. Sit down on that bed and listen to me, and don't fidget with that pillow it takes my attention away from what I want to say."

Mrs. Crantell allowed herself to be overcome and sat down, watching this strange Mr. Finchley with a growing curiosity and admiration.

"Mrs. Crantell," said Mr. Finchley, "I am a plain man and deal in plain answers and questions—"

"Would you mind telling me what it is you are talking about?"

"I've told you—marriage. Mrs. Crantell, I once decided not to ask you this question, but now that I have adopted the boy, I'm going to ask it, and I want from you a plain Yes or No. Mrs. Crantell, will you marry me?"

It was done. Mr. Finchley drew a great breath, the stairs and his talking had exhausted his lungs. Mrs. Crantell sat on the edge of the unmade bed, amazed. This man had stormed his way into the house, overwhelmed her with words and now stood waiting for a direct answer to a question which she felt every woman was entitled to meet at first with a gentle, pleasant period of equivocation.

"Well, Mr. Finchley," she began softly, "you know my feelings about marriage. We discussed the subject once and—"

"Stop!" thundered Mr. Finchley. "I don't want to know anybody's opinion. I want an answer. Will you marry me?"

There was a silence. Outside the street gave up its calls, the whistling errand boys, the cry of tyres across the macadam, the rattle of a milk cart, and then Mrs. Crantell answered, signalling her last moment of complete independence by refusing to give him his plain Yes or No.

"Of course I will," she said happily. "Why on earth haven't you asked me long before this?"

"You will!" Mr. Finchley almost shouted the words in his joy. Then his mood softened. "Oh, Mrs. Crantell," he said sincerely, "you have made me a very happy man and I will see that I never give you cause—"

"That's enough of that," said Mrs. Crantell warningly. "You wouldn't let me make a speech, and I'm not going to let you make one. I'd much rather you kissed me. It's customary, you know, on these occasions."

Mr. Finchley performed his duty with an awkwardness practice was soon to dispel.

"And now we'll go and tell Robert," he said. "He'll be unhappy for a while at not going to live on a farm, but I think he likes us both and we can soon make him happy again. Come on! Let's go now!"

"No," said Mrs. Crantell firmly. "Not until we've had lunch. Robert can wait an hour, and I don't mean to spoil the lunch I've got cooking. Besides, you could do with a good lunch to steady you down. You stop and have lunch and tell me all about Mr. Hammerton."

And Mr. Finchley had to stop. How simple it was, he thought as he ate, to solve life's problems when you went for them bald-headed. Well, perhaps straightforwardly instead of bald-headed, as that was not quite the metaphor for his use.

It was an excellent lunch, and it was three o'clock before he and Mrs. Crantell arrived at his house. The house was empty. It was one of those days when Mrs. Mohun did not call and Robert attended to his own lunch.

"He's gone out with Marie?" enquired Mrs. Crantell.

"No, that's not possible. She had a rehearsal for this afternoon. She told him that yesterday."

"Then he's probably gone for a walk by himself. We'll wait until he comes back."

But Mr. Finchley was not satisfied. The excitement of the morning had made him uneasy and restless. He was loath to accept any commonplace explanations. He went upstairs, Mrs. Crantell following him, and entered Robert's room. At once he knew there was something wrong. The drawers of the boy's chest were pulled out and empty, and a quick glance under the bed showed him that Robert's suitcase was gone.

"He's gone. He's taken his suitcase!" Mr. Finchley was conscious that his heart had begun to beat quickly and that he was trembling.

"And here's the reason," said Mrs. Crantell calmly from the dressing-table. "Here's a letter from our friend Mr. Hammerton. He must have written to Robert by the same post as the other letter. Evidently he didn't shirk from explaining his backsliding to the boy—that's a point in his favour."

Mr. Finchley took the letter and read it. Mr. Hammerton had written explaining that circumstances prevented him from coming to live in England and that Robert must do as Mr. Finchley directed, and that it was more than probable that Mr. Finchley would ask him to live with him.

"But why should this make him go away?" demanded Mr. Finchley.

"Never mind why," said Mrs. Crantell. "The thing at the moment is to find the boy. Have you any idea where he might go—did he have any money?"

"Not much—a few shillings. I can't understand. Wait a minute—there's one possibility. Yes, well try it."

Without explaining to Mrs. Crantell he hurried downstairs to the telephone and in a few moments was speaking to the gateman at the canal wharf. He learned that the *Milly Brown* had left the wharf that morning, and the gateman remembered a boy coming through just before it left. In fact, he knew the boy well; he was always hanging around the boats. Where would the boat be now? Well, it was going up through Watford. If they went to Watford and made enquiries they could tell whether it had gone through—should be easy enough to find it.

"Where are we going?" asked Mrs. Crantell as Mr. Finchley grabbed his hat.

"Watford, to find the *Milly Brown.* That's where Robert is, with Lanky Harris."

XXIII
In which Mr. Finchley's future is full of promise

ROBERT crooked one arm over the tiller of the *Milly Brown*, leaning his weight against it to counteract the pull of the horse as she plodded along the towing path. The passage of the barge sent tiny ripples fanning away to the canal banks where they tossed the water-buttercups and splashed enquiringly into rats' holes. It was good, he thought, to be on a barge again. But he could not understand why he still felt sad. He had done the right thing to leave Mr. Finchley. He could now marry Mrs. Crantell. Pépé had always said that the man who did the right thing was the happy man, for his conscience was clean. Nevertheless, Robert felt sad; though he did not let Lanky see his sadness.

The warm air of the late afternoon came back into his face, full of canal smells and the scents of the country. A moorcock moved daintily out of their path and a blackbird, dipping on an alder branch, cheered them. Faintly to their right came the occasional hum of traffic along the main road.

Lanky's head came from the galley, the marks of an indelible pencil over his lips.

"What rhymes with Mohun, Robert? I ain't never had that one to rhyme before?"

"Mohun?" Robert pursed his lips and frowned as he thought. "Why, spoon—"

"That's no good, the first line goes—'Oh, will you lend an ear, Mrs. Mohun.'"

"What about soon? Or croon?"

Lanky concentrated for a moment, then shook his head.

"It's hard, it's the hardest one I've ever had, but before we get to Boxmoor I'll have it. It's always the first two lines that's hardest for us poets." He broke off for a moment and then went on, pursuing another subject. "You're still sure you ain't done the wrong thing, running away from Mr. Finchley? He seemed all right to me—"

"He is all right," said Robert quickly. "I like him very much. That's why I ran away."

"That's a bit of a mix-up, ain't it?"

"Pépé always said—when you can't solve a problem, leave it. You would have liked Pépé."

"Maybe. I met a Frenchman once in a Tottenham Court Road pub. He did me out of five bob. I must say he did it neatly. Hullo, what's happening?"

He came out of the galley and looked up the canal. They were on a bend and two people coming down the path had stopped the horse and the boat was swinging gradually to a standstill. Finally it lost its momentum and hung in the still canal.

"Eh!" shouted Lanky. "What do you think you are doing?"

The two people came from behind the horse and Robert recognised Mr. Finchley and Mrs. Crantell. He jumped from the tiller and dived for the galley. But Lanky caught him by the arm.

"T'ain't no good duckin', Robert. You've got to face it. Afternoon, sir," he called, "and good afternoon to you, ma'am."

"Good afternoon, Lanky," replied Mr. Finchley from the bank. "We've come for Robert—"

"But I don't want to come!" Robert called back.

"But why not?" enquired Mr. Finchley. "I'm going to look after you now. You'd like to live with me, wouldn't you?"

Robert looked at Lanky, but he made no reply.

"Robert!" It was Mrs. Crantell. "You don't have to run away. Mr. Finchley and I are going to get married and we want to adopt you. Wouldn't you like to live with us?"

"You are going to get married!" Robert shouted excitedly.

Mr. Finchley nodded, beaming. "And we want you to live with us."

"Lanky, do you hear!" Robert turned to his friend and began to dance up and down with joy.

"Steady, there, steady!" called Lanky warningly. "Mind that grease."

But his warning came too late. Robert's foot slipped on a greasy patch of board, his legs flew from under him, and he toppled backwards into the canal.

"Robert!" Mr. Finchley danced agitatedly on the bank.

"Whooa!" roared Lanky, and catching hold of his boat-hook he fished for Robert and hooked the back of his trousers. With a mighty swing he lifted the boy from the water and dropped him neatly on to the towing path. "With the compliments of the captain of the *Milly Brown*!" he called, "and may I never land a better catch than you've got there!"

Mr. Finchley acknowledged the salute with a wave of his hand and then as the horse, obedient to Lanky's shout, resumed its journey and the barge moved away, the three of them watched it go.

"And now what?" asked Mr. Finchley, one arm round Robert's wet shoulders.

"Home," said Mrs. Crantell. The word bore a new significance for them all.

Preview

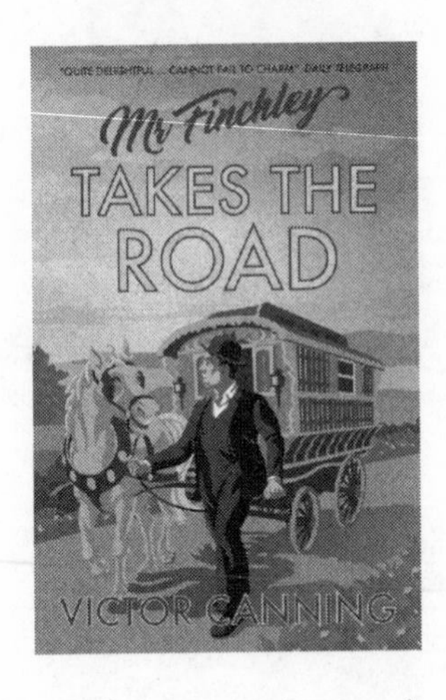

Mr. Finchley takes a fancy to a horse-drawn caravan that he sees for sale. His new wife does not relish the prospect of a caravan journey so goes to visit her brother, as he sets out to explore Kent and go house-hunting.

While learning to handle the horse and the caravan, he has various mishaps and encounters an array of country characters, viewing several unsuitable houses along the way. Gradually it emerges though that the caravan contains a secret – and mayhem ensues.

Mr Finchley, Book 3

Also Available

Mr Edgar Finchley, unmarried solicitor's clerk, aged 45, is told to take a holiday for the first time in his life. He decides to go to Margate. But Fate has other plans in store…

From his abduction in a Bentley by a cheerful crook, to his smuggling escapade off the south coast, the timid but plucky Mr Finchley is plunged into a series of the most astonishing and extraordinary adventures.

Mr Finchley, Book 1

OUT NOW

About the Mr Finchley Series

Mr Finchley is a middle-aged solicitor's clerk who takes a holiday for the first time in his life and finds himself in all kinds of unexpected situations across the length and breadth of England.

These gentle comedy adventures were a runaway success on first publication before the Second World War, and retain a timeless appeal today. They were serialized and dramatized for BBC Radio, with the 1990 dramatization regularly repeated.

Titles in the series, and further humorous works by Victor Canning –

Mr Finchley Discovers His England

Mr Finchley Goes to Paris

Mr Finchley Takes the Road

Polycarp's Progress

Fly Away Paul

Matthew Silverman

Fountain Inn

About the Author

Victor Canning was a prolific writer throughout his career, which began young: he had sold several short stories by the age of nineteen and his first novel, *Mr Finchley Discovers His England* (1934) was published when he was twenty-three. It proved to be a runaway bestseller. Canning also wrote for children: his trilogy The Runaways was adapted for US children's television. Canning's later thrillers were darker and more complex than his earlier work and received further critical acclaim.

Note from the Publisher

To receive background material and updates on further humorous titles by Victor Canning, sign up at farragobooks.com/canning-signup

Made in the USA
San Bernardino, CA
03 June 2020